T0319190

A Pebble In The River

Noufel Bouzeboudja

Langaa Research & Publishing CIG
Mankon, Bamenda

Publisher:
Langaa RPCIG
Langaa Research & Publishing Common Initiative Group
P.O. Box 902 Mankon
Bamenda
North West Region
Cameroon
Langaagrp@gmail.com
www.langaa-rpcig.net

Distributed in and outside N. America by African Books Collective
orders@africanbookscollective.com
www.africanbookscollective.com

ISBN: 9956-762-17-2

DISCLAIMER
All views expressed in this publication are those of the author and do not
necessarily reflect the views of Langaa RPCIG.

1

"See the sun's rays caressing the blossoms sprouting from the green grass. Green, life. And those daisies spreading their petals, a charming blanket, on the green field. Can you hear the robin chirping? He is probably marking his territory. Close your eyes and listen to all those agreeable harmonies. Take a breath, sigh and listen. Open your eyes! Hurry! Look at those Winged Princess ants leaving their nests. Are they gone for their nuptial meeting? See how they shine in the sky. Are they not like diamonds? There! There comes a swallow, whirling around. Is it the only one around? Where are his companions? Could one swallow make a spring? No. Go! Run after that butterfly. Hahaha! Don't be afraid of the bees. Bees give us food and honey. Go! Follow the butterfly and sing the spring's ecstasies!

Did you get up early to walk with the women in their procession to welcome the spring? The sun was rising and nature waking up. What did you see? The women! Throughout their procession, the walkers deposited in some places, small amounts of food. Why? The food will be eaten by birds, worms, insects. Not only there? Where the genius was thought to be dwelling? Ah, they say it is protective ingenuity. All this is just an omen for the coming season, and a blessing for a good harvest. You also sung with the farmers. Who was there? All the village's children, girls and boys! You went to the fields to give offerings and welcome spring. What did you sing?"

"*Spring! Spring! We flourish like spring. We grow like mist. Blessed by Gabriel the Mighty!*"

"The children picked flowers, wild roses, daffodils, thyme… and adorned their heads. Did you also adorn your head? Yes! And you rolled in the grass for the glory of the mother of the Gods Izi, the one your grand-mother celebrates through the tattoo on her cheek."

1

"Spring! Spring…"

"Where are the lovers gone? Where are they? Why do they hide? Tell them to come, to join beauty! Tell them to come, to beam and run on the fields, freely! Lie down at the top of that hill; observe that clear, blue sky. Yes, the sun is smiling at you. Not even a cloud to hide its shyness! Why is it shy? Because of you. Of your grace. It's time to flourish like spring!

Pick a lawn daisy! Pick off a petal, then another, and give your love a chance. He loves me…he loves me not…he loves me…no…he does, he does! Run! Jump! Yes, he does! He loves you. Call him and run!

See that wavy hair, that floating dress. Hear those enchanting laughs. Run after her and take her hand. Smile to her, smile, together, to life, to love, and be!"

Mashahu…Once upon a time…is this a dream or reality? *Mashahu*…The sun warmly caresses those majestic, proud and serene mountains. See how the villages, hamlets and houses are perched on those mountains! "Necklaces around their necks, suspended to the sky," says the poet. See how the mountains survive the passage of time! Those mountains are never spoiled. They are still there, witnesses of Man's joys and miseries. And whenever you call them - yes, the mountains - whenever you call them, they respond, echoing you. A far back in time echo telling you that nature's hands are of pure artistic essence. Should we not then respect art? Should we not respect nature? Put a hand on your forehead and observe that eagle flying over the mountains! What is an eagle without the mountains? A weak and fearful chick. What about those mountain men? Why did they choose the arduous mountains to live? We chose the mountains because a lot of swords, boots and holy books wanted to constrain us. 'Better be free in misery than wealthy under enslavement', is our daily bread. Those men are no better than the others are, but they are worthy of respect, just like the others. *Mashahu*… is this a tale? A legend?

2

"Mashahu, we spring through the chaos of history, spat by oblivion, vomited by a repeated denial. *Mashahu!* Even among hardships we know how to encounter little joys."

"Mashahu! Come back to love. Flame in the eyes! Talk to me about that flame and its bliss. Tell the lovers to come, to gather, to smile, to laugh, to play, to love, to kiss, to sing, to dance, to be!"

"Zira, my daughter… Do you like it when I call you my daughter? … You are grown up now, my dear. Look at you! Divine like Thanith, the Amazigh Goddess of fertility and war. Go! Go and run with them. Run! Is there a better thing than love?

Is this a dream? Then let me not awaken. Smile, my little girl, smile! There is no better remedy to pain than smiling. Better not think of pain in happy moments. Forget it! Live your joys fully, deeply, and forget your pains. Yours and mine. Don't pains interrupt joys? Then put them aside at least for a moment and be happy. Even for a moment."

Mashahu…

No! Not now. He can't break off this…dream… Or is he in this… this dream? He shouldn't do that…

The lamp! Holy God! Let me switch on the lamp. It was a dream. He isn't in my dream. He is again shouting and banging on the walls of his cell. Why does he snatch me from my dream so hastily?

"Yes, bang those walls! Cursed be it all! There is no risk at getting them down. Shout! Insult!"

One cannot rest even in his cell.

"We share, though separated, the same walls, and so, better stay calm. Stay calm and count uselessly the minutes, the hours, the days, the weeks. Count them as they slip away from your life. Our life. Cursed be it all! Please do not drive me into your rabies! Is it remorse and regret that lead you to all this ferocity? No need to shout or punch the walls, brother! Better dwell in grief than be consumed by madness and brutality. Shame on

3

me! How dare I blame you? Confinement leads to dreadful consequences."

But let me recall my dream. Spring, love, freedom, colourful fields, eagles, and mountains. Zira was smiling and running among the lovers. She looked beautiful. She was shining in the spring processions. She became a woman.

I wonder: How is she now? What is she doing? How is she doing in her life? The last time I saw her, she was a little baby. She could barely walk, but she had spoken that word that filled my heart with joy.Vava. Father. It was the first and last word I heard from her mouth. 'Vava' was the first word she uttered smiling wittily as if she was conscious of the good sensation it produced in us.

Cursed be these walls!

"Shout! Shout!"

He drives me crazy. What can I... The radio. Yes, let's switch the radio on. There it goes. Mmmm. No way! Louder? Nothing to do...

"It's three in the morning, brother. Why are you shouting like this? I want to sleep. Can I not? Let me lie down and try not to hear you."

"Close your eyes, Akli, and try to sleep... close the eyes..."

Impossible. It is even worse with the radio voices. Off!

"RUN! RUN! Let me help you brother. Let me shout with you. RUN! RUN! I don't even know who should run. Who is running, brother? Who would run at three in the morning? Whose soul are you calling, brother? We are alone here. You and I. Me and you. A wall between us. Calm down and try to sleep or whatever. Hear - if you are not tired of it - the night's silence. That's it, brother... Silence. A whisper. Huuuuuuush! Close your eyes. I close mine. A whisper. Huuuuush! Run! Let him run. Let the world run. Let the dream run, brother."

"*Mashahu...* Once upon a time..."

That voice again. Let it make way into my soul.

4

"Mashahu..."

I hear it. I feel it, sweetly, swiftly whispering. *Mashahu...*

2

"RUN! RUN! FASTER! FASTER! THE RIVER! GO TO THE RIVER! FASTER!"

We knew the area quite well. We grew up there. It was there that our troops had been surrounded and were almost totally wiped out. We were fifteen men. Only five survived that intense and barbarous fighting. The helicopters flew at treetop height and were shooting us down, one by one.

"RUN DOWN TO THE RIVER!" yelled Rabah, waving his gun, almost blowing my brain out. The bullets around us were buzzing like fast-attacking killer bees. The earth seemed to be shaking under our feet. Our chests were shivering.

"GRENADES! GET DOWN!"

Another raid. Explosions punched dust and earth into our faces and several times. I was sure this was my last moment. The air was stuffy. The frightening buzzes didn't stop. We were trapped. Rabah's knee was injured; he could hardly walk. We were all fleeing as fast as our strength could allow it. Fear mingled with the anger of knowing that we had been sold down the river. But who could rat on us? Fear mixed with the past undergone memories; fear mixed with the feelings of incapacity to get out unscathed from that ambush. A raging sprint between the trees and the rocks. Down the river, and along the stream, I dragged myself. I walked on bloated corpses mixed with cut down branches and trunks. Blood floods. I felt half-awake, half-asleep, drifting along the stream. I floated, sadly, endlessly, breathlessly, like a machine, hearing the silenced woods' sounds. I left behind my companions. Rabah and I were both behind a rock.

"Let's split up and meet the others down the river." He went left and I went right. Whilst running, I felt something hot penetrating my leg. I didn't stop. I kept fleeing. Then I heard a scream. Whose scream was that? It wasn't mine. Rabah's! He shrieked. An otherworldly shriek. I heard the buzzes around me and saw how the bullets rammed the ground. I couldn't go back. I kept running. I put my hand down onto the place where I was hit. Blood. I was bleeding, but I didn't feel the pain. My other hand was tightly holding my gun.

"You can't go back! Don't stop running!"

Don't look behind you. Better run than be killed! Better run than being both killed. Better die than surrender! Hold those tears for now! No use!

I didn't look behind. I didn't cry. Half-conscious, I plunged into the water. The fast stream took my body down, down, down.

"I should have stayed. I should have helped him!" I closed my eyes. Then, suddenly, a swift chill ran down my spine. Is it death's hand caressing me? I felt weak. So weak. I opened my eyes. It's not the time to die. I couldn't hear the helicopters anymore.

"Rabah is dead."

Was all this real? The stream was dragging me faster and faster. Where? I didn't know. A pain on my arm aroused. My brain was flustered. My vision blurred. I fainted.

"Akli! Akli!" A woman's voice awakened me.

I felt pain in my arm and leg. I opened my eyes. I couldn't move. I saw a bandage around my arm and another on my leg.

"You are safe, my brother," She added.

It was her. Saliha. Our unit's nurse.

"Rab…" I tried to say.

But Rabah was gone. He had already joined the other world. I closed my eyes. I felt pain deep in my soul. Deeper than what my tears could express. Rabah's life was a chopped bud. I mourned him because he was my companion, my confident, my role model, my brother. We were fifteen, but only five survived. We were young and fresh. We were thrown to life's serious course before even understanding it. We were aware of the consented sacrifice, sometimes without measuring its deep consequences. We were young, but our spirits weren't about charming or flirting with girls, although our age was that of love and adventures. We did not have time to play, entertain or amuse ourselves. It was time to fight. Fight for our country. Fight for our dignity.

"Twenty-six years, Rabah. Your twenty-six springs were ripped away by the French bullets. They were ripped away in the name of civilisation! In the name of fraternity, equality...bla bla bla. You could have survived that bloody ambush. You should have survived it. We were close to the liberation day, Rabah. If only you had waited a few more months, you would have survived; if only we had held onto our yearning to see our families a few more weeks, we could, all together, have made it and be back home and stay there forever. But we couldn't know what fate had in spare. We wanted to visit them for at least a tiny moment. And so, to grasp the distant glances of the father, the fine and learned movements of the mother, the smiles of the brothers and sisters; their voices, their embraces, their tears, their words. To grip, hastily, all those scenes and live them again and again, once hidden in the *maquis*. To consider again those faces, hear their words, their voices, miles away between the bushes and the rocks. To relive those scenes with nostalgia."

Driven by the instinct of survival, we couldn't even afford a moment of happiness that a gathering with our families would have given us. Such are the war's conditions. Our plan seemed unshakable. It couldn't fail. We knew the area nook by nook, inch by inch. But as soon as we heard the helicopters getting closer, we knew that we were sold. Who could do that? None other but Qiyas. We were hiding in the neighbouring woods when he came by on his donkey burdened with fagots. He saw us. He was the only one who saw us and exchanged greetings with some of our men. Who else could do that?

Rabah was our commander. He was a political commissar. He had abandoned his wife and his two daughters and joined the resistance movement. He hadn't seen his family for more than five years. How many difficult paths and impossible roads had he capsized? How many dangers, how much swaggering in the forests and mountains of Djwahra, Palestro and Thazruth? How many risks did we take? We never gave up or even thought of giving up. In those days, an oath was an oath, a commitment was a commitment! In those days, our country needed us, needed our word and our sacrifice. We said: "Here we are! In the name of these mountains, we shall triumph or die!"

"Rabah was foolish!" his wife Fatima told me once with tones of soreness. "He wanted the independence? See what we are up to now? Look, where is he today? Dead. Forgotten. And look at us! Me and his own daughters! Not even a decent roof under the wavering flag of this country for which he died!"

Rabah, oblivion engulfed your memory. "Forgotten," said your wife. "Do we not, in this land, possess the ability of burying the good and brave people? We indeed bury them, three times. Physically first, then in our memories, and finally, in the memories of our heirs. Do we not, in this land, have the ability of attributing honours to traitors and turncoats? Go and see their names! Yes! Traitors and *harkis'* names, engraved on marble slabs adorning the facades of the schools and the institutions of the state. Shame on them! They buried your bodies, then your names and memory."

We had made an oath towards the supreme cause: Freedom. We sacrificed everything for this land. Everything... What are the remains of that oath today? Words. Useless words. Words used to dazzle our children. What remained after the liberation is sorrow, the immense sorrow, the profound sorrow of war. Furthermore, the deep sorrow of having survived. We didn't expect any privileges or honours. We only wanted to live, free. Countless ordinary men and women rose against the enemy for no other reason other than that of living in dignity. We were afraid, horrified.

10

After the liberation, things had not quietened. The struggles' branches had not ceased swirling. We won the war, but not justice. Think carefully. Look at the present day. Look at our existence: pain, bitterness and despair. No relief! Justice had not been won. We won the war, but injustice, cruelty and inhuman savagery won too. Look carefully and think. Can't you perceive the truth? Instead of healing the wounds, we put back the daggers into the wounds, and stabbed unceasingly. Instead of healing the wounds, we added, and are still tallying other wounds. Is it useful to speak about the psychological scars? Those scars are to remain, forever.

But why am I thinking about that now? I prefer letting go of these thoughts. Thinking of these things throws me into so much torment and sadness. I don't want to ruminate about all this again.

Rabah was an excellent flute player. Out from the reeds along the river, he fabricated one. He spent hours playing cheerful tunes, or sad but harmonious ones. We were in need of some entertainment, mainly in between our missions, in time of rest. We thus used to improvise little parties. We danced, clapped hands and sang. Rabah used to play his instrument whilst some of us clapped and others played drums on the empty water gourds that we carried on the back of our donkey.

I just have to close my eyes and see all this. I just have to close my eyes and see Rabah. He was confident. He had achieved a fair balance between well-mannered self-esteem and irreproachable respect for others. Yes, I can see him. He seems delighted. He is blowing into the flute. He is smiling and seems happy to have a break from all the tumult we are going through. Blowing into that flute brings a sweet and melancholic pleasure - pleasure that swallows us into a trance within which our emotions of gladness and sadness arise and mix. A banquet of sensations. Let's dance then! Put aside those guns for a moment. Use your hands. Clap! Sing even if you don't follow

11

the rhythm! Let's dance, smile, sing, laugh before undertaking the arduous paths of fight. Even among the horrors of war, we knew how to create spiritual beauty to make it - war - less brutal and sadistic.

I still remember all those moments although forty years tried to wash them out. I sometimes recall them to the slightest detail.

"You are forgotten, Rabah. Fatima's tears wouldn't do anything for your memory. You left her a few months after you had married. You left her and went up to fight the French. She often repeats the words "I'm married to this country," which you told her before leaving her. Was it a naïve statement or a solemn oath? But what happened after all those years of fighting?

"Tomorrow's enemies are worse than today's enemies," you asserted once. How could you predict that? How could you know what was going to happen? I was a dreamer, a utopian? Didn't we share the same dreams of freedom? Did we fight with the consciousness that our fight's fulfilments will be robbed? Was our achievement a disgraceful success? A respectable failure? You were a clever man, Rabah. You didn't only teach us how to hold a gun but also instructed us about what was happening around us."

The enemy, in 1956, launched their 'Terre Brûlée', Scorched Earth operation, then 'Operation Jumelles', Twin operation. The napalm and fire had burnt our fields. People were obliged, a gun pointed to their heads, to chop down or put fire to their olive-trees with their own hands. The olive trees, which they had inherited from their parents, who had themselves, inherited them from their parents. The olive trees they kept safe from the Ottoman's greed. Hundreds of fighters were killed because of the 'bleuite' virus. They were suspected to be - wrongly or truly - collaborators. The psychological weapon is the worst. Colonel Amirouche was clever enough not to be fooled by the French commanders, but why did he order to kill

12

so many fighters? Abbane, the revolution's genius and restructurer, in 1958, was assassinated by those self-proclaimed freedom fighters based at the Moroccan border. They were enjoying the luxury offered by the King whilst we were suffering hunger and cold in our forests and mountains. Who trapped the best remaining revolution leaders, Amirouche and Lhewas, and left them to the colonial forces? Wasn't it those snakes that were established at the Moroccan border? The same snakes that, some days after the liberation, crawled towards the capital to build their nest. And we, the naïve, famished ordinary fighters, we just had the silliness of dreaming. We were dreaming of freedom, of the beautiful days amid our families, the stomach full and the body warm.

"Ah Rabah! Lucky you! You are lucky because you ought not to endure the ugliness our land is experiencing. Lucky, the thousands of fighters who were killed! Lucky them, they aren't here to endure today's sufferings. Yesterday's enemies were strangers, and whatever the level of inhumanity they reached, we could, with unforgivable indulgence, put up with it: They weren't from us. What about today's enemies?"

"Do you remember, Rabah, when we were detained in that prison? 'Is it possible to forget that?' you would you have said. Can one forget the electric wires clutching the nipples, the ears or the testicles? Can one forget those drunken litres of soapy water? We were gathered like sheep in that dark, stinking room. We were packed, naked, for several days and nights trembling from the cold. Sssssssss! I feel my whole body shiver."

When, for the umpteenth time, Le Peine put those electric wires to my testicles and nipples, I felt the blood getting cold into my veins. It was as if my body ran out of blood. My body was lacerated. I didn't feel the blood anymore. I sensed something strong within me. An inconceivable, indescribable feeling. I remained on that special table, chained, naked, stinking of piss and blood. Then, when the pain came back, Le Peine's words and insults turned slowly into burbles. He

13

shouted, increased the electrical shocks… My body answered him with an unremitting flickering. My mouth open, dry. No slobber, no word. Losing his nerves, he then started beating me, slapping me like a mad man. I fainted several times. I was unconscious for hours. And delirious. I was close to death, far from life. I opened my eyes and I saw his face. He was, every day, well shaved and perfumed. He put a special perfume that I still recognise whenever I smell it. The scent of his perfume, whenever it came through my nose, was a slight moment of freshness in that smelly room. Whenever I smelled it, it relaxed me a bit. It was like getting drunk with some strong potion. Le Peine seemed neurotic about his looks. Always tidy and checking for any probable dirt. He always stepped into the room in a fine and proud attitude. A gentleman. He was nice-looking, but I never noticed a smile on his face. Le Peine's face never left me. It will never leave me either. He still fills my dreams and nightmares, paralysing me on some night. I make the strenuous effort to free myself, to get away, but an unsustainable force cements me to my bed. I often jump, bolting, sitting upright on my bed, drenched in sweat, tears and sometimes, urine. Some other times, I scream, struggling, waving my arms against… nothing. Against the past.

Without any notion of war techniques, I joined the liberation movement under Rabah's orders. I was sixteen. Rabah was nineteen. At that age, we were already aware of what was happening around us. On our austere mountains, we reached majority at a very early age. I was already in charge of the little cattle that we had, at the age of twelve. The school of life brings us to maturity faster than any other school. At the school of life, the teachers are our parents, the elders, our friends, our enemies, nature, our village assemblies and paths, hunger, misery.

I had never held a weapon in my hands before. How was I going to go through that? War. War is synonymous with death. Did I realise what I was about to throw myself into? I don't think so. Yet, I had been politically conscious from a very early age, owing to Rabah's father, Ammi Ali. Rabah had inherited his father's bravery, intelligence and strategy. It was under the orders of the son that I met the father again. We used to work together at Fino's estate. Fino was a *pied-noir*. He inherited his property from his father, a colonial farmer, a settler, brought by the French after colonization in 1830. The land was taken by force from the true owners. The *pied-noirs*, encouraged by the French administration, took the place of the owners and turned the latter into the workforce often abused and inhumanly treated. Ammi Ali, fed up with Fino's injustices, gave him an unforgettable correction. Then he vanished, swallowed by the earth. Ammi Ali had burnt Fino's barn and fled.

"I joined the revolution," he told me, when I met him again. Ammi Ali defined himself as a communist, a Muslim communist. That's definitely something I never understood. However, since it did not seem to cause any harm, it was fine.

I was so pleased to find them both, the father and the son. Being at their side dissipated my fears and gave me enough confidence to fight. Rabah was never stingy in advice or help. He overshadowed my first steps, one by one. He taught me how to shoot, how to provide with first aid, how to coordinate an attack. I wondered how he could know all that. Where did he learn it?

"Like you, I was taught by some other fighters," he affirmed. "Beaten by the same stick, we must help each other, like brothers," he added.

Our common enemy strengthened our brotherhood. We were a family. Likewise, a family must stand up together. We had to start fighting and there was no other way than guerrilla strategy.

"Attack and save your skin! Attack, take the loot and run away."

Our armed groups were outnumbered. Compared to the second strongest army in the world, we - badly equipped and ill-prepared groups - did not have any chance to triumph. Heart and strategy were our only weapons.

Rabah was friendly with everyone. A natural trait that he preserved even in rough circumstances. He ensured fair and equitable treatment to all in the group, which positively influenced the fighters, enhancing respect and humility. He never behaved as an imposing repressive leader. We shared the hardships, the little joys, and our goals. He consulted everyone in the group about the tiny details concerning any attack plan.

"What didn't we share, Rabah?"

We talked about our worries and our dreams; we told jokes, made up others, we laughed together, and shared, when we were lucky enough to have them, a plate of couscous, a loaf of bread, a cigarette. Long walks during days and nights from a region to another. Together, we helped the population of this or that village. Elsewhere, we delivered speeches to gain people's support with regard to our cause. When we were resting, whether in the forest or the woods, we would tell popular tales or try to solve riddles.

Along rivers and up the hills, into the bushed and between the trees, to the top of mountains, we sung in one voice:

"Oh mother, dear, be patient, don't cry!
For you, we will die
Keep hope in your heart alive."

We also recited poems written for our girlfriends. Imaginary girlfriends, of course! Hahaha! It was a good exercise to avoid the torturing days of hunger and fear whilst we waited for things to calm down or waited for new orders or plans to execute. How did we manage to survive?

Poetry! Naïve poems for imaginary girlfriends. Hahaha! At that time, we were not like the soldiers that we see on TV nowadays. We didn't receive or send letters to our wives or girlfriends. We were, for the most of us, illiterate, and the recited poems were purely coming from our heads, following the tradition of Si Muhand U Mhand. An amazing poet indeed! He used to speak in verses. Rebel and troubadour, Si Muhand U Mhand travelled from one village to another telling poetry, exploring life and human nature. He walked very long distances, from Kabylia to Tunisia. His poems, even the wicked ones, never written until recently, survived thanks to the villagers' memories transmitted from mouth to ear, from one generation to another. I never managed to learn more than a poem or two. I wonder how he could speak in verses! From time to time, along with Rabah and the other brothers, we recited some of his erotic poems too.

"Oh, my heart, rejoice
When she came to dance
She bent over to take off her anklets
Her tits are apples
Musk she smells

17

Her hair is a brace
Wardiya, a morning star
Everything I will dare
Tonight let's take off the pants"

"Do you remember, Rabah? We laughed a lot about our improvisations. Was I not the French lover? Hahaha! 'French lover,' you used to tease me. 'French lover' because my love story with Martine was still vivid in our memory."

"Rabah, you never, not once, complained about anything. You were sacrificing body and soul without lamenting or complaining. How many dangers did you face? Also, during those gruelling nights and days in jail, enduring torments, you never showed a sign of weakness or relinquishment."

"During our detention, despite the collective torture we faced, you were silent. Deeply silent. Dignity did not abandon you even in merciless conditions. You never screamed or cried. You remained quiet, occasionally throttling your groans. I noticed that because you were the only one who didn't show any sign of suffering. Rabah, you were a man of unwavering faith and unusual conviction."

Everyone's help was needed to continue the struggle until the end. The end: death or victory. Our motivation was simply that of human beings refusing submission, refusing to be slaves in their own country. Our fight was motivated by our mere will to live free, to live in dignity and see our children afford a decent life on the land of their ancestors.

We, on this land, have been eternally revolted. Northern Africa seems to be cursed by its Goddess, Gaya, who seems powerless and unable to obstruct the way to the waves sent by the Greek Gods, the Roman emperors, the Viking Gods, the Arab princes, the Ottoman masters, the French imperialists, and then the successive corrupt regimes we have. Northern Africa accepted their different contributions, but never abdicated to any civilizational nor cultural substitution that wanted to corrode its being and deny its true identity, which

18

had existed 3000 years before Jesus' arrival. Go ask those sculptured rocks full of signs and symbols! It's not I who says it. It's science and knowledge. True knowledge, free from ideology and alienation.

What led us to rebel were our wounds. The wounds of our souls. Could we remain in our houses and swallow the inflicted humiliation? No. Obstinate and full of faith, we walked despite the obstacles. We walked through life, indomitable, trying to reinvent hope; the hope of our brothers and sisters; the hope of our forefathers; the hope of a torn motherland. Fervent hopes! We tried to recreate spring. Nevertheless, spring's path is better braved when righteousness is our travel stipend and justice our ambition.

It was not at school that we learned about sacrifice and freedom. We sucked the very principles of justice and freedom from our mothers' bosoms, transmitted from a generation to another. Aren't we free men? Thus, we ought to fight for justice and freedom. We fought because we, free men, wanted to be, no less and no more than free men.

I can still see, hardly opening my eyes, sweat beading on Rabah's tarnished face. His eyes were almost dislodged from their orbits. I felt a burning fire within my stomach. All the other organs were cold. Lifeless. I was at the doors of death. Rabah was facing me. I saw, at disparate moments, his silhouette. Suspended between the sky and the ground, my hands were bleeding, and my toes, the only parts of me touching the soil, were inert.

"Would I walk again?" I thought. Several times, I found myself screaming and shouting uselessly. But he was silent. Rabah remained calm. Rabah, you used to say, "The pain of a man is neither a scream nor tears. It is a silent complaint." Pain... a silent complaint...

I tried, in a herculean effort, to open my hefty eyelids to distinguish those half dead perched bodies. I saw their gloomy, disfigured faces, mouths half-open, dry lips, eyes closed or partially open. I looked towards Rabah. When my myopic eyes recognised him, I closed them for a moment then I re-opened them instantly to be sure that it was him. I looked at him, a mirror of my own agony.

How can I forget that smile drawn on his face? I was moaning. After a while, Rabah, with a deep smile, wonderfully fighting against pain, spoke to me from the depths of his being.

"We must thank God!" he said.

"Thank God?" I was lost in my own thoughts.

"Thank God!" My unique question was: "When is this suffering going to end?" They were abiding. I prayed God for death. Death was attainable, more than any other expectation. Death seemed to be the best remedy.

"Kill me!" I sobbed several times whilst the wires were burning my balls. "Finish it all up!" A minute was equivalent to hours.

In other moments, I tried to put forward lovely memories of my family.

"Think of something lovely, Akli," I frenetically repeated to myself, my body shaking, pulsating. Blank. As if during my whole life, I had never lived a sweet moment. Nothing was coming to my mind. I looked for my mother's face, my brother's, my father's, my sisters'... I couldn't see them. Emptiness. I could hardly see Martine's face, her smile. Martine, my first and unique love. Blank. My memory was dead. I was defeated. The creator! I had even forgotten my creator! Nonetheless, Rabah, who embodied my conscience, brought God into my heart. Can faith be of any help? God matters weren't really my favourite thoughts. But did we have much choice in those circumstances? Nothing else than spiritual force. And, in this life, if we need some hope, let's hope that God will be of any help. We, wretched beings, should hold on to something. That thing is God.

But in those situations, should we thank him or ask for his help and mercy?

"Thanks God! He added.

"We thank God," I mumbled with no conviction.

Then, as if he guessed my questionings, he whispered:

"We thank God because we are still alive. Because he gave us the force to accomplish our duty towards our land. Because he, right now, is giving us the courage to resist. Because we, all gathered here, are sharing the same pain, the same chains. Nobody is suffering alone. How would one have felt if he were alone? Nothing is worse than suffering alone, my brothers."

Truth came out of Rabah's mouth. It alleviated our pain a bit and gave us more tenacity. We were suffering, but together. We were listening to each other's moaning, glancing at each other. There was between us, an undeclared competition to stifle our pains, to never give up, and be an example for the others. Alone, one could have easily crumbled.

"May God preserve us from despair," he declared.

His words injected into our hearts, courage and confidence. You see why I adulate this man? You see why, although more than fifty years have passed, I still remember all these details? I learned a lot from him. There was no despair among us when Rabah was there.

Despair! Despair is the cause of our misfortunes, yesterday's and today's. Despair. The cause of our misfortunes and those of our children. Despair gave birth to fanaticism, terrorism, violence, banditry, prostitution, corruption, boat people...

"See, Rabah, what are we up to? We fought until the last day. We fought even after the liberation. But are we really independent? We had our liberation but we didn't have any independence. No rest. Permanent instability. Some people had spent days and nights celebrating the new fate, others returned to their wretched hamlets and cultivated their wretchedness until now, others hunted and killed the traitors or whatever they called them, others chased the settlers and their children, others seized palaces, wealthy houses, properties, and some

21

others got key positions through falsifications and bribes. Revenge became a rule. What we lived and are living today is a consequence of our ignorance and mutual hate."

Who would have imagined that the day would come where we would be witness to barbarities? How can a brother shed his brother's blood? And when? A few weeks after the liberation, a few years after the liberation, and even decades after the liberation. In fact, everything was going wrong even during the revolution. And our dreams ended up as illusions. Illusions patiently and passionately eternised. Absurd!

"Everything was wrong from the beginning. The oath, Rabah, our oath is betrayed. Today, confusion is set as a fatality and frenzy bonds our souls to stubbornness. Is there worse than an imbecility heightened by stubbornness?"

4

It seems that my neighbour is sleeping deeply.

"Snore! I can hear you from here. Snore! It's better than your screams and shouting. Better than banging on the walls."

Let me see what time it is. As if he did it on purpose. Five in the morning.

"You awakened me from my deep slumber, pulled me out of my dreams, then you slept!" Let me switch the radio on again. My unique companion. It is a pleasurable companionship, it cheers me up and, more often than not, lends my spirit wings to take me out of these walls. But it also fuels my frustration and stirs up my anger. This country's media is an instrument of propaganda and stinking populism. I already broke one. I furiously smashed it against the walls. I got up on that cursed morning and turned the radio on. The news presenter, in a soft voice, announced the new presidential measure. I was baffled, nailed to my bed.

"A new bill will be put to a vote," she said.

A bill pressing for the forgiveness of terrorists will be put to national popular vote. After a decade of bloodshed, the president wants peace and security all over the country... bla bla bla. They have the art of prettifying the ugliest of the deeds and facts. How? Very easy! They take some verses from the holy book... *Bismillah*... Allah, the almighty says... some words from the prophet's sayings... a solemn tone on TV and on the radio, glowing newspaper articles, special courses at school and, above all, sermons, sent on purpose by the ministry of religious affairs, to be bawled at the country's mosques. Done!

"Applauses, ladies and gentlemen! Amen, oh, Allah's believers! Vote and let the killers get down from the mountains. Vote for Allah's sake and thank the providence that has sent you the Neo Prophet who bears pardon in the heart. Look at him! He loves you. He taps his hand on his chest, his heart. Worship him! He is sent by Allah to lead this country. Those who protest against his laws, they are moved by a foreign hand, Allah's enemies, Satan's children, the enemies of this land, friends of the Jews, they must be repressed, sent to the dungeon, hung in public!"

Nevertheless, behind the President, there are nests of snakes from the mighty army order. Who doesn't know that? And do you know what? They create wind, rain and blood whenever they want. Allah, Allah himself, the one they use and exploit whenever they want, is less mighty than they are in this land. He seems unable to stop them. And now what? They press for a new bill to pardon the killers who committed horrible crimes. Did the killers ask for pardon? Did the snakes, wriggling for power, negotiate with the killers? Do they want to fool the people? Are people afraid? Manipulated? People were bored of a long decade of bloodshed. People are fed up with politics. They hate politics, it leads to blood and hatred. People don't vote anymore but the polls were in favour of the new law. The "Yes" has got the coveted percentage. Even the administration, commanded and manipulated by the snakes to cheat solemnly and secretly the polls, did not believe the results. The results it intended to fabricate.

Thanks to the prison principal, I got a new radio two days later. I didn't dare turning it on at the beginning, but I couldn't refrain my hand from switching it on.

The same radio speaker, with a soft voice, announced that 2200 terrorists would be released in the name of Allah, the Prophet and the "Saint President". 2200 killers will be freed from prison and a call, through mosques and TV, was made to those who are still gone astray to get down from the mountains to reintegrate the society again, no worries, no fear for their security, the state will guarantee it. The state could not guarantee its population's safety, so it guarantees the safety of those who were threatening the safety of the state and that of its population. That's a modern invention never found in any political system.

"Rabah, what would you have done if you had lived all this absurdness? You might have done what I did. But you are dead. I apparently have failed my challenges. Not even death wants me."

I am thrown here like a criminal... Yes, I killed! I killed a man, but I am not a criminal. I am not a terrorist. It seems better to be a terrorist. If I were a terrorist, I would have been set free by now! But I am not a terrorist. I killed a terrorist! And when you kill a terrorist, they don't set you free. They put you in a cell until your whole being becomes hollowed.

I killed a monster in truth and fairness. I have a clear conscience. Would I repeat it if the same circumstances would take place? Yes. If I killed under other circumstances, I wouldn't have mourned being cloistered between these four walls.

But today what enrages and saddens me the most is that these criminals are reintegrating their work, enjoying the privileges given by the state and roaming in the streets, provocative and proud. It tortures me.

"What would you have done, Rabah? Nothing! Would you have fled? A lot of people fled to France! Isn't it an irony? The same country we fought against for ages! And now, thousands are seeking refuge there. They are asking for asylum there. Others fled to Tunisia, Morocco, Canada..."

My thoughts torment me; and the remorse of everything taps my head and poisons my days and nights. What would a prisoner in his cell do, apart from spinning, stretching out, thinking, thinking, thinking? Dreaming about the sun, spring, the little paths in the village, the olive trees, the fig trees, the brooms. Loiter about through the alleys of the village, sip a tea or a coffee on the terrace of Thadarth's café, play dominoes. Get up early and take the ewe to graze, listen to the dawn's fighting and singing birds, watch the clouds in the sky, the trees, the brooks, nature, freedom, air, life. But all this does not belong to me anymore. I don't belong to it anymore. I would have liked ending this up at once. But I can't. I don't dare. And if I wanted to, how would I do it?

I'm in a hopeless search for the type of peace that a man only finds when he evolves in his ordinary environment, among his folks, in the village where he was born. Addressing neighbours, friends, family. Walk or wander freely between the houses. Smell, at the door of every house, the tasty different flavours floating out of the walls or chimneys. Stand for a little chat in front of this or that neighbouring house. Lay under the olive or fig tree and observe nature. Arriving to Thajmath, the village assembly, sit down with the elders, remembering the beautiful days when the village used to gather and solve its problems by itself under the aura of the Thadarth wise men. Thajmat stood as an institution itself. There, the decision could be made to clean the village or the cemetery, help a family in need, give shelter to a stranger, punish that man because of his offense to that woman. Punishment is never corporal but economical. All of that is done in a democratic way. Hands up. The Thajmath leader can't decide anything alone. And the Imam is nothing more than a simple citizen. People are free to talk, but humbly and respectfully. I miss those days. The best days ever! Childhood and youth days. Go once a week to Thizi Ghenif's market. Thizi Ghenif, The Hill of Pride, and meet old friends. Sit at a table on the terrace of a café, sipping a mint tea, facing the high mountains of the Djurdjura. Breathing the fresh air of a spring morning, and looking at the passers-by, going down or up. Observe their glances, sad and absent glances. Unhappy and preoccupied. And on the foreheads' furrows you can read: "Where have our dreams been diverted to?" People do not dream anymore. They lost the ability to hope. How? They were for a long time submitted to speeches full of promises. A lot of promises. Nice words. Only words, with a lot of beautiful adjectives. Then, nothing. Cynicism taught us hatred and thus, we became unable to love. We transmit this from one generation to another. Our children inherited hatred and the incapability of love. This is why they are violent and an easy prey to the whirling extremisms. Terrorism, suicide, self-immolation, drugs, banditry. It is a response to the diverted dreams. Ours and theirs. I don't question why they flee the country. Let them go and recover their dreams and loves under hopeful skies. Today, no one believes in promises. No one trusts those words and all those plans widely spread to subdue people and suck the energy left in them. Suck the energy left in our hearts, but mainly suck the huge energy that the soil of this country is providing. Nevertheless, the Western forces provide the snakes with help and speeches too. How our snakes like those sweet words pronounced by the Western governments! They long for them and do everything to hear them. And after that, they tell people: "See! See how we are good, and caring about democracy, human rights, welfare? Even the West salutes our efforts! Applaud!"

However, the nice words spoken and the promises made turned into open threats and brutal insults. And if this doesn't please you, you will receive threats, be harassed by the judges and the police officers, or thrown into a cell for years.

I laugh at our misfortune! I laugh at my misfortune too! I laugh! I am trapped between four walls, formulating nostalgic wishes. Is it the natural attitude of a prisoner? To reconsider all that he lived since the innocent days of childhood? Remember every moment of his life, happy or unfortunate! See again all the faces he met; all the smiles, the tears, the quarrels he witnessed. Reconsider everything…again, every detail. Imprisonment is double. First, it is the body living in a reduced space. Then, the worst part, it is thoughts drilling the spirit and racking it incessantly. I sometimes feel myself plunged into a deep, bottomless abyss, a hallucinating space, and I feel that my days, hours, minutes, waste away quicker than usual. It is true that pain makes one get older quickly? These walls are killing me. Slowly. These walls are torturing and consuming me.

5

I don't know why they repeat the same thing at every newscast. Go! Damn! Switch it off! No difference with their television. The only thing you are good at is singing the eulogies of a deceitful system. A mafia. It is an insult to the concepts of presidency and government to say that we have such institutions. We have nothing but a mafia. All those presidents, senile ministers, are mere comedians in the reign of falsehood and hypocrisy. The radio, like the TV, dedicates series to them, for the length of their mandates. They follow their parades, their shows, diffuse their talks, their imaginary realisations celebrated by blows into the *lghita*[*1] and onto the bendir. Their outstanding achievement has secured their positions for decades, and they rob, rob, rob. And if ever there is a change, they just shift from one seat to another. How? If you are a minister of education, you will be, in the next government, a minister of territory management or religious affairs. Some ministers are irremovable, not thanks to their skills, but to their vast knowledge of manipulation and bigotry. Thanks also to their ass licking abilities and their full obedience to the snakes' orders. Even the Pope resigned and quit because of illness and weakness, but our Popes, they are stuck to their posts as properties and not duties to accomplish, escaping from accountability, and going on without dignity and pride of serving the country.

Our little Napoleon, ill and worn out, is seventy-six, the ministers are about seventy, whilst seventy per cent of the population is under thirty. Is there bigger mockery than that? I sometimes hear on the radio, the age of other countries' presidents and ministers. Let me laugh! Laugh at our cynicism!

---

[1] Lghita: traditional folkloric flute.

The unique use of TV and radio is to broadcast their propaganda and alienate the population's minds with their cheap and silly programmes.

After years of Western programmes, they are now inundating us with those dubbed Egyptian, classical Arabic Mexican, and Turkish series and movies. They speak about national identity. Are we then Orientals? Arabs? Arabs from the Arabic peninsula? How is that possible? Aren't we Africans? Yes. No doubt the Arab invasion, like all the other invasions, left its mark, but it cannot replace the true North African identity. The Amazigh identity. Amazigh, the free and noble man. And those who pretend to be democrats and modernists whilst denying these countries, North African countries, their essence, languages, culture and heritage, are stupid and hypocrites!

On their TV, radio and newspapers, everything is nice, and life is beautiful and full of colours, and the country is successfully accomplishing the biggest projects ever, thanks to Allah and His servants on earth.

Well! I may be ungrateful to my companion! Is this little radio not the only thing keeping me company during my life's slow and painful moments? Turn it on again.

"I am sorry, dear. You know as well as I do that you are not the one to blame. You are a mere transmitter of voices. You are not the cause of my anger. I just don't want to turn dull and sluggish. You know that you are definitely not responsible. You are my dearest companion. It's not easy to be lonely. You know that."

Sometimes, whilst listening to those voices, I close my eyes and try to see their faces, their clothes, their complexion. When I hear them speaking, I almost feel their presence. I put a face and a character to each voice. I know by heart every voice's name and I can name them, voice by voice. Listening to the radio is a unique experience. It's so different from other media. One's imagination is stimulated and grows lush, not restricted to the director's visions, like in the movies. These voices draw smiles on our faces, provoke us, stimulate our deepest feelings and sometimes wet our eyes with tears.

God! What a silly lovely attachment I have to this little device! Without it, I would have been cut from all that is happening outside. The first weeks I came here, I didn't want to know anything. Removed from everything. Everyone. I didn't want to talk to anyone. I didn't want any human contact. I had my bed, my table, and these four walls. The prison's guardians wanted to exchange some formalities with me since they heard about my bla bla bla story, but I didn't even respond to their compassionate smiles. I was repugnant, I know. But I didn't want people to feel sorry for me. The prison principal often came to my cell, wanting to address me. But I couldn't tell much. He showed eagerness whenever I needed something from him. No visits. Neither lawyers nor friends. I wasn't allowed to receive visits and that didn't hurt me. They wanted to punish me as much as they could, but I didn't mind. I didn't care. I lost my capacity to react, to act.

Here it comes again!

"Spit out the same news again! Vomit it up! Yes! For the umpteenth time, for more than twenty days now. 2200 terrorists! 2200 criminals! Call them repentant or whatever, they are terrorists, killers, criminals, rapists. Oh, yes! Helpful demagogy, they are not called terrorists anymore, they are "those who were misled, the penitents, the returnees to Allah's path. Waaaw! Nice, sympathetic words towards the killers!"

Their language changes as much as they change their socks.

"Just like that! Good God! After all they have done to this country? More than 200 000 heartlessly assassinated humans! Release them and call those who are still in their jihad to come back home. Allah! Allah! Peace is back! Little Napoleon can chill out and be proud of his success. Stop it! Stop complaining and talking about..."

Let me calm down and accept my condition.

31

"Ah dear Rebbi...Allah, Dieu, God or whatever..."

But... I can't! Oh the rage in my chest! I want to screaaaam to hell!

They speak about pardon and the values of Islam. Values of reconciliation and love. Values of shit! They drive me crazy! They use those values only when it suits them.

I know, I know... I should not mention anything .. I did what I did, that is all! I gave up everything, my time, my youth, my energy, my silly love... Everything for this country, for its children. Its children, I, who never had children but always considered the children of this country as mine. Nonetheless, am I not lucky? At least, I did not leave any helpless family member out, in need. No one to cry me. To cry my absence. I didn't leave any wife, a son or a daughter... Zira doesn't know me. She was too young and I doubt that she would remember me. What about her mother? Who knows if she is dead or still alive? It is undeniably not only my freedom that is chained and castrated between these walls, but also my dignity, my pride! If at least she had a tomb on which I could cry on. If at least I knew that she is dead, I would not have any more hope.

I'm moping about. I lost everything, even my dignity. Dementia grazes my soul. Am I not already insane?

"See, Rabah, how fate mocks me! I, imprisoned within the same walls that you and I have touched, caressed and hated. The same prison. I remember every tiny detail of our stay here. I feel the cold penetrating my bones. Our cell, Rabah, is ten meters away from here. Number 62. A perfect coincidence! 62. The date of our compromised independence. Nothing has changed except the colour of the walls and the experience of my detention. From March 5th 1957 until December 23rd 1958, our imprisonment had a taste of bravery, but today, mine has the taste of soar indignity. At that time, we counted the days, hour after hour, having but only two wishes: to be released and go back to fight, or to be killed and not suffer the torture any more. Death was flying over our bodies laid on a table or, for the most resistant ones, attached to a chair. Urine, sweat, blood, and sometimes shit smelled in the very basement under my cell. A humid and huge basement. I came back to face my torments again. The acrid and brackish smell of death prowled along the corridors whenever the prison wardens approached. Fear. Pride. Rats. Cockroaches. Smiles. Cries. Intense discussions. Regrets. Absent eyes. Absentmindedness. Desolation. Despair. Fading determination. Hunger. Thirst. Cold. Humiliation. Torture. Emptiness. Cold, cold, cold!"

Ah, my memories! If I could dig a grave and bury myself. Bury myself to avoid rambling on about my afflictions and my unbearable regrets. Ay! I am condemned to live the same things every day. To crush the same thoughts. Saying the same mind-numbing words. Saying the same things. I don't live any more. The fire in my soul burns me, engulfs me, devours me.

Cursed be that day! I was proceeding, after an intense night of thinking and analysis, towards the *gendarmerie* station to ask for a weapon to defend my home and the whole Thadarth. I was walking on air. I was ecstatic. I had a disproportionate confidence. An exuberant self-assurance. Driven by the weight of my own truth built by intense facts and legitimate arguments, I walked there.

As soon as he was informed of my visit, the brigade commander, Rombo, received me with the respect I deserved. I was well esteemed among all the villagers and the authorities. Am I not Dada Akli, the veteran? People were as kind with me as I was with them. I was old and we show a lot of respect to our elders. Nothing better than an irreproachable attitude and attentiveness can speak for a man.

Rombo shook my hand tightly. We sat down side by side. He did not dare to get to his luxurious chair. His face showed regret. A *gendarme* entered and put the coffee on the table. He was quick. Rombo looked at me, showing grief and said, "I'm sorry about what happened, Dada Akli".

I didn't reply. I barely nodded.

"I cannot understand how our country could end up like that," he added, serving the coffee.

"The snakes come out of our bellies," I answered. He nodded handing me a cup.

Then, after a sip, he asked me why I came to visit them.

"I want a weapon to defend my property and my village," I replied swiftly.

Whenever I remember that, I feel foolish.

Rombo almost jumped by surprise. I could read his thoughts. How could it be that a veteran, at that age, wants to take up arms himself and fight the terrorists? I did not wait for another question. Therefore, I told him my motivations without delay.

"I am in danger."

He looked at me acutely. Admiration? Consternation? He probably was torn between both.

"But you… "

"I am old and I cannot fight?" I interrupted him. "This is what you want to say? Since the state is unable to protect its citizens, must we accept to be killed by those dirty bearded monkeys? Will we stay home and wait for death? Stay home and question where the huge amount of money given to the defence ministry is going to? Do we have a choice, weak as we are? No. So, we need…we must protect ourselves. This is why I'm here. They want us to die…to kill each other in this war? Let's kill! Let's die! They have themselves created this war because of their stupidity and greed. Let it be blood and tears. We will die, but we will die with dignity and pride. It will not be useless. Let me just to quench my rage."

Rombo remained speechless. He could not believe what he had heard. No one else would have dared to say what I said. Fear and cowardice became an accepted natural truth in the country. Second nature, shall I say. If it were an ordinary citizen who said what I said, Rombo would have leapt from his seat, jumped over him, would have beaten him and would have sent him to jail.

I am a veteran and my legitimacy could protect me from many troubles. They listened to the smelly truths coming out from my mouth with a smile on their faces. If you have power, you may say whatever you want. If not, you will be beaten, jailed or killed. Silenced. So simple. That is how this part of the world functions. I never used my status to get any privilege but, in extreme situations, I explode and vomit my poison. Yes! The war was wanted. When and where do the snakes thrive? In opacity and secrecy. In war and time of fear. Creating a civil war was the best occasion to watch us kill each other; the best occasion for them to make swell their bank accounts through the oil and gas business; and the best occasion for them to get international support, then constrain us under their boots. As simple as that! That is how this part of the world functions.

Rombo was confused. He understood my bottomless wrath and the futility of answering me.

"I'll be right back," he said. He left and came back, handing me a form to fill out. Fortunately, I had brought all the required documents. Bureaucracy is part of the daily routine in this part of the world. A modern absurdity! Whenever you file for any project or for the renewing of any document, useless documents will be required in three or four copies. Why ask for an identity card and a birth certificate knowing that the former is issued after presentation and verification of the birth certificate? People are able to name one by one all the required documents required to have this or that card, this or that certificate. But then again, the biggest absurdity is the time it takes for your documents to be issued. You will be queuing up for hours and hours. Sometimes for days. Tossed about between an odious administrative officer, an irresponsible secretary and a tyrannical security agent, one descends into a downward spiral. You may spend a quarter of your life queuing up, the mind drained and the spirit weakened. But things are different if you know someone working where you want a document to be issued. Things are different also when you know someone who knows someone who works there. It's even better if he or she, the officer, the security agent, the secretary, is a family member. No problem at all. Your papers will even be sent to your house. No queue, no quarrels, no stress. But the most successful option is without doubt paying for a "coffee" and have your papers. For that you must contact a medium who in turn will contact an agent, a secretary or the officer. Not seen, not heard.

Rombo gave me a pen. I took the form, filled it in, signed it. Done! He went out again, returning a while later, a Kalashnikov in his hands.

"Russian, he said with pointless smugness, then handed it to me.

"Russian? Evil is evil," I wanted to say.

It seems that God created life with a lot of necessary evil. His cynicism went far. He gave enough intelligence to some insane humans to exterminate the others.

"Russian, Rombo! The Russians and the Americans in a speedy race fabricate arms and we, weak-minded, we import them to kill each other! Be proud, Rombo!"

I took the Kalashnikov. I looked at it. I was unable to express what was going through my head at that moment. I looked at Rombo and saw the serious expression on his face. He then gave a military salute. I am sure he never did so as sincerely as he did it that day. His face was solemn. His eyes were full of tears. I wonder how that drop of emotion could leak from a man like Rombo.

I put the gun on my shoulder and went out. My feelings were bewildered. I was neither happy nor sad. I cannot name the feeling I had at that moment. Time was running. Fast. I went back to Thadarth. My pace was steady. My destiny traced. Resistance.

Nonetheless, in front of the *gendarmerie* station, my memory was sparked. I remembered the first moments of my enlistment in the ranks of the Resistance Movement against the coloniser. I was sixteen. Those days were particular, different. I was happy. Happy to serve my country against a foreign enemy. Happy to follow the path of those men who resisted the Ottomans, the French and other heroes about whom poems and legends were composed and recited all over Kabylia. My mother used to learn them through Thadarth's women who recited them at the public fountain, at home or by the river where they used to wash the clothes.

At that time, I was unemployed. I had been working at Fino's farm but he fired me. An old friend of mine at Thadarth had contacted me through a Liaison Officer, Said-My-Book.

"The Liberation Front needs you," he wrote.

That was an omen. A good omen, occurring at the perfect time. A few days later, the Liaison Agent came back.

"I'm ready," I said with confidence. After the declaration of the revolution on the 1st November 1954, the French army became more hostile and inhumane. A lot of people were imprisoned; villagers were harassed and intimidated. At Thadarth, the French army installed their barracks on a juxtaposing hill. The cruel proceedings of the soldiers struck me so much. They were arrogant and insulting. They patrolled daily in Thadarth and the surroundings. Many times, they broke into houses, forcing the families out, beating the men, insulting the women, searching, shouting, breaking what they could break, and sometimes setting fire to the roofs. It enraged me. I, since then, grew to hate French soldiers. Hate led to a will for revenge. How many times did they come to Thadarth? They lined up Thadarth's men and women at the village assembly, questioning and threatening them. I remember how terrified and frenetic my mother was when we heard the vigils' voices warning Thadarth about the arrival of the French soldiers. She used to run as fast as she could to our little barn, take some chicken, sheep or donkey excrement and apply it on her clothes so that the French soldiers wouldn't approach her. That act became usual for young Thadarth women to avoid being raped by the French soldiers.

Jacqueline, Fino's wife, had already taken her two children, Martine and Julien, and went back to France where her family used to live. Mr Fino, after the outbreak of the revolution, became more suspicious than ever. Paranoid. We could read fear in his eyes and in his attitude. He was scared even of a mundane gaze from any worker. Any innocuous exchange of words between two workers would stir his imagination.

"You are plotting something against me!" He was afraid that we, his own workers, would overthrow him. His nervousness doubled when Ammi Ali put fire to his barn. It contained the hay of a whole season. He held all of us responsible and threatened us.

"I will bring the *gendarmes* here. They will pull your trousers down," he screamed.

The news and the rumours about attacks against Europeans in the whole country intensified his nervousness. His wife and children's unexpected departure was a hard blow. He was alone. Abandoned. Forlorn and terrified. He could have been friendly and win the sympathy of his workers. But, no. That wasn't a personality trait of his. So, he took the other way around. His wife, before she left, no longer tolerated his mood swings. She was openly opposed to him abusing his employees. They often fought. We could sometimes hear them from the neighbouring fields where we used to work.

'The old fox', as we used to call Mr Fino, held me responsible for all the ills weighing down on him. He never wanted me to get close to his family. Finding me sitting at their table was an outmost outrage. But the worst was when he discovered that his daughter was madly in love with me.

Some weeks after his wife and children left, he fired me. I was fifteen or so. At the age of fourteen, I had to provide for my whole family. Fourteen years old, I was already the head of my family. I had worked at Fino's for about two years. I was the only one receiving a proper monthly wage. My father was in bed, struck by an unknown illness. He had himself started working when he was a little kid.

"What on earth should I do?" I was unemployed. "Should I find another job or join the Resistance?"

Even if I had chosen to work, finding a job would have been difficult. What would I have worked in? I was a stupid and uneducated villager. Thanks to Jacqueline who gave me some lessons, I could speak and read French properly. I was reluctant because of my accent though.

"Should I go and look for work in another settler's farm?" I asked myself. "Shall I go to the city to seek for work?"

I rarely went to the nearby city and I knew no one there. I had no training, but I was able to do a lot with my hands, mainly the hardest tasks. I was strong enough for hard jobs. If I join the revolution, who will take care of the family? It was said that a small sum is given to the families of the active fighters.

"But this country needs me! The revolution needs me." After a lot of thinking and analysis, I was ashamed having questioned my path. The resistance was a commitment, a sacrifice. Fighting is love. The love of freedom. Love for my land. It is revulsion towards enslavement and dispossession.

A faint glow appeared. Whilst I was tortured by my thoughts, my two brothers who used to take care of our sheep and work the plot of land we had, decided to emigrate to France where there was work.

"Those who went to France are very well paid. They send money to their families every month," the rumours held. Should I go to France too?

The solution did not take much time to be encountered. Because the family was going through a period of crisis, my father, as usual, gathered us to talk. We altogether sat around his bed. He was pale and spoke in a cavernous voice. His eyes were penetrating. They were ageless. He could hardly move. Eating was almost an impossible task for him. We gathered around him, my mother standing in the room. My sister was already married. She was sixteen when she left the family nest.

"Your mother and I always wanted the best for you. Alas, I am of no use in this world anymore and if it weren't for your mother's care, I would have gone," he voiced.

My mother was crying silently.

"It's a good idea to send you both to France," he addressed my brothers. "Akli will be staying home with us".

I was in a dilemma.

"Go, my sons, may God be with you. May my prayers and those of your mother protect you."

Parents are sacred. Disobeying your parents is a huge offense. I thought about what my father had said.

"What shall I do?" I didn't want doubt to come back into my soul.

"I'm joining the resistance movement," I declared, getting the bad news out. They all looked at me. I blushed, but the determination I had in my heart did not falter.

For a while, my father did nothing but look at me penetratingly. He then turned his eyes towards the front door. His inability, due to his illness, was a lopsided embarrassment. I read on his face a patent gloominess about his condition. All at sea, my mother's eyes started wetting again. Her plan, begun since my childhood, was, by a wave of the hand, falling apart. To marry my cousin Dihya and take care of them. If I go up to the mountain to join the resistance, her project will be delayed, if not ruined. My brothers were surprised. Confused. Did my announcement unsettle their plan too? Were their convictions shaken? Did they feel bad about their decision? My decision? I don't know. I felt that they were ill at ease.

Nobleness is a value transmitted from one generation to another. The collective spirit, mainly when our dignity is under attack, is proudly and feverously defended. What do we choose? The family or the country? Work and provide the family with a living, or going through the hardships of the *maquis* to liberate the country from France? Emigrate to France to find work? France, our coloniser! A coloniser who, in the name of fraternity, equality and liberty, was suppressing our basic rights. Life, freedom and dignity. But we were the vassals, the indigenous, the barbarians, the uncivilized... therefore all the crimes done against us were legitimate. I spare you the vocabulary used for that.

"The revolution..." said my father, suspending his word and avoiding me. My eyes were clinging to his face and its expressions. Silence became heavier and heavier. But my determination was stanch, though I was afraid of his reaction. I knew my father to be a man of goodness. A man who hates injustice and laziness. A man of principles and knowledge. Principles and knowledge nurtured by misery and a hard life.

"Curse hangs over our land since immemorial times," he assumed. "Whenever we want to rise, the curse comes rushing, bending our spines. All sorts of misfortunes flourished on this land until we kowtowed to their yoke. I no longer believe in anything, my son. I no longer believe in anything," he echoed again in a frail and heartrending voice.

"People are more aware of their situation today," I alleged hesitantly.

"There are things about our people that we will never understand," he replied. "I understand your passion. You are young and brave. You have always been responsible. If you believe that the revolution is what you should follow, so, hold on to your objectives until accomplishment or death. But you should know that you don't belong to your family anymore, you belong to the people's aspirations, you belong to your land. Be aware that this is an enormous responsibility. You chose your path, then God bless you, my son, take it! Now you are the son of your goals. Your goals are noble."

41

My father's words were flowing into me, one by one. I still carry those in my mind. I will remember them forever. My father was not convinced by my choice, but he was wise enough to accept it and encourage me to follow it. He wasn't convinced by my choice, not because he thought it wouldn't lead anywhere, but because his reasons were of a different nature. Curse. Curse is a word he often said during our talks. It is as stuck to his speeches as to the population of our country.

"There are things about our people that we will never understand," he said.

Wasn't he right? Was that intuition? The intuition of my father was forged by his experience about men and the history of the whole of Northern Africa. Did he foresee betrayal? Did he mean that men are hypocrites and even if one day they succeed, their success will have a sour aftertaste? In those days, I found his idea of the curse absurd. Today, I affirm that he was right. Today's enemies are worse than yesterday's. My father was an example of wisdom and knowledge, though unable to read and write a letter. But what is knowledge? Being able to read books? Typing on the machines they are making? Do the youngsters communicate with each other or are they alienated from each other through these new technologies? Well, they may be useful to a certain point? But abuse is always possible. We didn't have all this when we were kids. We had the *kanoun*, the fireplace, around which we used to gather every evening during wintertime. Then the magic formula comes flowing from mothers, grandmothers, fathers or grandfathers: "Mashahu, once upon a time, when the animals were able to speak... Mashahu, may my tale spread like a thread."

No radio, no television. We only saw images enthused by words uttered by learned mouths and brains transporting us to magical worlds. My mother and father's mouths had the wit to turn our ears into eyes. They had the intelligence to give our imagination wings to travel far, out of space, out of time. To a world where animals could speak and interact with humans.

42

From those animals and humans, we learned so much. Both my mother and father were perfect storytellers and poets. My father also used to tell us about his childhood adventures. But what particularly fascinated him was his own father's life. My grandfather, of course. I can still see his expressions when he spoke about him. He looked enchanted and moved. My grandfather was legendary in his eyes. His father, my grandfather's father, was a fierce opponent of an old-fashioned *Marabout*, a religious man. This man wanted to steal from him. He tried through many means. No way. Desperate, he sent his henchmen and had my grandfather's father killed. My father said that the *Marabouts* were charlatans who claimed to belong to the lineage of the prophet, whilst, on the other hand, they proclaim to be Amazighs. They did that to fool people, manipulate them, rob their land and force them into submission. Submission isn't one of my grandfather's values. Furious, he wanted to avenge his father. He then stealthily entered the *Marabout's* house, killed him and fled. Within the *Agraw* system, which is the ancient social code in Kabylia, no prison existed. People were pushed implicitly to exile. The power of the *Marabouts* was conferred by the Arabs, the Ottomans, and later the French who, in order to manipulate the populations, dared attribute them certificates attesting that they were the prophet's descendants. Don't the Moroccan king and other dignitaries in the whole of Northern Africa use this title until today? They pretend to be the descendants of Mohamed. Whenever anyone outside their *Marabout* group opposed their rules or authority, they informed the authorities about him. Whether it was a caliphate, under the Arab colonisation, an Agha, during the Ottoman presence, or a governor under the French occupation. And each of them knew exactly what to do when someone is accused. The soldiers will be sent to do what the *Marabouts* want and will imprison or even kill the accused if the latter is crazy enough to challenge them.

Well! For God, blood doesn't matter. It does not matter if you are from Mohamed, Jesus, Moses, Buddha's lineage. Or whatever other lineage. The unique parameter is good and evil. No other humbugs that they obliged people to gulp. Their aim was to dispossess the weak and miserable people who were already plunged into poverty and denial.

My lineage is neither from the prophet nor from Bachaghas, governors and whomever else had been sent to this land from hell. My lineage is this land I grew in. My lineage is love of the earth and the land my fathers lived on and fought for against the aggressors. My lineage is human love for nature and humans. My lineage is love of brotherhood and solidarity. My lineage is freedom and pride.

My great grandfather had refused expropriation and was killed by charlatans, in the name of Allah and Mohamed. He was murdered and cried in silence and fear. He left behind him a wife, children and a fugitive. They didn't have any news of him for years.

"He is sent by the colonial forces to unknown lands to fight," some news said. Indeed he enrolled by force in the French army to fight against the Nazis. He enrolled to fight in a war to which he was stranger.

"But under threats and fear of seeing the whole family exterminated, as the French army said would happen, he didn't have any other choice," my father told us.

He did not enroll to liberate France, "*La Mère-Patrie*," as the army was yelling. How can it be his *Mère-Patrie*? He didn't go to foreign lands to fight for the French republican values. He didn't even know what all those values were. France was not a *Mère-Patrie* but a *Mère-Colonisatrice*, plainly, like the previous ones. The Romans, the Greeks, the Phoenicians, the Ottomans, the Arabs. And that was obvious to everyone.

My father was never tired of recounting the particular episode when my grandfather deserted the French ranks during the Second World War.

"Whilst he and some other soldiers, North Africans, Senegalese, French… were gathered around an improvised fire, resting and telling tales, a fight broke out," my father told us. I recall every detail. A French soldier had insulted the Senegalese. The Senegalese, strong and rapid, rushed towards him, jumped on him and started hitting him.

"Let them!" shouted an officer.

"Let them fight!"

At the end, the Senegalese, singing so loudly the Marseillaise, unzipped his pants then pissed on the French soldier. When the officer saw that, he rushed towards the Senegalese and punched him on the face. Another fight started.

Shebirdu, as was my grandfather called, jumped towards them and tried to split them up. The whole camp was alerted and a huge crowd formed around the men. The officer, furious against Shebirdu, slapped him and shouted, "You, bloody dirty Arab!"

"Me… not Arab," cried back Shebirdu in a strong Kabyle accent. Me not here for France! Me here, not my country… I here for nothing… I fear my family. Me France not my country!"

"You will be detained, bastard!" threatened the officer.

"You say, let them!" answered Shebirdu. "The bastard you!"

The French officer couldn't stand that. So, the fight started again but ended as soon as they were split up. Sent to the infirmary, my grandfather pretended that his arm was broken. He could thus stay for a longer time there.

"He was a humble man who hated injustice," stated my father.

People who had known him said that he was peaceful, full of energy and very persuasive. But if ever you provoked him, you would eat dust and get his punch on the face. Shebirdu had a passion. He loved telling tales. He used to invent a few, drawing from his own imagination and fantasy. At the village, he used to gather people at Thajmath. They spent hours listening to him telling tales. He is funny! When he was a little kid, he went to a Zawiya to learn the Koran. He didn't go to learn the holy verses but to learn the interesting stories told in it. The Shikh ordered him to learn by heart some verses. Bored and not at all stimulated, Shebirdu couldn't learn them. When his turn to recite the verses came, he started reciting some dubious verses improvised at the very moment. Standing up in front of the Shikh, he recited his own verses in a solemn and confident way. The Shikh couldn't believe his ears. That wasn't from the Koran in any way! Frantic, using his long olive tree stick, he punished him ruthlessly. Shebirdu, furious, never went back to the Zawiya. A few days later, he took his revenge in an exceptional way. He robbed the Shikh's heaviest and promisingly tastiest hen. He then went with his gang to the neighbouring wood. They grilled the chicken and ate it, snickering at the story of the improvised verses. And, from time to time, imitating the Shikh's ways when he would discover that his dearest hen was missing. Hahaha! From Thadarth to the French-German frontier, his life was full of adventures. At the infirmary, my grandfather was doing well. He rested the whole daylong. The German doctor, the Bosch, as the soldiers called him, was taking care of him. The German was held prisoner there. He was a valuable doctor. The soldiers in the camp had already heard about him but had never seen his nose pointing out of the infirmary. Those who were treated by him said he didn't speak French. "He is dumb," said others.

Silent, the German doctor took care of Shebirdu. He looked affable and harmless. The gossips portrayed him as a savage Nazi.

"He sucks human blood," some nasty soldiers said.

Shebirdu was confused. He was in a foreign land, with foreign people, fighting for a country that was not his. By then, he was healed by an enemy of the same country he is fighting for. Why is he in the infirmary? Because of a fight he had with

46

a soldier of the army of the country, which is now colonising his own country. Who can make sense out of this? It was an absurd situation.

"Is the German doctor my enemy?" He would have asked himself, with no convincing answer. That war was not his concern. He didn't know what Nazism was. He didn't even know why that war was happening. He nevertheless knew that humans were constantly fighting. He also knew that good and evil were always at war and will be until the end of the world. Both him and the German doctor were in the same space, doing what they didn't want to do. Both were used by their common enemy. Both were experiencing exile. Both were in enemy territory. Is the enemy of my enemy my friend? My enemy? Shebirdu was careful and suspicious towards the friendly behaviour of the doctor.

"We change the bandage tomorrow," spoke the German doctor in broken French.

Surprise. He isn't dumb. He speaks French. He is friendly. He doesn't suck any blood nor does he eat any human flesh.

The doctor smiled and secretly winked towards Shebirdu. The nurses and the French doctor weren't there. The next day, whilst the doctor was changing the bandage, the two men were introduced to each other and started chatting. My grandfather discovered that the German was opposed to the war.

"I am forced to take part in it," he told him. "I hate Hitler and all his generals," he added. "I hate dictators and war."

A friendship sprang up between them from their intimate exchanges. However, Shebirdu didn't fully trust that doctor. But intuition and spontaneity helping, the two guys couldn't dodge the best human values of sincerity and brotherhood, despite the differences and the backgrounds. Shebirdu devoted more time to his new friend.

"His arm has an infection," he answered the officers whenever they asked about my grandfather's injury. They were both not allowed to leave the tent. No one could suspect anything to happen between an ignorant stubborn Northern African who barely speaks French and a haughty racist, dumb German. Those prejudices served their relationship. The situation they were in gave birth to a successful fleeing plan. One dawn, they ran away. They wore the French uniforms they robbed, went through the trenches and reached a huge forest. My grandfather fled south and the German doctor towards the north. My grandfather was fascinated by tales. His life itself was a tale. He ended up working in the Alsace mines. Then in the Parisian metro constructions. He came back to Thadart in the 1950's. He died under the olive tree in front of our house. He enjoyed lying on his back there watching the Djurdjura mountains. *Mashahu…* that was Shebirdu's story. I wasn't yet born when he died. I wish I had seen him and heard his adventures from his mouth. But life decided otherwise.

My father, compared to the majority of Kabyle fathers, was very tender and thoughtful. He never imposed anything to his children or wife.

My father never beat us. Whenever we did something wrong, he shouted: "You won't go out the whole day!" On the other hand, my mother was sometimes so cruel, and the best justification for her punishment was: "What will people say about us?"

My father laughed so hard the day when my brother, Said-My-Book, and I stole Ashur N Hmed's figs. He then, to calm down my mother, promised to pay the man back, as it was ordered by Thajmath laws. Within the Thajmat system, there were no prisons, no physical punishment. If someone commits a petty offense, he will simply pay a tax, and when the offense is considerable, he will be kicked out of the village. The biggest offenses were murder or adultery. But after the arrival of the French, the villagers' existence was spoiled by their administrative system, their offices and their justice. The laws of Thajmath weren't written. They were naturally transmitted from a generation to another. Known without formal instruction. They were a code of behaviour, a style of life.

"They are just kids. We all did bad things when we were kids," he said.

My father called me Shebirdu and said that I was like his father. He stopped calling me Shebirdu once I could finally go to the weekly market, in the neighbouring city, Thizi Ghenif.

"When you are fourteen," replied my father whenever I asked him to take me with him. It was a kind of tradition. Fourteen was the age of manhood, of a relative freedom to do certain things without asking the parents. I had heard so much about Thizi, but I had no idea how it was. Thizi symbolised a new world for me. We strangely called it, in French, "The Village". As if our villages didn't have the right to be named otherwise. As if in our villages we were sub-humans. As if our language didn't have the capacity to convey the same meaning. As if our villages weren't worth the vocabulary village. They were too poor and old.

We used to hear many things about Thizi. The adults who went there described it as a fascinating area. Big houses, beautiful villas with gardens, cars driven on the paved streets, pedestrians coming and going by, shops, cafes with terraces, a lot of French, schools. For the teenagers we were, going to the souk was like a pilgrimage. We wanted to accelerate time and age, to finally discover that part of the world, the city.

We, in our villages, became adults at an early age. At the age of ten, eleven, thirteen, the majority of us were already familiar with so many tasks and chores. Farming, picking olives, taking the sheep to graze in this or that field. Lead the donkey, with its different weights, water, wood or the washed clothes in the river, back home... etc., etc... We helped the adults with the different daily tasks as soon as we could. Going to the city was a dream for my mates and I. The ultimate dream of our childhood. A liberation from childhood. An entrance into the world of adulthood. An occasion to widen one's horizons.

The day I went to the city was extraordinary. The souk was swarming. My eyes were bouncing from a face to a building, from a window to a tree, from a terrace to a car, from a horse to a shop, from a donkey to a garden, from one object to another. I was glancing at all the faces my eyes met. I wanted to live everything, to see all of it. I was like in a wild twister that offset my focus. My father smiled at me whenever I looked at him. He smiled at my amazement. "Stay beside me," he said. There was a relentless stirring. Right, left, right, left! Crowds everywhere, unyielding noise, sickening dust. Shepherds guiding their sheep, old men on their donkeys, wearing their warm burnouses and big esparto made hats. Some people seemed to be in a rush. Whereas others had all the worldly time for strolling around, looking at products or bargaining them. A lot of images and scenes were revealed to the little boy I was, and assimilating them was a pleasant but hard task. Listen to the traditional healer yell, trying to sell some good or fake herbs. And those men sitting on carpets sipping tea or coffee. The crowd watching a man pretending to be able to tell fortunes, handing people an offering or a talisman. He writes on it and immediately puts it around the neck. Watching the dervish dancing on embers or putting a hot sickle on his tongue without feeling the burn. Stand by a farmer selling vegetables, fruits, sheep, goats, hens or eggs and hear his lovely poetic and loud shouts. The best one is the storyteller. He uses the right tone, the nicest intonation. He tells about humans and ghouls, about men and women from distant lands. *Mashahu...* Hear his hoarse voice. Many beggars were strolling or sitting on the ground, stretching their hands for a *dourou* or a loaf of bread. It was the first time I saw a beggar in my life. In Thadarth, we didn't have beggars. People showed solidarity and shared food with their poorer neighbours. We stood against misery together, sharing a loaf of bread, a nice word

50

and a sincere smile. Thala was open for all the villagers and no family suffered water shortages. Today, people even buy water.

The souk was overwhelming. Good morning, *salam alikum* and *azul* (peace, hello) were fusing from all directions. Embraces. Kisses. Greetings and greetings. And from time to time, a fight started between two sellers or a seller against a buyer, or a seller against a robber, between two people or even two groups… etc. Whenever a fight begun, people, curious, gathered around them. Some tried to calm the fighters, others, amused, added oil to the fire, as we say.

I was happy to finally discover that unknown face of the world where my father and his companions went every week. They didn't come back until the sun was set. I was glad that my horizons were expanded. It hence opened my mind and heart to new charms, new experiences.

"Where does the world end," I asked my father.

"There are a lot of countries and seas. It's huge," he replied with that ethereal smile of his.

The days before I went to the souk, I wasn't speaking or dreaming of anything else but that. I slept so little the night before. At dawn, my mother didn't have to wake me up. I was already up. I kindly refused the loaf of bread she handed me. I was too stressed. I couldn't put anything in my mouth.

"Take it with you," she ordered, "and eat it whenever you are hungry. The road is long, young man."

Young man. I wasn't the little boy anymore. I then loped out. My father was saddling the mule. My parents' vocabulary and attitude towards me changed. My life was changing. I was changing. I felt different. I helped my father to saddle the mule. My mother came out to the courtyard. She watched us. Her two men. Husband and son.

"Stay in peace," said my father addressing my smiling mother.

"Stay in peace," I echoed him.

"Go in peace," she replied waving her hand. Led by the mule, we walked down.

"We will find Mhand and Wali at the entrance of Thadarth," declared my father. They were both my father's co-workers. Their mules were loaded with sacks. Just like ours. The sacks contained the fruits and the vegetables they harvested whilst working at Fino's. Mr Fino was soft on that because the fruits and vegetables were of bad quality. They used to go every weekend to Thizi to sell their products. Their wages were so low. So, the products were useful to make some extra *dourous*.

"Errrrr! Errrrr!" yelled the men at their mules, and then we started walking down the hill. On our path to the souk, the three men didn't stop talking about the Finos.

"I wonder how, as grouchy as Mr Fino is, he had shut his eyes on that," commented Mhand about the fruits and vegetables.

If Mr Fino was fierce, his wife was definitely his opposite. The workers never stopped praising her qualities. Jacqueline is her name. Jacqueline had a natural affability towards all people around her.

"She loves my son, Said," said Wali. Said was her favourite. We both used to take food to our fathers at the Finos every day at midday. He was smart and funny. Jacqueline offered him a book full of pictures. It was the first pictured book Thadarth ever saw. Adults and children, men and women, girls and boys were amazed. Said loved the book. He took it everywhere he went, even to bed. Well! At that time, we didn't have any beds. We were sleeping in the same room on sheepskins or, for the luckiest ones, on homemade thin mattresses. The book Jacqueline offered to Said brought up a few problems though. The little boy didn't stop asking his father to send him to school. Poor him! He wanted to decode the sentences in his book.

"School is for the French," answered his dad, scolding him. "You must prepare yourself to work. We need food, not studies."

Whenever we wanted to meet Said, we knew where he was. Behind their house. He used to spend hours and hours there, playing and talking to the characters in his book, trying to soothe his frustration, imagining what the letters might say. He never wanted any kid to touch that book. Not even his brothers and sisters.

One evening, whilst we were all around him trying to get hold of that book, he fled holding it tight to his chest, screaming: "It's my book! It's my book!" We rushed behind him. A crowd of ten children. Boys and girls, shouting, jumping and clapping: "Said-My-Book! Said-My-Book!"

That is how he got his nickname. Ah, those times of light-heartedness and enthusiasm!

The sun, a wonderful and huge orange disk, partially hidden by the high mountains of Djurdjura, was setting when we were walking back, up to Thadarth. Whilst my mother was watching from the yard, my brothers and my sister hurried towards us. They were impatient and very excited. They, one by one, kissed father on the forehead then hopped towards me, talking to me all together at the same time. Questions, questions. I laughed at them. I tried to answer. Another question.

"Let me kiss my mother first," I begged. She caressed my cheeks and kissed me on the head.

"Blessed be my son," she pronounced. "Let's get in," she urged us. "I prepared a very good *berkukes* with chicken meat," she added.

And, of course, that was in my honour as the tradition stipulates it. That was a big event, so *berkukes* or *seksu* (*couscous*) with chicken were served. We also ate *berkukes* the day I shaved the little hair I had on my beard for the first time.

We didn't eat meat so often. That was a nice event. It made our mouths water. We were delighted, especially my father. Why? Because he finally got rid of the "nasty-rooster," as he used to call it. Why nasty? Because he often destroyed the vegetables my father used to plant in his small garden, behind our house. How did he get rid of it? Well, it wasn't himself actually who got rid of it, but my mother. The nasty-rooster ended up in our plates. Hahaha!

So many lovely anodyne quarrels took place because of that rooster. My father was chasing it all the time. My mother defended it.

"So, a problem less," said my father, teasing my mother.

"You still have to chase the hens," she replied merrily.

"The hens are useful," he added.

"If we didn't have the nasty rooster, she said insisting on nasty-rooster, what would we have served on today's occasion?"

"A hen," joked my father again.

The villagers used to have and keep poultry for eggs and special occasions. An unexpected guest would be well served. Meat was a luxury. We could eat it only in occasions such as births, marriages or circumcisions. The hens or roosters, sometimes sheep, were also reserved for sad occasions. Accidents or death in the family or the neighbourhood. When a familiar or a neighbour died, food is offered to the family of the latter. So, instead of being preoccupied by preparing the food, the family would only be tasked with receiving and attending to the guests coming to present their condolences and share their pain.

When I was a little boy, I was excited when my mother said: "Go to the hens' nest and see if there are any eggs. You will get one, but don't tell anybody." I then ran and often found the eggs still warm. The sheep we had were kept for sale. We used their wool for making clothes, pillows and blankets. My mother's fingers were made for art. Cooking, sewing, taking care of the vegetable garden, the poultry, the sheep, pottery. She used to make the most beautiful pots and crocks in Thadarth. She decorated them with very nice symbols. Only women knew the secret of those symbols. It is, more than an artistic expression, a language in itself. With no machine, using water and fire, she transformed that clay into pieces of art.

We sat at the table. We were impatient to be served. My father had gone out to relieve himself. At that time, we didn't have a proper toilet. Therefore, we used to go outside, in nature, to satisfy our biological needs. We used to take a bucket and hide behind a tree or a bush. Trees and plants needed to be fed, didn't they? Hahaha! After finishing his prayers, my father joined us. We started gulping down the tasty *berkukes* and the nasty rooster's meat. From time to time, we laughed at my parents' little teasing games.

Ah! Those were the happy days. We always found, despite our miserable life, breaching glimmers of happiness. But fate always comes back charging and bending our spine. Some months after, my father's backaches became excruciating. He hardly could walk. His absence from work preoccupied Mr Fino who pitilessly threatened him. "He will be fired!" said Mhand, repeating Fino. My father's job was our unique source of money. That source should keep feeding the family. "You are grown up now," affirmed my father addressing me. His strength was fading. I was fifteen. I was ready to work for the entire family.

"We will meet Mr Fino tomorrow," he whispered painfully. "I hope he will accept you as a worker in his farm."

A bent back, a wrinkled face, my father's expressions had lost their vim. I then realised that the big change in my life was not when I went to the souk for the first time. It was actually when I accompanied my father to the Finos. I felt sorry for my father. A sentiment of failure obscured his face. Sorrow was noticeable in his voice. At that moment, the only thing that I thought about was to show him that I was worthy of the task he assigned me to.

During the first weeks, he, as did his former co-workers, provided me with advice and instructions. "You must do your best to be recruited. Your words, with the Finos, should be limited to 'hello' and 'goodbye'. Do this… pay attention to that… don't do that…" He then blessed and encouraged me.

My mother, from her side, kept reminding me about my father's requests every morning. Nonetheless, I didn't only listen to the adults' instructions. I went to find Said-My-Book to understand the Finos better. He told me, more or less, how was life within that family.

"The father is rowdy, but the mother is very sweet and warm hearted. She speaks a beautiful and strange language," said Said.

Jacqueline and Mr Fino had two children. A son who, according to Said-My-Book, is a copy of his dad, and a daughter who was, along with her mom, the second pea in the pod. Julien. Martine. Those names sounded weird and wonderful to my ears. I tried, in my imagination, to associate faces to those names.

"Are they like the faces I met during my visit to the souk?" Their faces were white and their hair uncovered. Our faces were tanned because of the sun. And our men used to wear, on their heads, *lemdhella* or *thashashit*. Thadarth's women, if not covered with a beautiful colourful *mendil* showing strands of their hair flowing out like silver on their forehead and cheeks, they left their dark black hair move freely, caressed by the breeze flowing over those high mountains, along rivers and plains. And when they smile? When they smile, Anzar, the God of rain, comes down to glamor them. He kneels asking for their hand whilst a rainbow, behind him, goes up to the sky, enchanting the view. The rainbow's colours and design are those of the *fouta*, this particular attire covering the back of nice girls, down from their hips reaching almost their feet, revealing their sensuality and their femininity, full of elegance and charm. The *fouta* is tied around the hips. If the knot covers her bellybutton, the woman is single. Young men can ask for her hand. If it falls on the right leg, she is married. Be careful, she is taken. When it is on the left leg, she is divorced. Jewels adorning the head are used in a similar manner, either adorning the head or placed on the right, the left or the centre, or the breast, left or right.

Kabyle women are an exception in a world full of frenzied rules and sick fanaticism that require faces to be covered because of absurd beliefs, enticing holy beards with their streams of beauty, love, ability, words, smiles, making them doubt, leading them to hell.

Every region has its particular clothes' design and colours. A lot of colours. White like almond blossoms. Red like the flavoursome grains of a pomegranate. Blue like the sea. Green like juicy, succulent figs. Yellow like grooms' flowers, witnesses of beauty burgeoning from a thorny evergreen plant. Orange like fresh oranges. Black like olive grains, source of life to millions of families. Kabyle women are not a mere décor or an object of sensuality. If the man is the beam of the house, the woman is, as the proverb says, the pillar.

Is this nostalgia? What was I thinking about earlier? I suddenly went nostalgic and lost my line of thought. My memory jogged towards beauty and splendour. See where the *fouta* and the *mendil* brought me to?

What were that song's lyrics? Oh, yes! *"Come! Come! We have not met for a long time. Come! I ached and waited for you."* How does the melody go? On the table…Let me tap it. Dem dem dem! Tran tran tran! Ah, I still drum quite well. This table has a quite good resonance! *"Come! Come! I'm ill, heartsick. Alone without a family. Come! Neighbours, pity me. Patience became my companion. My soul pains are gazing. Dem dem dem!"* May God give Lhesnawi rest. How many artists have been buried in foreign lands? How many artists suffered the pain of exile? Isn't this a nice song?

Genius, Lhesnawi! He exquisitely interprets a woman's yearning to see her beloved coming back.

Well! Let me figure out where I was before I lost my line of thought. Where is the tail? Where is the head? Tail...Head...That's a nice verse for a song or a poem. Where is the tail...dem dem dem...where is the head?

Yes! The Finos! Said-My-Book! Isn't it an amusing nickname? Hahaha! Curious about how the French children were clothed, and how their faces and their hair were, we decided to stealthily go and pay them a visit. They were playing in the courtyard of their school. Their school was situated in the neighbouring village. When Said saw Martine from our hideout behind the bushes, he innocently declared: "I like Martine and I want to marry her."

"She is French," I replied. "Her father will never let you marry her."

"I'll flee with her," he said in a burst of enthusiasm.

"Do you think she will accept and come with you?"

That was a question with no response. He moved his head from side to side. He was unsure.

How fascinating is it that the human mind can remember such details! Why now?

Driven by an intense curiosity, I wanted to go to the courtyard of that school. It was built with bricks and cement and roofed with orange tiles. It wasn't like our miserable hovels, threatened to fall apart at any moment when it rained or snowed. I wanted to go inside the classrooms. Find out what those children were doing. We were hiding behind the trees. We couldn't get nearer. We were scared to be seen. Suddenly, a bell rang. Then, we heard the sound of chairs scraping the floor. The pupils rushed through the classrooms' doors towards the courtyard. We could barely see their faces. There was an enormous hullabaloo. Some children were jumping in circles, others running after each other, and others playing strange games. They were steady and clean. They were

58

children like us. Like me. Like Said. Like all the children in Thadarth. The only difference was their clothes, their games. Our clothes were dirty. The best among us was the one who had two worn pants and two mended shirts during his whole childhood. When one grows up, he passes them down to his younger brother or cousin. We used to play different games. We didn't have a ball, but we had other things to entertain ourselves.

The most exciting game we played was the donkey races. From Thadarth to Thala, we dashed as fast as we could on the back of our donkeys. We didn't win any prize. Just the pride to be the fastest. We also, secretly in a house in ruins, organised rooster fights. Oh, that one was gross! Who-will-piss-further-than-the-others competitions. Too gross! We stood on a top of a clod, unzipped our pants, prepared our little weapons, then, one, two, three! Vvshhhhhh! The most dangerous one was to climb the highest tree in the nearby woods. How many kids risked having their arm or leg broken. The river provided us with another game. Who can stay the longest underwater? The best and most rewarding game we played was collecting partridges' eggs in the wood. The one who collects the most would be the winner. He would take all the collected eggs. Our parents were against all the others games except this one. Eggs were welcome!

As children, we of course used to play, but we also used to work. The sheep should graze. Pick up elm leaves for the cow or the coat. The donkey or the mule should be tied in this or that field. Water should be brought from Thala, and wood from the forest... etc.

The French kids played funny, strange games. We laughed so much whilst watching them.

"Ridiculous and girlish," stated Said.

But they were full of life. They were laughing, dancing, singing.

"What are they carrying on their backs?" I asked.

59

"Bags full of books," replied Said.

Their bags were colourful and nicely hung on their backs around their shoulders.

Full of frustration and dreams, we left our hideout.

When I started working at the Finos, I noticed how they were enjoying the basic pleasures of life. They ate very well, they wore nice clothes. Julien and Martine, along with their mother, were running, laughing, dancing, with no stress, no fear, careless of what comes next. They were living life to the fullest. Life for them was like a fresh apple they easily ate. For us, the trapped 'indigenous', life was, for the majority, like a rock-solid black burnt loaf. A hard black burnt loaf that often might smash our teeth or throttle our throats. We were simply surviving. Being opulent was sometimes an outrage. An insult to good sense, knowing that the majority was starving.

I often, in my kid's heart, had asked a thousand of questions. "Why them and not us? Why is Julien, supposedly a foreigner in our land, enjoying life better than me, better than Said? Why can Martine have that sort of life and not my sister, not the others girls at Thadarth's? Am I not in my own country?"

"We recovered this land from the clutches of the Ottomans after decades and decades of struggle," my father told us. Then came the French, the Greek, the Italians, the Spanish, under the protection of the French army and administration, and took it again."

I was asking myself: "By what right do foreigners come and act as our masters? What right do these people have to exploit us in our own land?"

To my questions, I couldn't find any other concrete answer than this one: Injustice. All that disturbed me and hoisted me to have a complex. A complex complicated to express, to explain. A complex I felt but I could overcome years afterwards.

My father introduced me to Mr. Fino who, notwithstanding the exaggerated paternal praises, wasn't pleased.

"He is too young," he said.

My father insisted. Fino accepted to give me a chance. Besides, can he find any other worker that he could trust?

"*Confiance, confiance…*" mumbled my father in French.

Familiar with farming work and its derived tasks, I didn't have any outward trouble. My occupation got me away from the routine I was enduring. Working at Fino's farm was a new adventure full of promises and excitement. My life was being shaken from top to bottom.

I was the first teenager to work there. Accordingly, Mrs Fino was so opposed to it. She went to find my father, looking for explanations.

"*Mi madam, il dwa midi pasko mwa malade. An va pa mourir d'fa kamam!*" said my father in his own accent. "But, madam, he must help me because I'm ill. If he doesn't work, we will die from hunger!"

I blushed. Hahaha! Not only because of my father's special accent, but also because of Mrs Fino's presence. It was the first time I met a grown up French woman. I felt intimidated. She was near me. Looking at that strange teenager who stood there behind his father, daring neither to speak nor to look in her eyes. I could smell her scent. Her perfume was delightful. It woke all my senses. Her skin was as white as snow. Her arms and legs were bare. Her hair was red. She was there in front of my father, talking to him, no shyness, and no fear.

"She was arguing with him like a man," I told my mother when I came back home. "Dear mother," she said slapping her chest, smiling.

"It's their culture," my father replied.

"Such a thing is unconceivable for a woman here in Thadarth," replied my mother.

Women in Thadarth were so respected and never did a stranger, man, argue with them. A woman always argued with a woman. A man with a man. Wives too, they rarely argued with their husbands. The rule of submissiveness to the husband, the father, the brother, the father-in-law, the grandfather; in brief, to the male, was held sacred.

Whenever my parents argued, it was my mother who was admonished. Whenever that occurred, she kept silent and didn't openly argue. She was smart. Smarter than my father. She had her own ways to have the last word. Bloody mom! She used to stop talking to him for two or three days. Or, the best one! That was the smartest ever! She stopped cooking the dishes he craved for until he capitulated. Bloody mother indeed! The bed strategy was another option. It was the most efficient, I guess. We were astonished when all of a sudden my father, calm and wise as he was, became irritated and unbearable. The bed strategy!

"You don't want to talk with me? He shouted. Then don't talk! Don't…"

Then he left the house muttering between his lips some indiscernible words. I couldn't understand that at that time but once adult, one knows better. We were more astonished when, all of a sudden, we heard their laughs and voices chatting. Like nothing happened!

It took me a lot of time and courage to face Jacqueline without blushing. First, because she was bloody pretty; second, because I couldn't understand her words.

My father's encouragements convinced her.

"But he will only be doing minor tasks," she said and got a promise even from her husband.

I thus started working. Nevertheless, she watched me closely. Whenever she saw me doing anything she thought to be hard, she used to reprimand me even from far away. Sweetly.

"Akli, don't do that… Akli, drop that down… Akli, it's getting late… Akli, you are too early…"

Whenever she reprimanded me, I stopped and smiled at her. Wasn't she concerned about my health! Sometime later, I managed to understand and learn some of the words the Finos used. I also dared, whenever I doubted, to ask my colleagues. What does *bonjour* mean? What does *bien* mean? What does *merde* mean? *Merde* was stuck to Mr Fino's mouth. One couldn't miss the opportunity to learn and use it. The word *merde* entered Thadarth's daily language through Fino's workers. Whenever someone grumbled, *merde* popped out of his mouth.

From time to time, when Fino was gone to deliver the crops to Thizi's traders or elsewhere, my co-workers and I tried to imitate him, parodying his manners and trying to speak like him. When he wasn't there, the mice danced, but quite carefully because, even when gone, his shadow remained there! We enjoyed the moments when he was off. We rested, laughed, told jokes. We paused our hardships for that while.

Sick, Ammi Ali, Rabah's father, didn't come to work for two days. When he returned, Mr Fino, during a loud squabble, flogged him with his whip. Flog a man in his fifties? An outrage. Ammi Ali jumped on him. He beat him and was about to strangle him. We hurried and, as hard as we could, we pulled Ammi Ali away from him. Fino, cowardly, was begging him not to send his soul to the sky. He was weeping, his pants wet. As soon as we split them up, Fino rushed towards the *gendarme* office to indict Ammi Ali. The latter, since that day, vanished from the locality. The *gendarmes* went to the fugitive's house, evacuated its occupants. Fire spoke, half of the house was destroyed. The *gendarmes* left behind them Ammi Ali's wife and children crying. Fortunately, family and neighbours were there to help.

I met Ammi Ali again a few years later in the *maquis*. He was thrilled to see me. We weren't from the same village. He lived in the village where the Finos had a property. Ammi Ali, like my grandfather Shebirdu, fought against the Nazis.

"For France's freedom," he used to say ironically in his speeches. He talked to us a lot about what was happening in the world. He was literate and an ex-partisan of Messali Hadj. Ammi Ali was the first to stand against the revolution led by the Front. But afterwards, he was convinced that, "since France invaded us, weapon in hand; we must push her out, weapon in hand too," he argued. He changed his opinion mainly because the Messalists fought the initiators of the revolution. Thus the *maquis*, well after 1954, was witnessing a shameful civil war that soon ended with the defeat of the Messalists.

Everyday, Ammi Ali was trying to awaken our consciousness.

"I fought, against my will, for France, which is now free," he said. "France, which is today trampling my freedom. Our freedom. France is forcing us to be vassals in our own land. France took our land, the land of our ancestors, and gave it to the settlers who exploit and treat us worse than animals. See Fino! His horse, his dogs, his cows are better than we are. Does he treat his horse like he treats us? No! His horse is caressed, loved and eats well. We are well served! Hard work and a big deal of insults and humiliation for a handful of *dourous*. "But hope lies in our youth," he added, a mattock at hand, looking at us. "You are the hope, the future of this country."

His speeches filled me with enthusiasm and courage. Ammi Ali played a huge part in the awakening of my political consciousness. It was an advantage I wouldn't have had if I hadn't worked at Fino's. We often talked about patriotism, freedom, fight, independence, education, training and other notions and names that would have been strange and undiscovered if I hadn't had the chance to know Ammi Ali. May he rest in peace! Fate often separates us from the good people.

We are often left to ourselves, our thoughts, our memories. Thank goodness, some good memories pop out to freshen our spirits. It's strenuous to try and remain sane. Because the future is forbidden, I only live the bygone days.

But let me remember the beautiful ones. Let me enjoy them again. Let me recall those happy moments.

I was working in the fields under a skin-scorching sun. I didn't have a hat. There were no creams at that time. Martine innocently trotted towards me, a straw made hat in her hand, a bright smile on her face. It's useless to say that I blushed like a tomato that whole day.

Martine was not walking, she was floating towards me. She was wearing a short, colourful dress. The breeze was lifting it, waving it. I could see her beautiful legs. Her skin was milky white. I was motionless, amazed. I never saw a young beautiful woman's legs so close. Not once in my entire fifteen winters. At that age, we did not know what these parts of the woman's body looked like. Still we fantasised about them. We talked about them secretly in the absence of the grown-ups. We could not talk about sex with them. It was taboo to talk about sex. We even were ashamed when we saw a donkey's hard-on or a sheep mating with a ewe, or a dog with another. Each time I tried to imagine the intimate parts of a woman, everything turned blurry. Adolescent, curious and excited, we tried to spy on our cousins when they showered or went to satisfy their biological needs, but we could not see much. Our female cousins and neighbours did not wear short dresses and our parents, afraid of any misstep, kept trying to keep us far from them. Said and I used to hide up on the mound overlooking Thala to see some fresh skin. Thala was the place where women, away from men's observing moustaches, dwelt freely. They often took a shower at Thala, but without taking off their dresses unfortunately. It was maybe more arousing than without any clothes on. Women often gave freedom to their mouths there. Thus, we could hear streams of wicked words addressed to each other. We could hear their mockeries, their secrets and foolishness. Said and I discovered the best place to watch and hear them. We held it top-secret. No one knew about it. What we saw and heard nurtured in us intense desires. Desires, which we tried, sometimes in vain, to quench in secret, intimate and brief moments. Wicked! We were too frustrated, holy God! At least we were not like those who were engaged in sneaky and perverse practices. They tried the donkey, a goat or a sheep, even a friend, neighbour or cousin. Fortunately, it was not so often. Those were tender youth's errors. Anyway, there were lucky, yet very few, young men who could, on the sly, share with young women some kisses or caresses in a barn, a house in ruins, between the bushes, in the neighbouring woods, etc... But be careful not to break that holy thing. That holy fine and delicate thing must be protected. That fine and delicate holy thing is the honour of the entire family, the entire tribe. Do not break it, says the tradition. If you do so and are discovered, the rifle, the axe, or whatever sharp object will, if you do not flee, end your life at once. If this does not happen, you will get into the court's labyrinths. Thus women, limited to their organs, live their whole youth with an absurd obsession. Protect the holy fine delicate thing. What are you talking about? Love, passion, freedom! Let me laugh.

Martine was shining. How can I forget that smile? Her smile for me. ME. Her mother was observing her from the porch. She was laughing. Her eyes brightened. Proud of her daughter. I stood there, in the middle of the field, observing that little creature running towards me. "My co-workers!" I looked at them. How, inquisitive as they were, could they miss that? They did not miss anything. I knew that for the next hours my name would be in all the mouths of the village.

She handed me the hat. Without thinking, I stretched my hand to take it. Could I refuse anything coming from that beautiful girl who revealed charm and generosity? No. Refusing would have been an insult to her beauty. To beauty.

If I close my eyes, I can see it again... I see my hand stretching out, I see the hat, her hand. Her hand was small and white. It was not concealed under a brownish tan like my mother's, my sister's or my cousins'. Martine was not allowed to work, to wash the clothes, to bring water from the fountain, to clean the house or any other task Thadarth's young girls were accustomed to do. Not even Jacqueline did because they had an Aisha. An Aisha, as the French called her, was the indigenous woman cleaning, cooking, washing, serving. Martine's hand was, though we had almost the same age, different from mine that was hardened by work. Her hand was different from that of my cousin Dihya, my promised wife. Why them and not us? Why us and not them?

Frozen, the hat between my hands, I was looking at her running back towards her mom. I felt a cold sweat drop rolling down my forehead, ending up on the tip of my nose before falling onto the ground. Martine stopped abruptly. Her mom was telling her something. Martine looked at me then at her mom. She dawdled for a moment. Then I saw her running back towards me. Once in front of me, she puckered her brows. She spoke to me. I couldn't understand. I did not move. I didn't understand. I shrugged my shoulders. At that moment, she took the hat from my hand and, straightaway, put it on my head. Another sweat drop rolled down. I felt warm. Burning.

Serenely, that creature smiled at me. She turned to her mother. The latter did not stop laughing. I felt ridiculous. I peeped at the workers. They were holding back their laughs. Could they miss that show? I was dazed and paralysed. That was so much kindness towards me. For a few days, I mulled over that day's scenes, moment after moment. I recalled Jacqueline's laughs. I could see Martine floating towards me. Her elegant gestures. Her little fine face. Her smiles, her eyes, her mouth, her white teeth. Her precious, growing breasts. Her hair swaying in the wind.

My ardour and enthusiasm were stirred. My mind went far. It went to the realm of dreams and cravings, the realm of charm and senses.

The Fino ladies' heartwarming care was unusual for the peasant, son of a peasant, I was. I was nailed to the ground. I did not even say the "*merci*" I had just learnt. Whilst I was re-living that unexpected moment of kindness, word of it had already galloped to Thadarth. It preceded me home. At Thajmath, a counsel in my honour or, better said, in my dishonour, had been held by Thadarth's teenagers. Said-My-Book was the leader of that movement. I was avoided for quite a few weeks. Only a few teenagers talked to me. I was guilty. Of what? I didn't know. I became the "French lover". I unwittingly caused Said's jealousy and anger. Martine was the cause. Or the reason? He stopped talking to me and went as far as purposely walking on the other side of the road to avoid meeting me.

However, fate led us both to a common path. A few years later, the *maquis* united us. I was surprised when he contacted me. "The revolution needs you," he said. I was relieved to find him enrolled in Rabah's group.

"Those were childish whims," he replied when we spoke about Martine and his jealousy.

Yet, for me, those were not merely childish whims. It was intense, delightful.

Martine murmured into her mother's ear. She was looking at me. "What is she telling her? Who knows?" I was there, standing, feeling silly. I didn't move from my initial pose. The afternoon breeze was cooling up the sweat drops I had on my skin. It was blowing the hat off my head. I finally moved an arm to adjust the hat. The Fino ladies laughed. Were they mocking me? Impossible. I was mortified.

"You fool! Get back to work!" I heard Fino saying. He came out of nowhere. Martine and her mother walked indoors.

"Get back to work," repeated someone among the workers. I did not dare look at anyone that day. Neither at my workplace nor in the village. I did not want to look anyone in the eye. For several weeks, I was, by chance or because of Jacqueline, the talk of Thadarth. My name was in every conversation. People would start speaking softly, whenever I walked past.

That episode with Martine went all wind. Monstrous details were added to spice up the gossips and entertain people for days. When the hen lays an egg, the roosters feel pain in their asses. People had a fertile fantasy. It went from "He kissed her" to "Slept with her," "Raped her"...

Happy and full of what I lived a few moments ago, I started digging the ground again. Carelessly. I was clumsy. Was I aware of what I was doing? I must answer 'no'. That same evening, on my way back home, whom did I meet? My mother! She was on her way back from Thala. She scolded me.

"There you are," she said from about fifty meters away. "You will marry, whether you like it or not, your cousin Diyha!" she said, before I even kissed her on the forehead.

"Don't hide that hat! I already know everything," she added.

Hahaha! She noticed the hat I was awkwardly hiding behind my back.

"None other than Dihya!" She started again, her finger pointing at me. "She... tatabatata, tatabatata."

I sheepishly listened to her lecture. I guessed why she was in that temper. It seemed that word of what happened with Martine had reached Thala too. How? The hen... lays the egg... the rooster's ass... you know the rest. Did my mother know that her rage was unnecessary? Did I do anything wrong? I was just offered a hat. I was not given the opportunity to explain or tell her what happened. It was like if I was prevented from owning a moment of my own life. I was reminded "the traditions," "the oaths," "rich," "poor," "French," 'Kabyle," "Muslim," "Christian".

After my mother's reprimands, came those of my father, those of my grandmothers. Yes, both. My aunts', my neighbours', my friends'. Even people I did not know or who never addressed me before joined in rebuke. My relatives paid a special visit to talk to me, or, better, to blame me, I must say. About what? About something they did not know, they did not witness. My life was not my life. It was my family's, my neighbours', my village's life.

Since then, a shield was built around Martine. Her only sin was offering me a hat to protect me from the sun. I was guilty because I was the one who had the hat.

My mother walked away and headed home. I watched her for a while, then I threw the hat to the ground!

"Traditions, poor, rich, Kabyle, French... Damn it all!" I angrily mumbled.

What in hell did we do? If something had happened between her and me, wouldn't it concern only Akli, Martine and me? Did it not concern two adolescents who did not have any idea of nationalism, religion, class struggle... etc.?

Hell! I'm not a Kabyle! I'm not a Muslim! I'm nothing!

But I must say that all the fuss happening around me was not affecting me as was the struggle within me. My feelings for Martine were beyond all their empty speeches. I was confused. I was gratuitously driven to a dilemma by those circumstances. "Should I agree with the views of the people around me? Should I open my mouth and say that all that was a huge fuss stemming from their suspicions, their imagination and foolishness?

I looked at the hat on the ground. "What shall I do with it now?"

I took it, shook it. "I will hide it somewhere," I thought. I hid it in a bush. I checked if it was well hidden. It seemed so. Then I went home.

In all that story, only one person behaved sympathetically. My father.

"I hid it somewhere," I answered him when he asked about the hat. Once home, he wanted to talk to me. I sat on the floor, by his bed.

"Keep it," he replied. As a sign of gratitude to Mrs. Fino, you should wear it. But don't mess around with the Fino daughter," he insisted. "We aren't from the same social class, my son. Do your work and that's it."

My mother was listening behind the door during the conversation with my father. With my father, I didn't feel any need to justify anything. He didn't ask me about what happened. He just talked wisely about the responsibility I had with regard to the family.

I brewed over all what happened. I felt proud of my father. He was graceful. What I was living was a moment of notoriety for me. A moment of unpopularity among my friends. But I decided to avoid any confrontation, any explanations. I didn't reply to any reproach. I was fed up. I played along with being "the French lover". When I saw the results of this, I was quite sure of what I should do. Thus, I prepared my retaliation. I wore the hat and walked, head high, whistling romantic songs. I even exaggerated whenever I walked past any group of teenagers. A few weeks after, those who had stopped started talking to me again. The hostility had passed. Glory replaced it. I savoured it enthusiastically. My strategy worked. And those who talked behind my back, I left them there. Behind my back.

I must say that Martine fuelled my fires. But I didn't think about anything serious. I mean, a probable affair. I only had fantasies as a teenager would. Well, that was at the beginning. You would say: "To every story, there is a beginning!" To every story there is a spark, and maybe some oil thrown to the fire. But was that fire about cosily warming me up or thoroughly devouring me? Did I think about love at that time? No. I didn't even know what love was. Did I feel love at that time? I don't know. Maybe they were mere carnal desires of a frustrated teenager. That fire, I felt within my chest, lit my lonely nights and plunged my soul in sorrowful pleasure. At dawn, after a sleepless night, I closed my eyes to scraps of innocent and indecent dreams. There was no gossip in my dreams, no intrusions. I could smell Martine's scent. I could taste her flesh, feel her breath, touch her hand and run in the fields, run to the river. Away from indiscrete eyes, away from inquisitive minds susceptible of spoiling beautiful moments lived by innocent creatures.

"Let's swim," suggested Martine who already started taking off her clothes.

"Do you think the water is warm enough?" I said, blushing and looking away.

She jumped into the river and laughed. She kept laughing.

"Is the water cold?"

She was waving at me.

"Come!"

I couldn't take my clothes off. I was shy. But wasn't that a great opportunity? I took my shirt off and put it on a rock. Take off all your clothes, I cheered myself up. But something was preventing me from enjoying those moments. I could have seen her naked. I could have been naked. I could have jumped in right after her and stopped thinking about whether the water is cold or warm, whether people would speak about it or not, whether the sky is blue or green.

I could understand her. I could perfectly understand her words. I could communicate with her. It felt amazing! Which language was that? Was it French? But I didn't speak French! "Akli, come!" Heavens! She called my name. Then, I hesitantly jumped in. The water was perfect. Bla bla... is the water warm... bla bla... is it cold... How silly I was, even in a dream!

We swam each towards each other, slowly, swaying, floating, closer and closer...

72

"Get up! It's time!"

"Hell! What is my mother doing there? No, it's a dream!"

My mother's voice suddenly snapped me out of the most beautiful dream I ever had.

I woke up. I thought, for an instant, that I still have the capacity to talk with Martine the way we did in… but… it was a dream. We could talk and that was a fabulous dream. Do dreams have a special language in which humans can understand each other?

"It is just a dream's trickery," I realised. Unexpectedly, whilst taking off the blankets, I felt a wet spot on my pants. I used to sleep with my everyday clothes since I only had two trousers. Ha! A pyjama? Not for us. It seemed that I didn't manage to stop my invading nightly desires from making me wet my pants. Disgusting! Fortunately, I was alone. My two brothers were already in France. We used to share the same room and the same blankets. "No one shall see that," I told myself. I went out hiding, under my *burnous*, the wet spot. What a shame! I felt ridiculous. "The river! I thought. Then I went to the river where I washed my pants and hid behind a bush until they were dry. Thank God it was a sunny Sunday.

Was I falling in love with Martine without knowing it? I wanted to approach her, to talk to her. "But would she understand my language? I didn't speak French. I felt frustrated. I needed to learn French to tell her my feelings. The feelings I had, I lived intensely in my mother tongue. Could I have done it in another language? I could dare a "*Je t'aime*" in French, but it would have sounded so wrong and would have been too early a declaration. "Why, I sometimes naively thought, did God not provide humans with only one language?" We would have understood each other and avoided loads of troubles. "A letter! Why wouldn't I send her a letter?," I asked myself. I couldn't write even in my own language. I never went to school. Our language was not taught at school

73

and still, until today, only a few schools teach it! How could that happen with a language spoken for thousands of years? I don't know. A lot of us could write Latin, Arabic, French and were great thinkers. Apuleius, Saint Augustine, Ibn Khaldoun, Memmeri and others. But our own language wasn't taken seriously until lately. This language, in other circumstances, would have been a pride for the whole of humanity, thanks to its persistence and endurance. It survived orally whilst other languages, influential and written ones, disappeared. The Arabs came, they killed, raped and Islamised the majority of us. "The Koran is in Arabic, Arabic is the language of Allah, Allah gives access to heaven. So, those who don't speak Arabic are denied access to heaven." Aren't these nice sermons? Sermons from the dark ages. Arabic was thought to be a language of knowledge. As if there are languages unable of transmitting knowledge! As if the other languages were not created by God. Islamised, arabised, we don't know who is who. Who is Arab, who is Amazigh. Those who rejected the sword and slavery fought, fought, fought, and when they couldn't fight anymore, they took refuge in the high mountains. The mountains preserved their honour, life, and language.

I needed to write a letter to Martine. "Who in Thaddart could do that?"

Slimane Uhemu! He was Thadarth's public writer. He wrote letters to the whole village's children who went to work in France. He was in charge of reading my brothers' letters. "Why not? But Slimane Uhemu wouldn't write that letter!" What if in front of him, the words I have to say wouldn't come up? No! My words are too intimate to be written by him. He would mock me and my feelings. He probably will tell the whole of Thadarth about it and I will be subject to mockery again.

I hated the attitudes of the adults who mocked the youngsters. Things didn't change even now. If someone is to teach you something, the aim is not teaching you, but to show that he knows better than you. That he is better than you. It is regrettable that among prominent persons, doctors, researchers, journalists, teachers, there is a lack of wisdom. Being literate isn't enough. It is important to know how to think and how to transmit the knowledge one acquires. A spoon is well shaped but it doesn't know the taste of soup. Same thing with a learned fool. He has a position, nice clothes, but doesn't have and know the taste of wisdom.

Anyway! I don't want to stop thinking about Martine. When I think of her, I become ageless. Eternal. I started hating the linguistic barrier between her and me. I wanted to burn or destroy the school in the neighbouring village whose access was reserved for the French.

"Why not us? Were they super humans and we sub-humans?," I questioned. "Why couldn't they speak Kabyle? Yes! Why?" Had they not lived here for decades already? But they were the 'masters'. We were slaves, in truth."

Martine's love was enslavement. A sweet enslavement for the teenager I was. She never left my thoughts. I wondered what I was thinking about before Martine invaded my soul. She never left my mind, my dreams, day and night. She lived in me. That she loved me too was the fruit of my imagination. And whenever I saw her, I suffered. A beautiful yearning. A pleasurable suffering.

What is the secret of her eternal joy? She had a naturally cheerful face. Her eyes smiled all the time. I would have given up everything, religion, nation, traditions, and all this nonsense, to kiss her eyes. She is here, with me. In front of me. Her face blushes. Ah, that shyness on her face! She can now hear, understand my warm feelings. She can now feel me. Eyes and hands tell love. She is excited, moved. I spin around her like a butterfly around a beautiful flower. I hold her hand between my hands. Hers is moist. She blushes again. Suddenly someone horns in! Other traits. Different traits. My mother's voice. "Never a French!" Martine's face was blurring at intervals.

Dihya! My cousin. "She is your wife!" My mother's voice again! Dihya's face replaces that of Martine at intervals. Martine's smile becomes veiled by the sullen and angry look of Dihya. Was I dizzy because of the sun? My day's reveries stunned me more than the sun's rays.

"Your body is here but your mind is there in the clouds," Mhand said to me every time he found me daydreaming.

At sixteen, Dihya was already a woman. Beautiful and fresh, although strengthened by everyday tasks imposed upon her. She was in constant movement during the day. She was like an ant. She was responsible and devoted to her work. As the proverb says, "Every finger is gifted". Thus, she was, as were all the girls of her age, a perfect future housewife. Women weren't destined to any other fate than that of being housekeepers and their husbands' servants.

For days, weeks and months, I kept dreaming and thinking of Martine. Then, it might have been by the force of thoughts and dreams, the day I longed for finally came. For weeks, the sun was scorching earth and beings. An incomprehensible and divine punishment. Together with my co-workers, we had lunch. A handful of dried figs, a few sips of whey, a mother's handmade bread, a fresh onion and some olives. Then everyone went to rest. Some under a fig tree, others under an olive tree. The whey, thick as it is, went not down to the stomach, but up to the head. It weighed our brains and bodies. A *siesta* was more than welcome. Let's lie down until the sun gets mild. I was leaning against the trunk of an olive tree, ready to take a peaceful nap. I was yawning sporadically and smiling at the view of my friends already asleep. Wali was already snoring. I covered my face with my hat. The hat. As soon as I closed my eyes, Martine's silhouette struck me. A dream? I saw her lips approaching mine with chilling poise. Wake up, fool! It's not a dream. It's the truth. Or a dream coming true. She pressed her lips against mine. The sun was high in the sky. It was hot, burning hot. And from everywhere around there were sounds. Flapping wings, singing birds. A breeze came suddenly that freshened up our lips already wet. I sighed. I could hear my sigh. I could hear her breathing. I could feel her breath. I closed my eyes. I was feverish. There was no dog barking, no hawk shrieking, no donkey bawling.

We lost ourselves instantly in the gentle tension that our lips were causing in our bodies. Two hovering souls joined. They were heading to a spring gorged with wholesomeness and lust. That was our first kiss. My first kiss. Her first kiss. Behind a barn. Yes! We secretly kissed behind that barn. That kiss was my first act of love. I loved floating in its memory. I relived it as much as I could in my dreams, day and night dreams.

Isn't it funny how I can remember every detail? Her looks, her hair, her lips, her shyness. Everything. Her eyes, her faded eyes, her rosy cheeks, her movements, her hands. I didn't notice her when she came form behind me. I was cleaning the barn. I hated cleaning that barn. I learned to love it because it became our secret place, witness to our first kisses. Witness to the beginning of our infatuation. I had abandoned the idea of sending her a letter. However, I went for another. A deed. A deed that would prove my passion. Or was it madness?

"A rose," said Said-My-Book. "To show love for girls, we can offer them roses".

"But where on earth can I find a rose? I thought. Those of the Finos were untouchable. His wife used them to decorate the living room. At Thadarth, rare were the families that planted roses. Usually, we planted, let's say, useful plants. Vegetables and fruits. Those that we could eat, perfume or decorate the house with. Utility preceded beauty. We had no time to spend musing over beauty because we were hungry. Between roses and potatoes, we picked potatoes.

"Where could I find roses? And, let's say I found a rose to give her, how would she take it? What would be her reaction?"

I was afraid of rejection. Was I not a mere worker in their property? An illiterate. This word, indeed, hurt me. I was desperate, illiterate. Ignorant.

But things were set to be exceptional. Jacqueline came to the fields to find me. I saw her coming. I was lying down, as I usually did, on 'my olive tree' trunk. I got up. Then when she arrived, "Ɛalxir!" She said in Kabyle.

"Bojor!" I replied. She was no better at speaking in Kabyle than I in French. The letter Ɛ almost hurt her throat. Hahaha.

"No *siesta* any more," she said in a lovely but intimidating tone. Then, with her arms, fingers and her face, she tried to explain what I should do: "You come here twice... Monday and Wednesday..."

I repeated these last words. I knew the days in French.

"Monday... after weekend... you learn French... you... you... here... You should come! No absence!" She added with an imposing finger and a false grimace. Sheepish, I stood in front of her not quite understanding her words and gestures. French... *siesta*... Monday... weekend!

Fortunately, Wali was not far behind. He therefore tried to explain what it was about. She wanted me to learn French.

"But would Mr Fino agree with that?"

Jacqueline's idea was impracticable. I had to go to their house twice a week after the lunch pauses. Me? At Fino's? I went to their house the following Monday. I was astounded. It was the first time I entered a house. A true and modern house. There were tables, chairs... a lot of furniture. She welcomed me. Words, sounds, gestures and a lot of smiles. She invited me to sit down. I looked at the chair.

"What an invention!" I thought. I saw people sitting on them when I visited Thizi. I never sat on a chair before. It was my first time. As soon as I sat down, she showed me a book. It was open and there were many images. She sat down near me. I smelled her perfume. She put the same perfume that got my senses up when I met her for the first time. Thadarth's women

78

used different fragrances. Natural and fresh ones. They used to hang to their hair some mint, basil, a geranium, pennyroyal or others. These same herbs were used for cooking and perfuming the house too.

Jacqueline showed me a picture and pronounced, several times, the corresponding word. She then made me repeat after her. I did. I was finally about to decipher the secret of those letters and sounds hitherto unintelligible to me.

"Fantastic! A good excuse for getting closer to Martine," I thought.

Learning her language was a good opportunity to be able to talk with her. It was also a good opportunity to see how a French family lived. I started learning French from those colourful books. I thought about Said-My-Book. I was lucky. I could learn French. I could see Martine when she came back from school. I was happy. I was sad for Said.

"A, B, C, D… Like that! Again! No. U not OU! Try again. Open your mouth this way. Round your lips… again!" Each letter corresponded to a picture of an animal, a plant or an object.

Oh Jacqueline, how thankful I am!

However, as I expected, these lessons upset her husband. At that time, their relationship was already failing. He was knocked for six when he saw me for the first time there - in his living room, sitting at his table, next to his wife. Mr Fino raised his voice but Jacqueline didn't react to his provocations. I was sitting there, between them, scared and feeling guilty. It was not difficult for me to understand what was going on. The context, and Fino's tone and looks were enough. Fino left. Since then, I never saw him during my lessons. He stopped replying to my usual morning greetings. My presence was undesirable and he made it obvious.

Thadarth knew about my lessons. Thadarth gossiped, gossiped. My father smiled. My mother advised me.

"Jacqueline is a communist," I once heard Mhand telling my father during one of his visits. I knew that Mhand was watching me and was reporting everything that I did and did not do to my father. I didn't understand what the word communist meant. I didn't dare to ask. "Co...mun...ist," I tried several times to break it down. At Thizi, there was '*la commune*', the municipality, also called '*la mairie*'. I tried to figure out what was it but I couldn't until that day when I heard the Finos fighting.

"There is no harm in teaching this boy a few words," I heard Jacqueline whimpering.

"How silly!" he answered mockingly. "He is here to work not to learn."

"He is a child. You are exploiting him!"

Silence.

"You like exploiting these people, don't you?" She went on. "In their own land!"

"Madam wants to civilise these dirty, ignorant people," he replied. "This people, without us, cannot do anything! You know what their proverb says? Give him a finger, he takes the whole arm. This is what you are doing with this boy."

"Monsieur knows their proverbs! So they aren't ignorant and uncivilised, are they?"

"You'd better stop your charade. What would our friends say?" He replied.

"What will your friends, looters, say? What will your friends, exploiters, say?"

"Enough with your disgusting communist speech!"

She smiled faintly. He then spoke his mind.

"In life, there are masters and slaves. The master has strength and power. The slaves must be obedient and submissive."

"Is this the speech of a civilized man?," she burst out. "In life, there are humans and nobody must be superior or inferior. Where do you put Equality, Fraternity? Would I dare to talk of

Liberty with someone who treads on people in their own country, trying to force them into assimilation and acculturation? Ah, all these concepts are meaningless to you. You know what this is called? Exploitation. Hypocrisy. History will one day judge you like it did in Indochina and other parts of the world."

"I'm fed up with your moralising speeches!" he said rushing out.

"You are unable to hear the truth!" she ended.

I was listening eagerly. I could understand almost everything. I had a hidden little notebook. I was writing everything that I did not understand. I went over the difficult words once home. Jacqueline had given me a dictionary. I used to spend hours reading from it. It helped. The word communist didn't exist. It might have been banned? Or was the dictionary a simple and concise one?

My co-workers spoke about that fight.

"Yes, she is a communist," said Mhand again. She defends the workers and their rights. Ammi Ali is also a communist," he added.

I recalled Jacqueline's words. They matched Ammi Ali's. Since then, I loved the word communist. I loved Jacqueline who was defending me. I loved Ammi Ali for his intelligence and dignity. I wanted to be a communist without even knowing what it actually was.

But let's go back to the roses. Well, the flowers. I was walking back home when an idea popped up in my brain. "Dihya, my cousin. She loves flowers," I thought. "Flowers could help. Yes! The geraniums behind their house".

She was the one who took care of them. She watered them every morning. "Geraniums aren't roses!" I said. "But let's take a look behind their house! Who knows? There may be roses?" I smiled at that idea. Steal my promised wife's geraniums and offer them to Martine. A hint of regret stung me. "It's just a bouquet," I convinced myself.

I went to my cousins' and furtively looked at the geraniums. They were bright, reddish pink.

"See you tomorrow morning," I happily said to them. I could have taken some the same evening but I should take them fresh. "Martine should have them fresh like those fresh spring mornings," I thought.

The next day, as the first sunrays lit my room, I woke up quietly. My mother, awake early as usual, scolded me because I didn't wait for her coffee and left with an empty stomach to work. I took the path towards the Finos without thinking about it twice, exchanging 'good morning' with the women coming back from Thala. I expected meeting Dihya but she was not among the group she used to go with.

"Is she home? Did she comeback earlier? Is she there yet?" I reached their house. I looked right, left, behind and in front of me. No one around. Hop! I prudently walked to the back of the house. The geranium leaves were covered with dewdrops. The soil was wet. Dihya had already watered them!

"Stop there, you robber!" shouted someone behind me as soon as I picked the flowers.

I was caught. She was standing by the corner of the house, a jar on her head, her hands to her hips. Did she read my thoughts? I blushed. She blushed.

"Since when do you like geraniums?" She asked.

I stared right into her eyes. She avoided my gaze. I made her uncomfortable. She blushed again.

"I just want to see them," I said, uselessly trying to hide my embarrassment.

My voice, my words sounded silly. I felt silly too.

"You want to steal them, right?"

She then crossed her arms, looked at me insistently.

"What about those you are hiding behind your back?" She asked.

I mumbled something I myself did not understand. She added, "Do you think that the French girl is better than me?"

82

In one quick movement, she put the jar down against her breast and held it tight. She looked at me again. It was not a stare. It was a reproach. My words clung to my tongue. I was about to mumble some other thing but she did not wait for any answer. She disappeared behind the back wall of the house.

It was unnecessary to answer her. She would not have listened. I felt sad. I felt anger. I did not know what to think anymore. The entire Thadarth was against me. Dihya was reproaching me something I was not responsible for. Should I feel sorry for her? I was showing her sympathy whenever we met. Compassion? She did not want any compassion. She wanted me to consent to the promise our mothers made without our consent. She seemed jealous after all the rumours about Martine and me. She probably loved me. Was it just an absurd compliance to an absurd oath? I couldn't love her the way I would a girlfriend or a wife. She was my cousin, a sister. I couldn't go beyond that. It was out of question. I was fond of another girl.

I was seventeen. She was sixteen. The pain she felt was caused because of gossips. Nothing happened between Martine and me at that time. We weren't in a relationship. I was the only one aware of what was happening. Martine did not know about what was thought and said in Thadarth. We lived in two different worlds. The only connection we had was that made through preconceived thoughts and many prejudices. We both refused to approach each other. Fear and difference were the main reasons. We lived together, but we could not know each other better and could not appreciate each other. The majority of the French wanted to be our masters and subject us to their orders. Fed up with their enduring injustices and devoured by resentment, we did not want to put up with them in our own home too.

I loved Dihya, of course. Yet, I loved her as a cousin, as a sister. I am not trying to justify anything. It is just because we both grew among brothers and sisters, like a brother and a sister. Martine did not spoil in any way the love I had for my cousin. Martine gave me the strength to force things and rebel, within myself first, against my mother's oath. If Martine hadn't come into my life, I might have accepted things as they were. I mean, I would probably have married Dihya. But things took another turn. A turn I could not suspect.

The geranium bouquet in hand, I walked towards the Finos. I walked telling myself, "I am crazy! I am a fool!"

My feelings were fighting against my logic. My head was full of doubt. My knees were weak.

"We are not the same. We are different. What if she rejects me? I will feel ridiculous. I already feel ridiculous. No, I can't do that." I stopped walking.

But... the geraniums... what if I met someone on the way? I should hide them. Hide my ridiculousness. Hide my spontaneity. Hide my innocence. Hide beauty. Hide it all from prejudice and inequality. Hide a nice geranium bouquet, my sign of love, from the bad eyes, the bad mouths, the bad minds that would mock or hate me. They would be less mocking or hating if they found me stealing or even committing a murder. Where shall I hide them? Geraniums are so delicate.

"My hat! Yes! I put them under my hat, hoping that they would arrive safe and fresh.

I hurried up holding my hat. I didn't want to think about: "hows, whys, ifs..." Doesn't men's bad luck come from their fear and hesitation? I wanted neither.

The Finos were on holiday. They will not get up early, I thought. I had a plan. A plan I came up with after days of thinking and calculation. "Get up early, rush to the Finos and knock on Martine's window." I know, I know, you may say that this is a simple plan and it does not need any calculation. I was a kid. I was afraid. It was indeed a simple plan that required a lot of courage and ardour. I stood there. In front of her window. I was not afraid any more. Well! The truth is, I was anxious...just a little bit. Or maybe a lot? I was surprised by my own courage and the excitement of what I was feeling and living. It gave me even more courage. I looked at the geraniums in my hand. "Not bad. Not bad."

"Knock, Akli!" I encouraged myself. "No! What if… Stop thinking! Stop hesitating!"

I stretched my arm out through the window bars. "What in hell I am doing here?" I closed my eyes. "Take a deep breath, Akli. Remember her smile, her lovely smile, her sweet eyes, her gleaming lips, her delightful skin. Hear her laughter, like a spring breeze in the colourful fields. Don't you dream of all this day and night? Knock, Akli, knock! Knock and let the window be open. Open, Sesame! Open that heart of hers full of kindness and tenderness."

I knocked on the shutters. Once. A second time. Again. No answer. "Maybe she is sleeping in another room?" I was sure to be standing in front of the window of her room. She used to spend hours sitting on the sill of that very window, reading books and singing songs.

I knocked again.

"Who is there?," whispered Martine.

Her voice heightened my excitement. "Why doesn't she open?"

In a hurried and awkward tone, I replied, muffling: "Akli!"

That tone was embarrassing. Was it mine? I should not fall or trip. Not now anyway! I was preparing myself. "The hat! Adjust your hat. No, not this way. Yes, that's it. Good." Adjusting that damned hat on my little head became an obsession. "The geraniums! Not bad, not bad. They are still… somehow fresh. Dihya! Oh Dihya! If you saw me standing here, your geraniums in hand, trembling in front of Martine's window! I should not think of that now! What if my words didn't come out? What if my throat does not allow me to speak up? What if my tongue betrays me? What now? Sh… knoc…"

Suddenly, the shutters opened. I saw her hand pushing them. I followed the movement of her naked arm. My eyes were locked on her face. She tried to look at me, but the light entering the room blocked her view. She put her hand over her forehead to block the sunlight. She had sleepy eyes. Her hair was messy. Through her transparent nightgown, I could see her divinely sculpted forms. The cleavage of her firm breasts delighted me. Her breasts! An exquisite promise of feverish nights. I watched that exotic splendour. A woman's splendour I never saw before. A woman revealing her private self. I looked at the bars separating us. I wish I could open them at once! She was inside. I was out. Yet wasn't it I who was trapped behind the bars of the feelings I had for her? She was free. She was as free as the soft breeze caressing her flesh on which goose bumps formed. Was she cold? Afraid? Excited?

I looked at her and smiled. I was not the same person at all. Her face lit up when she saw the geraniums, or what was left of the geraniums.

"Is this for me?" she asked, looking at me. I looked into her eyes spasmodically. Decency? How could I be decent when I had in front of me such a sublime creature? I could not get my eyes off her, her beauty, her chest, the milky skin under her nightgown. I was not decent, not according to traditions.

Martine smiled. Did she notice that I stared at her breasts? I tried to hide my nervousness. I snapped out of my trance. I was there for something, no? For what? The geraniums! I gave them to her. "Yes, these are for you," I said timidly, elegantly.

At least this is how it felt. What really transpired is another thing.

Gently, she held out her hand and took the bouquet. I realised that my hand was sweating.

"The geraniums would be wet," I thought.

"Thank you," she said, bringing them to her nose. She smelled them. "That's very kind of you, Akli!" she added, warmth in her eyes. I dared. I stared straight into her eyes. My mother always told me that I had beautiful eyes. It was my mother's unique expression of her love for me. "My son has beautiful eyes." Wasn't it a good reason to muster up my courage in front of Martine? I thought that if I used them I could show Martine my flame without saying a word. Would it be French or Martian? My mother's compliment gave me more confidence, but if she knew what I was up to, she would have kicked me out of the house.

Hahaha! Thinking of all this amuses me.

I looked straight into Martine's eyes. She was already looking deep into mine. "Can she read my thoughts? My feelings? Does she know that she fascinates me?"

We spoke with our eyes. Mine told her what my tongue could not say. We stood there staring at each other. An everlasting soul embrace. There was no need to talk, to say, to speak in French, in Kabyle or any other language. We just needed to forget, for a moment, one tiny moment, all the meddling around us, and look into the depth of our souls to express our feelings. Whose hand had brushed away all the complications I was seeing in that relationship? Was it God's hand? A glimpse of mercy? Martine seemed to have feelings for me too. Weren't her eyes saying so? Eyes do not lie. "Is this a dream?," I thought. Nothing on earth would have been more marvellous than being loved by Martine. My mother's warnings, Fino's cruelty and Thadarth's gossips were gone from my mind. Nationalities, languages, taboos, religions, cultural differences did not matter. They were a hindrance to love, to the enjoyment of beauty, to the soul's truth.

"Martine!" We heard Jacqueline's voice, waking us up from our sweet languor.

Panicked, Martine hopped. She mumbled a '*merci*', and she sneakily closed the window on me.

"I should get out of here," I thought. This magical moment was over and I did not steal even a kiss. I walked away, my back glued to the wall of the house, like a thief. I could lose my job. I was gambling away my family's survival. I was running the risk of causing my mother's wrath and Thadarth's cruel judgements.

"The workers are not here. Go to the back of the barn, jump over the fence, and run into the wood, then go down to the path leading back to the Finos. All is well! 'Good morning, good day! I am going to work'."

Martine's eyes, her looks and what happened that day and afterwards occupied my mind. Forever. Well this is how they say. Forever. Since that morning, our love grew. It was true love. Mutual love. Secret love. We had to hide to enjoy it. Were we doing any harm to anyone? No. Yet, love between Martine and I was sacrilege to my family, a nonsense for Thadarth, and an aberration for Mr Fino. Hiding our love for each other increased excitement even more. I never expected, "the studious and wise boy I was," as my father said of me, to be drowned in that kind of passion. A dangerous passion.

Once at work, I spent the entire day daydreaming. Working in the fields, serene and happy, I wanted to plant love in all the furrows of Mother Earth so that the flowers that grew in them would diffuse happiness and joy to all souls. I felt love in the soil, in the breeze, in the leaves, the sun and everything I saw or touched. I heard love in birds' songs, in cows' moos, in roosters' crows, in donkeys' brawls. Yes! Even donkeys' brawls sounded lovely!

But surely not Mr Fino's shouts. I was feigning ploughing the soil in front of the house when he called me. I actually was not doing any work. I was just waiting for Martine to come out. I was waiting for our second meeting. Mr Fino's shouts interrupted my daydreaming.

"*Na3din rebb-ik!*" (Cursed be your God's religion!), I swore silently. He had not talked to me in ages. Why now?"

Without greeting or looking at me, he screamed: "What in the hell are you doing? Go and clean the barn and around it immediately!"

I hated that barn. I disliked Mr Fino. It was a harmless disliking though.

Silently, rage in the heart, I walked towards that shitty barn.

"Wait till I finish what I have to say, idiot!" He added.

I stopped, frowned. Did he know about what happened at Martine's window? I was certain no one had seen me. But with that old fox, Mr Fino, one must be very careful. Fortunately, my nervousness did not show. Nothing to be afraid of. Fino was living in another world. The world of exploitation and reproaches.

He uttered the word "idiot" as he breathed out. I was his favourite target when it came to saying 'idiot, broken arms, lazy'. I was the idiot whenever a task was completed, duly or not. I was deaf when I did not listen to him. I was lazy when I was late. I was stupid when I came to work early. He seemed enthused with blaming me for everything whenever we met. He had the gift to twist everything in his favour. Wasn't he the master after all?

When Mr Fino was absent, I was invited to have lunch or tea with the Fino ladies. Julien, the son, never sanctioned that. He kept threatening his mom and me.

"I will tell my father," he kept saying. He never told Fino about it. I actually tried many times to speak to him but my attempts remained unsuccessful.

"I don't want to be your friend!" he once told me. "Who are you? You only work for my father."

"I am a boy like all the other boys," I answered assertively.

He laughed at me and replied: "You aren't like me. Look at you! Your clothes are dirty and you don't speak good French."

"My clothes are dirty because I work. You don't work and you don't speak Kabyle," I answered.

"I can speak Kabyle," he said. "I know 'azul' means hello, 'akhir' means good morning, 'aghrum' means bread, 'aman' is water."

His Kabyle accent was far worse than my father's in French. He tried to remember other words. I tried to help him. "I don't want to learn your language," he exclaimed. "I don't want to be your friend."

"I don't care about your friendship," I replied proudly. It felt good for a moment. I could argue with him and I did it in French. I always thought that whenever someone can speak a language, it is his. For me, learning French was a way to get closer to the French, a way to understand them better. It was not a way to avoid their evil deeds or thoughts. It was a way to get closer to them. I learned French to understand my Martine, to be closer to her, to talk to her, to love her better. I wish she could do the same, with my language.

Julien was jealous because both his mom and sister were friendly to me. They showed me a lot of kindness. I do not think that he hated me. He was just jealous.

I was reliable at work. No one could reproach me anything.

"I won't make of the two Fino males the cause of my troubles and worries," I established.

After I finished with the barn, I began cleaning its surroundings. Martine's eyes occupied my mind when I was pulling out the weeds. I felt like I was floating on a cloud. I often used to lie under a tree and think of Martine, feeling that wonderful sensation, floating on a soft and fluffy cloud. It raises me out of the surface, fluctuating gently in the air. The cloud is moist, fresh, and my body warm and heavy, sinking into it. The sky is bright blue. Everything around is slightly hazy. I close my eyes and feel the sun's warm rays, just enough, on my face. Then a soft breeze, caressing my hair, opens my eyes. The ground below me looks like a makeshift quilt. Green grass, golden fields. Patches of water, rivers and lakes. I see the shadow of my cloud below, on the ground. It moves silently. But... a twin shadow. I can see another drifting beside my cloud's shadow. Where is... its cloud? There! Beside me. So close to me. Comfortably sat, Martine smiles at me. I stretch out my arm… My hand joins hers. Our clouds join too and together we float, float, float…

What a wonderful feeling. I feel like I am still floating even when I wake up from my fantasy, wiggling my toes and fingers. I shrug my shoulders, stretch out my arms and legs, open my eyes, ready to go back to work, full of energy. I sometimes try to relive this feeling down here in my cell. I float, but I never see Martine again.

"Was she moved by the flowers? Should I trust the look in her eyes? How would her attitude be towards me after all that? Could it be that I was just fooled by my emotions and saw only what I wanted to see? Wasn't it just an illusion? Was her look something other than affection? Was it a one of compassion?" I languished. I lingered over my doubts the entire morning.

I was ploughing the soil behind the barn when, unexpectedly, two hands covered my eyes. Drowned in my sweet daydream, I had not noticed anyone approaching me. The hands were moist and soft. A woman's hands.

"Who could it be? Martine?" No word. I heard her breath. Then suddenly, she burst into laughter and let go. I turned around. Martine! She stepped back. I smiled. She blushed. I did too. Her eyes were sparkling. She looked into my eyes and came closer. Closer. She was still looking into my eyes. Our noses were almost touching. I looked at her lips. Open. Moist. I felt her breath. She took my hand. The other one dropped the shovel and took hers. I was frozen. Taken by surprise. It was dazzling. Forget the barn, the world! Forget God, hell! Forget mother, Thadarth, Fino! Forget everything!

She softly pressed her lips against mine.

"Is this what we call a kiss?" Then, yes! Martine kissed me.

"What am I supposed to do now? Close your lips and let her do it."

At that time, we did not have TV or any book explaining or showing how to kiss. I sometimes saw the Fino parents kissing, but never close up. My parents? That is unlikely! I always asked myself how they were in their intimacy. We never spoke about love. Sexuality? Sexuality is the biggest taboo ever, ever! I never heard my father saying lovely words to my mother and vice versa. In the secret of the night? Perhaps. Their relationship was reduced to: "Do this! Don't do that! Serve me!" Orders. It was no more than a marriage of convenience. She was the housekeeper, he was the food provider; they should give birth to children and live together. Both their families had agreed to their marriage and that was it. My parents, no doubt, loved each other. I could feel it but I never saw any burst of love or tenderness coming from them for each other, nor even towards us, their own children. Their relationship was not patriarchal, but it was a kind of competition. My mother knew how to have the final say. So many times my father swore, pointing at his moustache: "If you do not do what I say, I am not a man, I will shave this. May Thadarth laugh at me, if...! Etc." However, the next day or a few days later, we realised that my mother had won the argument, refusing to obey my father despite him threatening to shave his moustache. Those were the night's secrets! They were so charming and we enjoyed their competitions. False tensions! When I grew up, I understood that those tensions were mere games they were playing as part of their secret pleasures. Still, it would have been splendid if they put words to their love, a few caresses, some affection. That would probably have delighted us and taught us to see life in colour, with love. Some would say: "These are our ways, our lifestyle!" Others would say: "We are Muslims, we aren't Europeans to do so."

Is it a matter of being African, European or American? It is a matter of love. The parameter should not relate to culture or nationality but to appreciation. Doesn't spring feel good? Don't birds show and sing love? Don't we appreciate it? If we don't, it means that we are callous. If we do not appreciate it, it means that we have lost the human in us.

I closed my eyes and tasted Martine's lips. She pressed hers against mine, she gently bit my bottom lip, and ran her hands through my hair. My hat fell.

Martine's kiss threw me into ecstasy. I did not care about the virgins in paradise or any other consolation. Her lips kissed mine and it felt like heaven. Whilst Martine was fearless, I was clumsy. Clumsy but blissfully stirred.

"Let me fly, high! Let me sigh, live or die!" We both floated, floated, floated.

So was our love. Thrilling. Thrilling but frail. An unpromising love. I was enthusiastic, virile and strong, but alone and naive. I defied the existing standards. Secretly lived, my love to Martine was more exciting. Since then, I knew that love exists. Above all, I knew that love was not sex. I knew that love goes beyond the bodies. It goes into the realm of the spirits that no standard, no norm, no harm, no evil, no wickedness can destroy. Martine was my first love. My last love. Due to her family's problems and the history of both our countries, our love went up in smoke, not to the clouds. She went, along with her mother and brother, to live in France. Jacqueline took her children and left Mr Fino.

I met Martine again forty-six years after the liberation. It was during a summer morning. The sun was already melting our brains. The cicadas were already buzzing. They replaced the lovely birds' morning songs. They added more gloom to the villages plunged into endless bloody fights.

"An old woman and two men are looking for you," I was told. I was trooping, as usual, Thadarth's avenues and its surroundings with my comrades in arms.

"They are French". French? How can it be? How do they know me?

It was Martine.

"Martine? Martine Fino?"

Her brother Julien and his son.

93

"See, Martine, what happened to me? How fate's hand played with my life? You left without saying goodbye. You left with your mother and brother without a word. You did not have the time to. You did not expect it to happen. You went to France where you did not know anyone. You left the land that fed you, that saw you grow. The land where you were born. But what are you doing here? After all these years? Visit? Visit when death is afflicting the whole country? Visit when death is as effortless as a good morning? Visit when neighbours are killing each other? Visit when brothers are slaughtering each other? Aren't you afraid? These are not times to visit. But since you are here, "Welcome". Did you come to cry the past? Your properties? See what is left today of your father's property! Where are those tall trees, those green hectares full of fruits and vegetables, those fat cows, those healthy horses? Where are those sweet scents of orange trees, fig trees, roses and flowers? Even the soil smelled good and was fertile in those times. See what it turned into! Slums invading the whole area in the name of the agrarian revolution, as they named it. The agrarian revolution for self-sufficiency, about which they spoke proudly on TV, radio and newspapers. It was actually not a revolution but a mere razzmatazz in honour of our Stalin. Besides, we never produced anything. We import even nails from foreign countries. We import everything and nails are just a meagre part of the ninety-six per cent of our importations. What is left from Fino's farm? Open sewers stinking and spreading bacteria all around. Abandoned arable land invaded by weeds and rubbish. Arable land waiting the eternally postponed verdict of one judge or another in favour of this mayor or other corrupted notary."

My woe was deeper than that felt by Martine and Julien. Julien talked with respect and reverence to me.

"The past is past," I told him when he said, "Sorry. I know I was a bad kid."

"Don't be sorry, my brother. There are scars between us but we are old enough to understand that we should look at things in a different way, in a positive way. These scars must remind us of our stupidities. We should both accept them in order to live better."

We spoke about the present links between our two countries.

"Today's harms are provoked by both sides," I told him. One, frustrated, wants to glorify horror, and the other, by demagogy and mass manipulation, wants to remain in power. The enemy is not us. The enemy is them! There is no difference between the past and our present because we are stuck with precariousness. We surrender for some time, and then we explode again. After the explosion comes the implosion. Then everyone tries to eat the other, in the name of everything or in the name of everyone he can use; God, the prophet, the martyrs, religion, the values of... etc."

"How is it that people are living like this, Martine?" What can I say? We wanted to be free. Free from the colonialists. But it seems that today's enemies are worse. Snakes. They are snakes coming from our own blood, from our own womb.

"Your visit drove me into deeper despair, Martine. Yes, what you saw is not what we wanted to establish. No, it is not what we fought for, Martine. I feel ashamed. I feel ashamed because we did not succeed despite the thousands of deaths and exiles. Despite the sweat, the blood, the tears, the hunger, and the cold. You know, Martine, that our war was just. Your mother was aware of that too. Our war against the French was just. Now? Today? You are asking me about today. I don't know. What did you say? Why am I holding this Kalashnikov? Resistance, Julien. Resistance. See! We never rest. Wars are uninterruptedly running towards us. Do we have any other choice than to resist? No. No rest. No life, just the struggle. Rest is not for us. Resistance is written on our forehead. Look! You can read it. Read it on my forehead, in my tired eyes. Do not feel sorry if you read, yes, on that same forehead, sorrow. Our prayers, our arms, our sweat, our blood and our tears could not rub off what is written on our foreheads. God has abandoned us. We maybe abandoned him. Whatever! He does not seem as great as he pretends to be. Well! These are his secrets. Why is he so cruel? I told you, these are his secrets. Has he forgotten us? Has he become deaf to our prayers and our cries? Has he become blind and cannot see our sufferings? I cannot answer that. I don't know. I wish he could be as great as he pretends to be or, I must say, as great as they present him.

Yes, Martine, I took up arms against the French and now against these savages. What would I have done? Accept my brothers' suggestion to go to France and live with them? No. Not for me. Tired and old. It is my duty to fight, to protect my property, to protect my village. I am neither an idealist nor a hero. It is a normal duty and a natural deed when danger is rambling around. Before the liberation, some occult forces gave birth to these snakes misleading us. Some people spoke about your dear De Gaulle himself. Did he give birth to the snakes that are spoiling our days? Who knows? These snakes are from us, turned against us. They are mighty and have the country into their pocket, deciding whether it would wind, rain or shit on us. God has forgotten them too. He cannot take away the throne under their asses. They overpowered him. I did not take up the arms to protect the snakes or to play their game. I took them up to protect my village and myself. I took them because my dignity and honour forbid me from watching my neighbours being humiliated, killed or raped. I didn't change? No... Yes... Hahaha! You make me laugh, Martine. I laugh though laughing has become an effort. Our eyes and minds are full of horrors. These horrors prevented our lips from smiling and our mouths from laughing. We saw beyond what should ever be seen. We lived what no country lived. It is needless to tell you the horrors we saw and lived. They are too painful to be told. Telling them does not alleviate our pains."

"I didn't change," you said, Martine. Thereupon, gazing over the hamlets and the hills, you hid your emotion. You wept. I felt bitter, Martine. I feel bitter. Martine, it is hard to meet forty-six years later. Forty-six long years. A whole life.

Julien was recounting the past to his son. Telling him stories and life. His son is living with a Kabyle girl, Martine told me.

"That's good. Good. We are all from the same family now. The human family," I told him tapping him on the shoulder.

"Did you hear when he greeted me in Kabyle? 'Azul'," he said. Then he explained, yes, he explained what *Azul* means.

Martine, we were looking at them when they were up there in the woods. Julien was excited. You looked at me. Tears were running down your face. You had a blue handkerchief. Blue, your favourite colour. You were not wearing glasses.

"You didn't change either," I told you.

We both didn't change but times have changed. I took your hand and I cried too. We both cried like two little boys. What did we cry, Martine? Our love? Our kisses? Our past? What we could not live? Or, we cried our present? What we missed? Martine, I also cried when you left. I wish I could read those letters you had sent me. You sent them after you left, you said. I never received them. I was in the harshest parts of the *maquis*. Maybe it is your father who received them? You wrote about the lovely moments we had together. You also wanted to keep in touch with me and receive news of me, you said. But, see! Things went differently. You said that your father probably tore them up or burnt them.

You know, I came to work the morning of your departure. I only found your father. I did not know that your mother planned to go, to leave the country. Things went so fast, so badly. The house, the farm became empty and so became my soul.

Forty-six years later. We sat at Thajmath and cried. We cried our love, our furtive moments in the barn, our secret escapes to the river, and our caresses under the table when her mother was teaching me French. We cried the beautiful orchards where we used to hide, sharing tender moments. See now what they have become. See how those trees are! Ashes. Why? The army decided so. They say it is in order to get the terrorists out of the woods. Then it became a ritual. Every summer, hectares are burnt, and the air becomes unbreathable. They do so to stifle us, yes!

We cried our past. I cried our past and my present.

"Only pebbles remain in the river," you said putting your frail hand on mine.

My hand was holding my weapon. What did I tell you? Yes. I said: "It's terrible for a man when he, helpless and powerless, witnesses the river getting dry." After the river dried out, blood flowed. Then we watered it with tears. Lots of tears. Drought came again. Look, now! I am nothing but an insignificant pebble in that same river. Nothing more than that! Lucky are those who did not watch the river dry out, every single day, feeling powerless and disgraced. You left. You were right when you left. Jacqueline, your mother, was right. She was a just woman. You mean my French? Not bad. I still have my accent. It will never leave me. You laughed at that!

You told me that you married twice. Divorced once and three years ago you became a widow. Me? It is a long story, I told you. Telling it hurts the old man I became. See, in that respect, we have changed. We are tainted. We are now old, weak and bitter. When we get old, our happiness has the past as its address. Though that past was tough, the older we become, the rosier it appears. Why did I take up arms? Again? It is a long story, Martine. Telling it makes me sad and torments me. You kept asking until I told you the whole of it. Then we stood up. We were sitting on the grass. I helped you. We got up together. "You are still strong," you whispered into my ear. Julien and his son walked back and joined us for a walk in Thadarth. The neighbours who remembered the Finos came and said: "Hello and welcome". They also said: "Go well and come back again". When the visit was over, I stood up, there, at the Lqahwa's terrace, waving sadly at you, watching you going down, away. You went away, Martine, taking with you some of my pains, fragments of my soul.

I could not help it. I saw you running. I was also running, just behind you. Your laughter rose, setting loose the birds hidden in the bushes and trees. Your dress brushed the trees and the grass blissfully. In those times, there were no bearded wild boars to slaughter the lovers or kidnap the beloved from her lover. In those times, there were no savage policemen to imprison lovers because they aren't married. During those times, there was no *sharia* imposed on people.

Yes, only pebbles remain in the river. It is everything that this old woman, beloved Martine, left behind with a lot of bitterness and regret. I still feel the touch of her wrinkled hands. I still feel the touch of her fresh and young hands. I still feel the moisture and tenderness of our kiss. My first kiss. Our first kiss, there, at the barn.

Martine, how it is that your eyes did not lose their spark? Your eyes, mirror of your tenderness and kindness. You left again. You left...

Don't be sorry, Julien. Let us shake hands and be friends. You also dared a few tears! We don't need cries now. Please. We have cried enough. Let us be glad because we meet again, in better spirits. Don't ask for forgiveness, Martine. What for? You didn't do any harm. You taught me love and your mother reinforced my convictions to fight for dignity. Love and dignity, the same principles which my parents, relatives and friends wanted to feed me with. Love and dignity beyond any limited mental or geographical borders. Love and dignity, the principles for which we, the colonised, aspired to when we fought against the colonisers. We had in our hearts the strength of the conviction and the strength of justice to realise them. Alas, the river has been diverted and ugly things were born.

You left, Martine, and took with you, my words, rags of my life. You insisted to hear about what happened. "I want to have an idea of how is your life after all these years," you tried to convince the guarded man I am. "It is important for me," you said in a deep and frail voice. I then told you my story, my pain and my hopes. Your tears, your words could not fill my heart with enthusiasm, Martine, nor could they console me.

6

I was the first to take up arms in Thadarth. Rombo's face was serious. I still remember his classy military salute. I took the Kalashnikov and went back to Thadarth. It was on 5 April 1995. It had been a long time since I had touched a gun. I was excited, determined. I was so sad too. That same day, I wanted Thadarth to know what I was about to do. I wanted Thadarth to see that I am not a man who gives up even after what happened. I did not tell anyone about my intention to fight against the terrorists. For years, my interactions were limited to 'good morning;, 'good evening' and other little insignificant exchanges of words. I was leading an ordinary life. Taking care of my sheep, my house, my dog, and my plot of land, which I farmed as I could. Old, I had few relations. Moreover, the tensions, after the beginning of the civil war in 1992, had changed people's attitude a lot. One should stay discrete and careful. Careful because the blow could come from, not only the enemy, but also the brother, the closest relative. At Thadarth, beards had begun to darken the faces and the minds. Islamist extremism grew among the neighbours.

I went out and walked through Thadarth's streets.

"Nana Ldju will spread the word," I thought. She was excellent at that. She used to spend her days gossiping from door to door, from a gathering to another. We called her 'Nana Ldju the radar'. Nothing at Thadarth could be kept from her. When she tells you about this or that person, this or that family, she mentions every detail, as if she were living with these people. Still, she was nice to people and she did not do any harm. I had found her at the village assembly, Thajmath. She went speechless for a moment when she saw me carrying a weapon.

"What is this, brother Akli?" she asked. I then told her. A while later, feigning having something urgent to do, she left shouting back: "Stay well, Akli!" She then walked through Thadarth's avenues, barefoot, since she never wore shoes in her life. Her spine was bent by time's hardships and by the gossip she bore from mouth to ear. Within hours, Thadarth was informed of my intentions.

Then, I came to you, Rabah. I came to your tomb. I wanted to talk to someone. I realised that I had no one to talk to, no one with whom I could share my pain, my doubt, and my feelings. You were the right one. You are still of a good help, Rabah. Even if under the earth, you give me a lot of comfort. You must be happy not seeing all the chaos that is taking place down here. I envy you. I envy you and I would have wished to be there, with you. Of death, I am not afraid, but of dwelling between these white and cold walls girdling my desires and thoughts, I am afraid. Bored. Death, I wish for it! However, I cannot offer it to myself. I am probably not man enough to kill myself. I can do it. I can use my shoes laces or any other trick. God forbid it! Isn't it terrible to think about suicide? My faith cannot comfort me. I sometimes pray but my prayers become ever more like robotic movements. No depth, no feeling. I cannot concentrate anymore. Did I lose faith? Or is it faith that can't ease my soul any longer? I sometimes rebel against the creator, name it God, Allah or whatever! There are many things I do not, I cannot understand. I have a brain and this brain, given by him, tells me not to follow blindly God's or whomsoever's sermon.

Rabah, do you remember when the helicopters were bombing our unit? Despite your injured leg, you were not afraid, you could run. We were in a net of bullets! Hell was set loose in the woods that day. We had to reach the river. We could not retaliate. We were outnumbered. Running was the unique way out. Everyone ran for his life. I was running behind you. I was terribly frightened. We ran in the woods, up to At Ichir's hills. My feet were bleeding but I did not feel them. I did not even feel the bullet planted in my arm. I was hearing my breath, interrupted by the bombings and the shootings.

"The river! Get to the river!" Then suddenly, silence. You stopped running. You hid behind the enormous rocks. I came to you. You smiled at me. A mysterious smile. Your trousers were torn up, your leg was bleeding.

"It's time for me to join my father," you told me. Then, you started reciting that song... Let me remember the words! Oh, yes! "Whenever...whenever someone dies, others will carry on, carry on the fight... " Then you said: *Thamurth Thilellit*. Free country. Our unit's password. Free country. These were your last words. Your attestation of faith. Is there a better declaration?

Life in those days was held to a fine thread. It happened so quickly, so savagely!

You died, Rabah. I survived. I survived, worn out by eternal grief. Do you think these images, these memories, will one day free me? Free country, you said. The country was liberated, but only from the French. The country was liberated for a few days, a few hours... No, the country has never been free. The snakes came, Rabah. You knew that! They came and took hold of the throne. They crawled on all fours, in force, tanks and fire; killed hundreds of people then took power. They had a plan. They crawled whilst people were, unaware of the games of power, celebrating in the streets. The opposing forces were very soon eliminated, and the snakes swore on the holy book their obedience to the principles of the revolution, they swore their deference to the brave people of this country. They swore on the holy book, in the name of Allah, in the name of blood, the martyrs' blood, to fill their bank accounts and bring the country to its knees. A better position for the French, the Americans and the others to screw it. To screw us actually.

When people started to be aware of what was really happening, in the 1980's and 2000's, spring came several times.

In 1980, 1988 and 2001. Our spring wasn't funded by the Qataris nor the Americans. It was fuelled by our consciousness and will for justice. We did not get up for bread and sugar. We got up for social and economic improvement, for culture, for identity, for human dignity. But in this part of the world, spring always turns into a winter. What comes from a snake? "A snake never gives a kiss," my father used to say.

The snakes know how to swallow the spring's flowers. They, whenever spring comes, give birth to monsters. These monsters, with swords, guns, sermons, threats, assassinations, oblige people to wear beards and veils in the minds. There is nothing worse than that.

At the beginning of the nineties, change was obvious. We were watching how things were daily and gradually changing. I went every Friday to pray at Thizi's mosque. Age, and fear of death and of the after-life were the cause of my spiritual practice. However, I always wished I could worship God in another way. I would love to worship God not because of fear but because of love. But fear is human, natural. Peace is an illusion we aspire to, constantly.

I went to Thizi's mosque because, naïve as I was, I thought that a collective prayer is better awarded than a solitary one. I followed the logic of 'one good deed is awarded ten favours.' In the case of a prayer, the collective one was twenty-seven times better! I, silly, followed without knowing how and on whose side of the balance all those favours were put. However, since it gives people the assurance (the illusion?) of being awarded and the confidence to go to heaven, never mind... Let them collect rewards for the after-life. Still, is our relationship with God as simplistic as that? Is it based on an absurd counting system? How can we count faith? Is it not a deep feeling of ease? The values of religion are all about peace, love, goodwill and amity. Why do we then have so much zeal when it comes to some insignificant gestures and practices? 'Pray, arm on the chest! No, not on the chest, it is not in the *sunna*!

Enter the toilet with your right foot. A long beard is blessed. This is halal, that is haram... Spirit, damn it! Some spirit!'

Good God! Let me change my position on this bed. I need more space, for heaven's sake! Let's be quiet now. That's it! It feels good on this side. A little bit more. Better. What about the notion of the 'chosen ones'? In every religion, God, Allah or whatever, states that the people he sent the books to, are the chosen ones. Is this right? I mean, we are all humans and the only parameter of judgement would be good and evil, not something else. Would it not be more simple and practical to live together and accept the others whatever they think, according to their standards, not ours? Why do we not accept the others' beliefs as they choose to believe in them? Sometimes, I doubt of all these things. Sometimes, I have a feeling that problems come from the words, the holy books themselves. God should have sent only one book for all of humanity and simply set things in a clear way. Better, why does he not, by the simple blink of an eye, change our hearts and make us the way he wants us to be? Obedient and doubtless. Isn't he the almighty? I sometimes wonder why in Kabyle we swear 'by all the religions or oaths? *Jmaa liman!*' It is true that in these vast lands of Northern Africa, we were Animists, Jews, Christians, Muslims and we still are from all these religions. How is it that some ignorant morons try to limit us to one current of thought, or in one religious practice? These bearded cannibals want to introduce their ideas into our water and bread, into our looks, our coughs and sighs, brains, our sexes, our shit.

Let me get up! This bed seems to be rejecting me. Where are my sandals? Here. I used to go to Thizi, and there, I noticed those weird cloths worn by those... the word 'men' does not fit them... by those 'apes', I'd prefer. Apes are far better than them. They were arrogant and proud. Their beards were grown and full. A long beard and an ugly brownish stain on the forehead were among the other parameters to get into

Allah's heaven and win the forty or seventy promised virgins. If they were not mentally ill, would they have thought about that? Sex! If they were not perverts, would they have thought about their libido whilst dealing with the after-life? Do they think of other things than the pleasures of the after-life? Rivers of sweet wine, milky white skin virgins... etc. They come and talk to you. "*Salam alikum*, brother! Why don't you keep your beard long? You must keep your beard long! We must follow the prophet's ways, acts and sayings."

Growing a beard was their primary social, agricultural and political project for the society. The second project: veil the female kind to avoid Satan's seditions. All women over ten. Isn't that a life project? Ah! An after-life project! Whilst other people are growing their wealth, sustaining their economic system, these morons are preoccupied by their ugly beards!

In the name of freedom and democracy, one couldn't say anything against them. These germs use freedom and democracy to dirty countries and infect them.

You are free to have a beard on the face or on the ass, boy! But, go away! Go preach your 'truths' elsewhere! Do not force me as you want me to be, as you are. Wear whatever you want, according to what you want, but do not force me to wear what I do not want to wear. I only understand one thing: these people are not a party in the democratic game, they are a problem to solve. They infected our countries. See in the world where there is the most chaos, poverty and violence. Now, they are at the doors of other countries.

Things went worse at the beginning of the nineties. Lots of indoctrinated young men used to gather on side roads, after and before the *muezzin* calls, discussing, threatening, stopping people and forcing them to hear their sermons. Some ran after women and little girls threatening them and preaching the necessity of wearing the scarf.

However, savageness reached its height during the nineties. The *jihad* by the Shikhs, supported by other foreign Shikhs, was ordered against the regime and all that symbolises the regime. Militaries, policemen, *gendarmes*, teachers, writers, journalists. Blood flowed, and still flows, in a savage and disproportionate way. Thousands of innocents were killed. Thousands! They cut heads, slain throats and burnt people alive. They didn't spare women, babies, children, animals. They raped women and little girls. They bombed public buildings and even mosques. They robbed, tortured. *Jihad*, they said! They persuaded kids, teenagers, women, entire families. Thousands of people adhered to their fanaticism and savageness. The snakes rejoiced and took advantage of the situation and, adding oil to the fire, they played the victims in front of the world. The snakes manipulated some extreme terrorist groups and did what they are best at: eliminate the opposition. Thousands of intellectuals were killed or sent into exile. Doctors, teachers, architects, journalists, singers, comedians, writers, poets… Thousands of voices were silenced. Thousands of lights were switched off. How can people see today without those lights?

7

I'm tired and I must rest instead of getting angry because of bygone futilities. I'm tired and starving. Ten minutes to eight. Time for dinner. Yuva might be working tonight. This man is a bag of laughs. His laughter is raucous, like a gorilla. His colleagues call him gorilla. He sometimes laughs even before I open my mouth. As if he had the capacity to anticipate my jokes. The door! Someone is opening the door. It is with no doubt him. He always knocks in the same manner. I have learnt it. Two sharp knocks. One, two.

"Hey, Yuva! How are you, my boy? Hahaha! You are a bag of laughs, man! Better to laugh than cry, you are right. I just asked you how you are. Fine! How is your wife? Fine! Your little boy? Fine!"

Yuva doesn't talk so much.

Are we late? Where are the others? There are no prisoners in the corridor. Ah! They must be starving. What are we eating today?

The food is not bad and often I have an extra portion of dessert offered by the chef. Fortunately, there are good men here. We sometimes talk. Yuva and the chef are nice men. They don't look at me with sorrowful eyes. They talk about work, about the low salaries, about their eternal strikes, about the workers robbing from the kitchen.

"The worst is the prison director," once whispered the chef in my ear. "He takes boxes of food destined to the kitchen and sells them on the black market. Go to Thizi's market, you will find his son selling yogurts and juice packs there."

Corruption, it seems, has reached the roots. Better said, we are corrupted to the roots.

"Olives with beef sauce, ha? That'll be delicious. For which occasion are they offering us this? The workers have got their wage raise. So, this is why you are smiling from ear to ear tonight!"

Everyone here respects me. They certainly had read the newspapers that had reported my case. I was told that petitions were also signed in the country and all over the world. Organisations, associations, human rights activists. I don't care anymore. After more than six years in prison, I don't care about any support, any compassion, any pity. My soul is hurt, and the fire I had in my heart turned into ashes. I stopped reading the newspapers. Mainly those produced by the regime's clans to bark for them and sing their 'Democrazy'. If I knew a general or a colonel, I wouldn't be here. If I were a colonel or a commander, I wouldn't be here, treated like a piece of thrash. I am left here whilst terrorists are free and given protection. I am thrown in here whilst ministers, mayors and state representatives, with dozens of scandals on their back, are maintained in their posts. I should have been a terrorist; it would have given me a lot of privileges. A salary, a job, and protection by their laws.

"You won't stay to eat with me, Yuva? Never mind. See you later. Hahaha! Keep laughing!"

How funny is this man? His laugh is contagious.

"Hello, my brothers. Can I sit down here? Thank you."

Their wages have been raised, are saying the prisoners. This is why we have a tasty meal tonight. Poor them! They were on strike for weeks.

In this country, better be a young entrepreneur affiliated to any army general or any minister who will facilitate all your investments. You will receive bribes from foreign firms and work with the richest dignitaries of the country. You initiate false import operations, fraudulent bank loans, false customs taxes and the law will protect you. Better be a seventy-four year old minister. The state will work for you and offer you the privileges you would never thought to have. Look at me! If I followed the stream of those fighters who, literate or illiterate, integrated the political and administrative institution, I would have had companies, corporations, banks. I would have had large shoulders, and would have integrated a regime's clan to go above and beyond the laws. I'd have full bank accounts in many foreign countries. I would have bought luxurious apartments in the most exclusive districts of Paris, or a *hacienda* in Latin America, or a palace in Abu Dhabi or Dubai. I would have offered my children the most expensive cars. Arrogant, they would have exhibited them in the streets of the capital whilst their countrymen or women are picking up pieces of bread from the trash. I would have had, my children too, a double nationality so that I can travel and live wherever I want. I would have had mistresses covered with my money, with chic jewels and clothes. I would also have fans, many fans, to whom I would throw a few bank notes in order to have them do everything I want. I would have been loved and feared by everyone. I only have to be arrogant. Banish smiles from my face. Easy! Justice? Justice would be a stick in my hand against all the midges buzzing around. Whenever a risk pops up, I would flee to a foreign country. Paris, London, Geneva. It's there where I would have gone whenever I have a headache or a stomachache. I wouldn't trust our own medical system. Well! What about being president? I would have robbed billions and billions and disappear. Then suddenly, negotiating in deep waters, I would become president. The most powerful clan among the snakes will promote me and give me almost all the powers. I will bring in my brothers. I will get my revenge and eliminate all those who criticise me. With the oil's money, thanked be God who had given us a lot, and the bones of the martyrs, peace be upon them and may they never come back to earth. I will corrupt everyone and everything. I will crush any opposition. I will double the salaries of the police and the *gendarmes*! They will then beat, put in jail or even kill anyone or any group going against my wishes. The Western governments, so-called defenders of human rights and blablabla, won't say anything. Do they not like me mainly when I sign off the huge contracts they propose? Gas or oil, any profitable market, they are ready to take the deal and shut their mouths but also censor their TV and radios. They will then surrender to that universal truth: 'Thus is the third world!'

I like them so much, those Western governments! They make speeches about democracy, about the huge steps taken by Kaddafi, Ben Ali, Mubarak, etc... whilst plotting with them. The funniest thing ever is: When they don't need them anymore, they come up with new speeches full of double moral standards, attacking them and accusing them of all the miseries their countries are living.

On TV, I, President, will show that in our republic, everything is well. I will show beautiful sexy women, but also a lot of Islamic propaganda programs. I will fill their heads with Egyptian, Syrian, Mexican and Turkish series and soap operas. Millions of families will be amused all year round. They will then imitate their favourite stars. Women will fall in love with the handsome guys in the soap opera, and men with the gorgeous women. They will even name their newborns after their favourite actors.

And the city hall would accept to register those strange names. The city hall doesn't accept to register Aksel, Massinissa or any Amazigh African name, rooted in our history and identity. Our ancestors, the Gauls, arabised our family names. Our other ancestors, the Arabs, are imposing on us the language of Allah. No, the city hall is not racist. The republic is not racist either. The republic wants us to grow cloned and be something that we are not. Clones of our human brothers in the distant, distant, distant lands of the Arabian Peninsula. They are sure of it. They claim it high: "God is Arab, he speaks Arabic". We'd better prepare ourselves for judgement day. Heaven! The virgins, the virgins, brothers! We'd better speak perfect classical Arabic! Ooo! I'm disobeying the constitution! Oh what about the president who tailored it as he wanted, to stay another five-years in power? Ah! I must bow to the state. Yes, the state bows to God himself! The state uses God and the saints for its interests.

Aaaaa! I feel like jumping out of my skin. Words! Words! Words! Politics! Politics! Sometimes, I have the impression I am losing my mind. More than ever, when I am caught by all these memories. Images, faces, words, come to me unexpectedly. Then I feel like I am burning. A scorching ball comes up my throat, suffocating me. Then, I start shouting, saying things I am not aware of. Screaming, shouting, insulting, banging the walls of my cell. In situations like these, I am able to snatch his heart, drink his blood... yes, drink his blood... I... become savage! Yes... yes... savage...

Here come my tears betraying me yet another time. Don't think that they are those of a coward. No! They are tears of a desperate old man, but not a coward.

"Oh, yes! The food is spicy. You help me to stand up, Yuva? Thank you, my son. Thank you! Did you thank your wife? Delicious! She is very good at preparing pancakes. Next week? Send her my greetings. See you tomorrow. Thank you. Go well."

114

8

When concealment and lie are claimed as principles, a country becomes subject to tyranny and injustice. Freedom and justice become empty speeches. Demagogical speeches. My speech within these walls is the emptiest ever! Yet, I still unwillingly build them up, as if I were preparing a public appearance, as if I were elaborating a political plan. We are reduced to analysis. We don't live, we watch and wait. We wait and, for the whole day, we comment on what is happening around us, within us, about us. As if our lives are not ours. They depend on the flunky and corrupted politicians. Analysis is a faculty we acquired through years of unemployment, misery, and decades of empty speeches. It is probably a good thing to comment instead of going dull or crazy. It is better to speak out, to get all our frustrations out. But... but isn't it a waste of time? The problems need solutions, not talks. If we talk all the time, we will become insane. Like I already must be.

Again! He screams again. This man has fire in the brain.

"Take those walls down! I'd prefer hearing you singing like last night. Shout! Shout!" Yesterday was the time for songs. Romantic songs... la la la la... jovial and funny tone.

"Sing, my brother! It's better. Sing."

Did they not give him his medicine again? He cries again. He started that a few weeks ago. Piercing sobs, loud laughter mixed with some mysterious words. The first time was during a silent night. His shriek arose from darkness, tearing the walls' silence. He roared in an inhumane voice. I woke up panicked. My cell was dark. I jumped out of my sheets. A few minutes later, I understood what he was up to. He was lunatic. Gone! Crazy. Wild. As his grumbles continued, I couldn't sleep. What if it were I? Is it because of confinement? I got up, walked to the door. I walked. Walked back and forth. Trying to avoid listening to him. I went back to my bed. I closed my eyes and covered my ears with the pillow. A light wind passed through my ears softening his screams for a while. I couldn't stand it. I tried to cover my ears with my hand this time. Another sleepless night. A night I spent musing. I never met him at the canteen.

"He is too dangerous," the nurse told me when I complained.

"Why isn't he under specialised treatment?" I asked. I told the same thing to the doctor and the principal.

"Bureaucratic problems," I was told.

"He is condemned to perpetuity because he killed both his wife and her lover," Yuva informed me. He lost his mind when he found them fornicating in his own bed. He went to the kitchen and took an axe then suddenly ran towards them and, frenzied, started hacking their bodies; eyes shut, shouting God knows what.

The story of the prisoner in the neighbour cell was not very credible, mainly when Yuva ended it with a laugh.

"Why don't you calm him down with some pills?" I asked again.

"See, Dada Akli," said the nurse, "the doctor in charge of this prison is going to Canada soon. He doesn't care about what's going on here."

"No one cares?" I asked. They are thousands of doctors fleeing to Canada and France. After years of studies in their country, they do not even receive a decent wage. Better go abroad.

I did not complain anymore. Everyone in this country seems to have something to complain about.

Confinement drives one crazy. The pangs of loneliness are rough. Loneliness turns into desperate and sometimes suicidal thoughts. Regrets and remorse become inevitable, unbearable. I feel the space shrinking. I need some air. I want movement.

The truth is that I had my own moments of craziness. I wonder if it wasn't I who provoked that of the prisoner in the neighbour cell. The nurse gave me some sedatives when my nervousness started. But what can sedatives do? They don't calm me down. Idle, I am spinning around the whole day in a compact space. Three paces by two. A bed. A table. A chair. A sink. A mirror. A toilet. Me. Alone. Abandoned to my memories. The only thing not failing me. For the moment. What if I went to France when my brothers asked me to do so? What about my sister? She went with her family to live in Morocco. Morocco, so far, so close. With Morocco we have the longest closed frontier in the world. A frontier separating families, friends. Why? Shame on our common snakes! The conflict between the snakes on both thrones is an 'idiocracy' extended by human greed.

My sister wanted to visit me, but she couldn't. She sent me a letter written by her little boy. "Everything is going well," she said. She is in deep sorrow. She can't even visit me.

"Even if the borders between the two countries are closed, I could have come to visit you," she assumed.

Since visits are forbidden, she can't come. She has a family now. Two boys and two daughters. I never saw them. I don't even know their names. I don't even know their faces. With my brothers, all the same. I don't know even their children's names. They must have changed a lot. I also received a few letters from them. Always the same words.

"We are doing well, we miss you, courage, don't despair, you are a brave man."

I replied three or four times. Of course I never wrote about how I feel here.

"Everything is good here. I don't need anything. I eat well. I sleep well. I miss you." Then they stopped writing for a while. It was maybe their letters that couldn't reach me for one reason or another. When I started receiving their letters again, I stopped opening them. I kept answering anyhow. Automatic

117

answers. Absence of ardour, of hope. The last time I saw their faces was during the first days of my trial. Yet, I didn't meet or talk with them. They were waving their hands from the benches they were sitting on. I hardly recognised them. They used to come to Thadarth for holidays. But during the bloody decade of the 90's, the risks were big.

I had nothing to say to them. As if we stepped back from what was a sensible consideration: daily life. It was a brotherhood with tones of something else. They had their life in France. I had mine in Thadarth. They have their life in France. I have mine in prison.

I have lived a big part of my life alone. No friend, no confident to tell my feelings, my despairs and hopes. As if the moment we came back from the *maquis,* everything had stopped. We wanted to have the braves' rest. We showed a lot of enthusiasm, but anguish was noticeable because the revolution had many strategic errors. Many fighters made big profits from their status. They came back home and took goods and women. *Conquistadors.* After years of sacrifice and suffering, the frustrations were wanted quenched, often in a perverse way. I remember a lot of them having five or six weddings per a year. I refused to be a headmaster of the school where Martine and Julien studied. Si Wali, illiterate and idiot, took the job. He was married to three women. "Historical legitimacy," he said. When we started to ask about the future, the nightmare came. Everything was paused. Stopped. Then, speeches came. Speeches. No work, no electricity, no water, race towards the throne, war between the departments, fear, torture, killings. Life was horrible, but we said: "We are independent now, it's a natural development." We were lying. We lied to ourselves. Things went worse.

I didn't want to get involved in any institution or political work. I could have been a section director of the ruling party. But seeing what many politicians were doing in the name of the revolution, I wished earth could swallow me. Some self-proclaimed unique heirs of the independence dispossessed families of their land or destroyed them, and executed all those who rebelled against their greed. I had my pension. I retired. I became, like the majority, a spectator. A spectator of our gradual fall. I lived alone. All people in Thadarth were friendly. I didn't have any secret. I sat down with them at Thajmath, I received visits, and I helped, as I could, those who were in need. I didn't have any problem with anyone.

Things turned out to be more complex than I imagined. Yet, the deepest frustration, I carry within my broken heart follows me like a shadow and, at my lowest, injects me with shots of pain. I couldn't make a baby. A creature. I couldn't have a child. I will never have a child. I married my first wife, my unique rejoice after the independence. Nana Ldju, the radar's daughter, also called Nana Ldju, chose for me, one from her acquaintances. "She must have strong calves and be a good housekeeper," she said. Confidence and respect, she added. She then went to Thala, the public source, to look at the girls down there. She followed them up to Thadarth, to see how strong they were. She chose the one she judged to be the best match for me. Is there anything easier? Nothing at that time. I yielded to the traditional conventions. I followed my parents' example. I did not think much about it. Martine was a faraway memory and Dihya was already married. She had many children. My mother followed my father three years later. They both died when I was in the *maquis*. I fortunately could secretively come and see their faces before they were buried. When the war was over, I went to their graves, talked to them and cried. It was then that I realised how lonely I was. Alone in that house. Full of memories. Full of sadness. Some three years after the liberation, Nana Ldju had found a beautiful wife for me. I was young and strong. Having children was my dearest hope. I didn't know that God or nature didn't provide me with that natural and legitimate function. Make a baby. When I was in the *maquis*, I could have erections, I could ejaculate. I used to hide, to quench my frustrations. The only way to get our sexual frustrations out was through 'madam five'. Five, the fingers of the hand. We did not have any other choice.

Nana Ldju's choice was on Malika whom I married a few weeks later. She was patient and caring. Almost all Thadarth was invited to our wedding. There was no telephone at that time. I couldn't invite my brothers and my sister. I had sent them a letter telling them the news. A year went by. A second. No results. My seed was useless, hopeless. Malika tried traditional medicine. She tried amulets and foreseers but nothing worked. Three years after, we were separated. I didn't actually wait for a miracle.

"You are free," I told Malika. "You are young and your womb, fertile. Go and be happy."

She gently opposed my decision. Nonetheless, there was no other way. We separated. My unmet desire to have children resuscitated. I believed again in miracles. Thus, I wanted to try with another woman, another wife. So I married Fetta. But my hopes were dashed when I ended up by visiting a doctor. He ascertained my fears. "We must try a therapy," he uselessly tried to convince me. What therapy, dear doctor, when the French electrical clinches had bitten my testicles during days and nights? What therapy, doctor, when the electric waves penetrate you until you fall unconscious? I since then lived cursing my French torturers and the fate I was and am enduring. Whenever I see a little kid, I feel weak, sad. Whenever I see a little kid, I remember those electric wires. I remember Le Peine and his sergeants. I remember the soapy water, the dirty stinking basement where we were held prisoners. Whenever I see a child, my heart trembles. What else can rejoice a man like me more than a little baby, a little girl or boy? I was young, strong. I was healthy but unable to procreate. No heir, no future, no hope. All the other life's joys became sour. I lost my smiles. My face became rigid and stern.

Fetta and I separated three years after. Then I lived alone. Alone for a long, long period.

9

I want to sleep. If I could sleep for one last time. I want to sleep deeply, then go. No agony, no pain. Do people at the threshold of death feel pain? Even when they sleep? Who knows! That's impossible to know. If I were a writer or an artist, I would have written about that. But what for? An artist; it is a classy thing. One can be as he wants without being obliged to give any explanations. Art is the explanation. The artist sublimates life and recreates it to live better. Whenever he doesn't want to walk among people, he spreads his wings and gets higher and higher. His flight makes him happy. I would have accepted the melancholic enjoyment of an artist to my bitterness. Or perhaps, it would have been better if I were an idiot! Hahaha! An idiot doesn't understand and doesn't care about life. He therefore suffers less. He doesn't ask questions and doesn't have much regret. I have no talent to be an artist. I am so conscious of what is happening around me, so, I cannot be an idiot. The worse of it all is that I cannot stand and watch. I react. I don't shut my eyes, my mouth, and, whenever it's required, my gun's mouth either.

I never knew anything other than fighting. Fighting is the search for truth. A search for improvement. Is this not what artists do? Is that not what all humans do? I hope, before I die, not to sink into insanity like the prisoner in the neighbour cell. Am I still sane? If I can think about and tell nice things like these, I think I'm still sane. Let me laugh at myself. But until when will I stay sane? All day long, I am repeating the same words, the same silly and futile sentences, the same insults. All day long, I am speaking to dead and absent people. Am I still sane? I hate when the night comes.

I often have nightmares these days. Whenever it happens, I switch on my radio. It distracts my demons a little bit and brings sleep back. I keep the radio on for most of the day. I cannot break that habit. I don't know what to make of life between these walls. Over seventy years is no age. Not here. I don't feel energetic anymore. But when I listen to the news, it no longer has the same effect on me or on my views of the world. Maybe there is something wrong with the news, the way it is reported. And for heaven's sake, there is too much happening in the world. However, I love when those clear voices flow in my cell. They seem to be coming from far away, detached from the device that diffuses them. Those voices sooth my soul for a while. I listen to music, documentaries. Turning the radio on is the first thing I do when I get up. Then I walk towards the sink, face the mirror and shave my beard. I became a maniac. I sometimes shave twice a day. I want no single hair on my chin. I keep my moustache though, not as a sign of manhood or anything else. Just because I like it. Stylish! Hahaha! Since there is no woman to kiss, it doesn't really matter. I wonder if women like moustaches. No! Old fashioned.

When I shave, I take my time. I stay in front of the mirror for about one hour. Sometimes thinking loudly, others quietly, others unconsciously. I talk to myself, to God, to nothing.

He is shouting again.

"Calm down, brother!"

Should I try again? It sometimes works. Let's bang against that wall? Let's try.

"Please, brother! I want to sleep. I can't sleep."

I'd better switch on the radio. Fill my cell with voices. Try to cover his shouts.

"I don't blame you, dear brother. We are struck by the same stick. I also have my outbreaks."

I had one once. I started trembling. I never trembled like that before. I was shuddering. My teeth were creaking. I felt exasperated. A piercing cry came out of my throat. The loudness of it surprised me. I swiftly, brutally and in a sort of superhuman effort, jumped towards the door. I banged it hundreds of times. Shouting, banging unceasingly, fiercely for ever. I was sweating, suffocating. I wanted to go out, into the world. The door was easily hindering my assaults. I banged again, again. No way! I fell by the door, breathless. Everything became dark. I could not see nor hear. I fainted. When I came to, I found myself on the infirmary's bed. I heard some voices. I opened my eyes.

"Yuva!" I said, when I saw him. He was holding my hand. The nurse was talking to wake me up. My muscles felt inert. I did not move. I could not move.

"Do you feel better, Dada Akli?" the nurse said, kindly.

Since then, I understood that I was no longer the same man. My faculties had lost their verve.

"I am… as you can see, doctor," I replied undecidedly whilst I felt warmth gradually getting back into the marrow of my cold bones. My skin felt cold for an instant. The warmth brought my body to life. Yuva helped me to get up and sit.

"I want to go to my room," I said. The nurse refused but yielded.

"Take these pills. Twice a day," she insisted.

I wanted to be by myself. To go back to my cell. My fate. I needed to return to the space of my frozen wills. The space of my cumbersome thoughts. Yuva assisted me. He was of a huge help, especially during that period.

A few hours later, the prison director visited me.

"I want to see the sunlight, the blue sky, breathe some fresh air," I replied.

"Let's go at once," he replied.

Together with Yuva and him, we went out to the yard. I was craving for some air, open space. I wanted to walk. I left both men at the door and I walked a few minutes. We go to that yard twice a day. One time after lunch and another before diner. Only for thirty minutes. I don't go to the yard so often. I don't want to meet people. I don't want to talk with the prisoners. I am too tired and many things become insignificant to me.

"*Allahu akber!*" The muezzin's call. I wanted to start praying again.

"It will probably give a sense to my life," I thought then. What kind of sense? Am I going to pray God because of what I am going through? Would he get me out of here if I prayed him? Why does he not get me out of here without my prayers? Does he need my prayers? Is he not the almighty? I should maybe pray the Gods of this country. Kneel before their boots to get me out of here.

"*Allahu akber!*" Again! Another muezzin starts from another mosque. What I never understood is why the four muezzins do not call out to the believers at the same time. There are four mosques in town and every muezzin makes the call at a different time. Their calls often crisscross. A huge and unbearable nuisance. We are now in modern times and every believer is able to know at what time he should wake up or go to pray. The only thing that is not in crisis in this country is the construction of mosques. Instead of using the money to build mosques, they would have done better filling the people's starving stomachs, or building roofs at least to hide their misery. I can see from my window three huge minarets. What for? To reach God in the heavens? The money of these three minarets could have paid for two apartments. A few decades ago, we didn't have all these mosques. Is faith in mosques or in our hearts? Is faith in the mosques or in the dirty avenues of our districts? Is faith in the mosques or in our violent attitude? Since the Baathists started blowing their parasite wind over our land, people seem plunged into frenzy. Instead of building universities, hospitals, airports, factories, they are constructing mosques! I heard the news about a new mosque that the Chinese will build in the capital. Our little king receives healthcare in the Parisian hospitals, and instead of building a hospital here, he builds a mosque. The biggest mosque in

126

Africa! The third biggest in the world. Maybe they want to purge their conscience full of blood and tears. Definitely! Thus, they will have a percentage from the prayers and the benediction of the believers. God will forgive their crimes. People will go to pray, in thousands, millions, not to fall sick. No need for hospitals. We will pray God to give us work, to send us food through the tall minarets. The biggest in Africa. Thousands of Chinese are coming to build the biggest mosque in Africa. What? Work for our jobless kids? They - yes, our jobless kids - will see the mosque as an insult to their youth, to their intelligence. There is no God but God! May God accept your prayers.

I was living my faith with no zeal. For the Friday's collective prayer, I went to Thizi. It was the whole day's priority. We were in the mosque that day. I couldn't understand the Imam's sermon. He was speaking in classical Arabic. The sounds were buzzing in my ear because the loudspeakers were of low quality. Anyway, I could understand a few words, always the same words: "We are the chosen... We are the best nation given to earth... May Allah curse the Jews and the Christians... "

I was, in truth, always disturbed by those words. Why is adversity held as a doctrine? Can we not accomplish our faith independently from the Jews, Christians or non-believers or whatever? But the scriptures are full of: "We, to paradise. Them, to hell..." All the scriptures. The Koran, the Torah, the Bible. Yes! You bring up love and peace whenever it suits you. Empty, sweet speeches. Then, consciously or unconsciously, you charge again with: "We, the best. Them, the inferior..."

As a good sheepish believer, one must hear and keep silent. A good believer mustn't protest. Doubt is the ultimate sin, the biggest.

I doubted. How can God curse other humans, his own creation? How can a human being pray God to curse other human beings? Is it not God's business? How many people were killed following the view of 'We are the chosen'?

Have I gone astray? Then kill me and sing peace and love. Then kill me and send me to hell. Then kill me and Allah will put it on the scale of your good deeds. Kill me, Allah will send you straightforward to the opened legs of seventy-three *houris*.

It was in the spring of 1994 or 1995. I can't remember very well. The mosque was overcrowded and the believers were sitting tightly in straight ranks. The Imam was telling his sermon in a mechanical way. He was like a robot telling a boring speech sent by the minister of Religious Affairs. Some were listening, others seemed lost in a long reverie, others were sleepy, others were evoking God's name silently. The Imam's voice, through the loudspeakers, was too loud. People were silent. It is forbidden, a sin, a bad deed, to speak when the Imam is speaking from above his pulpit. Then, abruptly and violently, the mosque's door opened and armed bearded men erupted forth inside.

"STAY WHERE YOU ARE! NOBODY MOVES!" they shouted. Some others were hiding in the mosque waiting for the attack to start. They took out their hidden guns. Two terrorists guarded the two exits whilst others flooded the ranks, preventing the worshippers from reacting. I didn't move.

"What's happening here?" shouted the Imam, panicked, walking down towards the four men who walked belligerently towards the pulpit.

"SHUT UP! SIT DOWN!" they shouted at him. The Imam tried to argue with them but he got the nose broken as soon as the butt of a Kalashnikov hit him.

Suddenly, a voice from the loudspeakers came out. During that whole mess, my blood was boiling. We were trapped like rats. If anyone moved, a probable massacre would have happened. Then the speech started: "*Jihad*, Allah, the prophet, paradise, hell, fire…"

The man was over-excited. He was scowling. He promised punishment to those who would refuse to support the *jihadists*.

"We must get rid of God's enemies! Kill them all, the Christians, the non-believers. We must get this unjust and miscreant regime down; *Sharia* must be established in this country." He forbade alcohol, cigarettes. "Women must stay home and mustn't mix with men. Men must grow their beards and women must wear veils." He forbade going to cafés, playing dominos. "Bars must close; churches must be transformed into mosques. All those who don't conform their habits and life to what Allah and his prophet said will be killed."

Meanwhile, not a sigh was heard. Peril was looming. Everyone stayed huddled in his place, listening to that sermon calling for death. I was torn between fear and anger. Do not look into these monsters' eyes. Yet, I was afraid of something.

"If they stay for longer, the others will arrive and things will go so bad," I thought. The 'others' are the police, the *gendarmes*, the army. They were deployed along the main streets in the biggest cities around the country after the regime stopped the electoral process, when the Islamists won the polls in 1992. They installed check-points everywhere to control traffic. People who had hunting rifles gave them back to the authorities. It was at that time that I stopped hunting. Many Islamists were killed and others disappeared or were placed in concentration camps. They were protesting every Friday. Were they right? Were the elections democratic? We know that the snakes are the best fraud organisers ever. Even dead people vote in our elections. Many political parties were created after the 1988's riots. They named that 'democratic process'. People were suspicious. It could be another trick. Only a small percentage of the population voted in the local elections in 1992. The Islamists won the majority of the seats in the local assemblies. Misery fed extremism, extremism increased misery. Extremism does not have a social or political plan. The unique plan it has is selling you a place in heaven. They then started closing down cinemas, theatres. They intimidated people and threatened those who opposed them. The monsters were born from the snakes' bellies. Then bloodshed started. People were trapped between the snakes' jaws and the monsters' swords.

What I was afraid would happen, happened. Uncontrollable shooting started. We could hear them from within the mosque. A general panic arose. The terrorists panicked, shouted "*Allahu akber*" and ran towards the exit. We heard screams. Then explosions outside. Helicopters were approaching. Terrified, the worshippers fled in a huge chaos. Shootings. The terrorists mixed with us in a hellish confusion. The shootings increased! The terrorists at the exits were retaliating.

"HE'S HIT!" screamed one among them.

"DON'T MOVE! DON'T MOVE!" shouted some. Bodies fell because of the hustle and others, because of the shots.

"GET OUT! RUN! GET OUT!"

I got up. I did not have time to think about where I should go. The waves of people took me onto their stream. Gunshots covered people's shouts. I suddenly found myself outside, in the street, running, barefoot. I was nearly trampled on several times. I ran.

"Where? Don't think of that now. Keep running. Save your ass."

I jumped over bodies on the ground. Screams, roars. Bloody bodies. Inert bodies.

"RUN. Follow your instinct or intuition and RUN!"

We had to avoid the shots. From the terrorists, from the military.

"RUN!"

I flowed and followed the others. No clear destination. I saw an old woman waving her hands far away, urging people to get into her house. A few men went in through the small door. The old woman seemed alarmed but did not stop telling people

130

to enter. I ran towards that door. It could not be a trap! The old woman seemed harmless. I entered. I was panting. There were a lot of men gathered in one room, lying on their bellies. They were looking anxious, shocked, dismayed. I was afraid. Lying on our bellies, we could hear our breaths and the sound of heavy guns bursts. Explosions were shaking the ground below us. The fight had lasted for hours. It lasted the entire afternoon and night. Memories from the revolution war sprung into my mind. Was it because I was exhausted?

The French artillery and their aviation, rapid and energetic, were devastating every inch of land. We were hiding in the forest of Beqqas. Heavy mortars, cannons, long-range bombers, helicopters. We crouched into our holes, trembling and empty.

Musa was the most nervous. He stood up. He lost his nerves.

"MUSA, NO! DO NOT GET UP!" shouted Wali. He then started laughing, tearing up. He could not stand it anymore. Pale and shivering, he got up, walked, and then ran towards the French soldiers, firing in rage.

"MUSAAAA! NOO! GET DOWN!" we shouted.

We watched him helplessly. He did not hear us. He could not hear anymore. He was already in another world. Then, all of a sudden, he fell down. Distress was in full swing. At every movement, death could seize us. We were firing back, furiously, desperately. A scream tore the sky and the hearts. The throne of God would have trembled at Musa's last cry. I did not dare looking at him. We did not dare to look into each other's eyes. We just retaliated. We just swallowed our bitterness. We should not succumb to our emotions. Action was needed. Action more than anything else. If we succumbed to our emotions, we could have been killed that day.

"Leave horror and desolation for the end. Now, shoot and try to escape this furnace."

I was firing and weeping at the same time. I could not wipe my tears. I saw the soldiers at a distance. I fired with hatred, with vengeance.

"Everything will be right, my brother," said the good woman, a hand on my shoulder. I wiped my tears secretly. I felt confused.

I looked again at the men in the room. We were sitting this time. We kept silent. The good woman was offering us water. We drunk from the same jar.

We were enduring the same fire... and under that rain of fire, we were crouching into our holes, behind the rocks. The explosions were closer. We should run. Flee. We could not afford any other loss. Shoot and run! Cover the others and pull back. Run and hide. Pray God for the sun to set sooner. The night was our rescuer. We fled before the French soldiers set fire to the forest.

The good woman offered us food. She gave us some bread and tomatoes.

My memories were shaken. Images from the war against the French coloniser propped up into my mind mingling with what I was living at that moment. I could not sleep for that whole night. I felt dizzy and confused. I saw terrorists, fire, blood, the French soldiers... I saw war, the liberation days. I saw the brothers capsizing, fighting, sharing pieces of the same loaf, offered by the hands of women in this or that village.

Back then, the monsters were known. They had a uniform and were different from us. We could easily recognise them. Whereas today, the monsters come from our own bellies. They are our sons, our brothers, our neighbours, our relatives. The curse went through our history. Our fights have all the time been transformed, used, perverted.

"This is worse than during the occupation," declared the good woman. "O mother dear," she was pleading incessantly, "what is happening to our country? Brothers are killing each other! We are at doomsday's doors. It is the end of times."

132

The gunshots ceased. Outside, we heard the soldiers' boots running in all directions. Then tanks drove by. I looked at my watch. Five in the morning. The mosques did not call for the dawn's prayer. The old woman offered us coffee. I kindly refused. We did not stop thanking her during the whole night. She did not stop lamenting and praying. We did not ask her if she had any family. She was alone. She probably lived alone.

No one dared to go out. Silence was deep, traumatising. It is until we heard the ambulances' alarms that we understood that the nightmare was over.

"My wife and children must be worried," I heard someone saying. I was thinking how was Zira my wife? I never, even for one night, slept outside of my home.

I was married to Zira. Zira was sixteen years younger than I was. I married her out of fear. Fear of loneliness. She was frightened during the mosque attack. Nevertheless, she followed my advice. She invited Nana Ldju to keep her company and sleep at our house. Nana Ldju was a mother to the whole of Thadarth.

The alarms of the ambulances stopped after about half an hour. Outside, we heard people talking. Chitchat started. We could hear kids playing and laughing. It was over. But what was over that day started to last for a long, long time. We hesitantly went outside.

"Stay well, aunt!" we all wished to the good woman. We thanked her again.

"Go well, my sons! May God be with you," she wished back.

Her little house gave refuge to about fifteen persons. I immediately went back home. I took a taxi. I avoided Thajmath. I knew that the news would have reached Thadarth. The curious people often went to Thajmath for the news. Once home, I found my wife, Nana Ldju and a few neighbours waiting for me on the porch of the main door. As soon as Lulu

133

saw me getting closer, she barked and ran towards me jumping up to my knees.

"You are happy to see me back, little girl!" I said, cuddling her. So were my wife, Nana Ldju and my neighbours. I thanked them for their concern and went inside, followed by Zira and Nana Ldju who, as soon as she heard the news, apologised and went to do what she did best. Tell Thadarth what happened in Thizi. The newspapers reported fifteen dead persons and more than twenty injured ones.

A few months after, fire and fear were sown all the over the country. The terrorists attacked state institutions, killed soldiers, policemen, *gendarmes* and destroyed all the state's symbols they could reach. Terror and doubt gained the minds. We didn't know who was who. Who is a terrorist, who is not? Who is an ordinary citizen, who is an agent of the secret services? Who is a policeman, who is a terrorist?

The fever of Islamism reached the villages. Some youngsters grew their beards and did not accept praying at Thadarth's small mosque.

"The Imam is ignorant and what he is practicing is not the right Islam," they said. Therefore, they gathered into a different group and went to pray at the same mosque separately.

Things went so fast, awfully. People were forced to give their rifles to the authorities. I had a hunting rifle. After the liberation, I used to hunt. During the seventies until the beginning of the nineties, hunting was my favourite activity. I had a group of friends. We took mules, donkeys and dogs and went into the woods of Thadarth's hills. We hunted hares, partridges, starlings and wild boars. I love wild boar meat. Succulent! It is so delicious, especially when it is grilled. A slice or two with a nice red wine would be pure bliss. Those were the beautiful days! We were carefree. We lived the moment as we felt it.

"They are praying alone," said the village assembly's supervisor, Slimane Uhemu.

134

"Then what? Let them pray," I answered, sceptical.

"They are bearded," he added. "Give them a finger, they take the whole arm," he said.

I did not know what to say. I was suspicious too. All those weird transformations were about to have heavy consequences. People did not know what to do. At school, they were taught about doomsday, hell, earthquakes and afterlife punishments. School put fear into the hearts of our kids. School did not teach them anything, but filled their brains with hatred and violence. School filled their spirits with doubt about themselves and their abilities. It does the same until now. At home, there was no communication. Most of the parents were ignorant, and the only thing they did was recriminating their heirs. Lovely words were rarely heard. Misery was a big reason for that. Children denigrated their own fathers, working or jobless, because they could not offer them even a decent meal. Then, religion became a refuge. Religion became a consolation for a better life. A better life in the afterlife. Baathism, Wahabism, Salafism exploited that misery and injected their venom in the minds and the hearts.

A few weeks later, Slimane Uhemu came to visit me again.

"There are serious rumours," he said alarmingly. "Some of Thadarth's young men went up to the mountain for *jihad*," he added.

The irony of fate. They took over the same hills we did during the revolution.

"The rumours," I told him, "say that there are also some who are secretly active within Thadarth".

The rumours were smoke hiding the impending fire. The rumours were a truth. Five young people joined their shitty jihad movement. Three others were informers and money collectors. They were living among us, among their families and no one could suspect them or accuse them openly. Pointing at their beards was not enough evidence. A few days after the rumours spread, the *gendarmes* started visiting and inspecting Thadarth. A few young men were arrested but they were soon released. A few months later, military camps were improvised here and there to avoid any attacks on the civilians.

Three of the five recruited young men were martyrs' children. The *gendarmes* constantly visited their families. They often harassed them. In a few months, the quiet and peaceful Thadarth became frantic, full of suspicion and fright. Before that, we rarely saw *gendarmes* coming up to our villages. People did not dare to go out, mainly after sunset. Not long before, young people played music until late in the night and families visited each other without a shade of fear.

In all that mess, I was confused. We did not understand. We did not believe. Trapped behind our windows and doors, we were witnessing how horror was growing. What to do? Hold the stomach and wait. Thadarth showed me a lot of respect. However, I never accepted to take any official responsibility. I wanted to live as any villager does. I am a man of action, not responsibilities. I was fully dedicated to my herd and my hunting activities. I liked going into nature followed or guided by my dog, a little black Labrador. I always had Labradors. I loved them without knowing why. They all were females too. They are good at hunting. When my first dog died, it hurt me so much. I did not dare to adopt another one. Lulu spent her whole life with me. Nine years. Day after day. But I did adopt another one. Lulu again. We became attached to each other and it felt like never a creature, not even a human being, was so important to me than my dog. Loneliness? Could be. Maybe it was a way of making up for my failure to get through with the humans living around me. It was maybe a materialisation of my will to dominate and master, since I could not do it with humans. Hahaha. Whenever a Lulu died, I had another Lulu. I adopted her, but never dared to change the name. I wonder: How is Lulu now?

I seldom went outside. After the mosque attack, fear and despair got hold of my soul. I used to go out just to buy food at Ali Lwenas or Jabril's shop. I seldom went to Lqahwa's to have coffee or tea. "Good morning or good evening, give me that or this, here you go, thank you, stay well, go well." We stopped talking at Thadarth. Even those little chitchats one could have at the corner of a street, under an olive tree, at Thajmath, at Thadarth's café, between the houses, stopped. But the news kept coming. Nana Ldju was the source. The best source. She often came to visit us, Zira and me.

"They are threatening all the women going to Thala," she reported once. "They say that women must stay home and never go out. These people are taking steps beyond reason."

"They want to change Thadarth's habits," replied Zira.

Zira did not go often to Thala. She just did to help Nana Ldju with her jar. Nana Ldju wanted to have a daily jar from the fresh source. She did not like the water we bought from the tracks that came to Thadarth. There were people who could buy water; others, short of money, went to get it from Thala.

"Times are rotten, brother Akli," she said. "'We brought the true Islam, they say.' *Jmaa liman*," she swore angrily. "They will never stop me from going outside. I have no one to take care of my ewes, no one to go to Thala. Let them kill me if they want. I will never wrap my head as well. If I did, I would not be a Kabyle!"

Zira and Nana Ldju whispered one by one the names of the persons responsible for these threats. I could not match the faces with the uttered names but accordingly I knew their fathers, except one of the four.

At that time, the village assembly was almost dissolute. The problem Thajmath had with Hmiti was a fatal blow. Hmiti threw the principles of Thajmath down. Egoistic and greedy, he pretended that Thala was his inheritance. He even stopped people from taking water from there. Thala was the unique source of water Thadarth had had since decades. According to the laws of Thajmath, no one should go beyond the assembly. The decisions made at Thajmath are sovereign. No one should trespass them. Thajmath was Thadarth's organisation, Thadarth's assemblies, Thadarth's court. It was the sacred authority recognised by all the villagers. It was the space where they express themselves and vote the decisions. Hmiti, shattering the laws and the traditions, sued Thajmath to the court. After years of court appeals, Slimane Uhemu, the representative of Thajmath, won the trial and got Thajmath its rights. But things did not go onto the right side since Thadarth split into groups. Those who, secretly or openly, supported Hmiti, on one hand. Those who sought the good of all Thadarth, on the other. Since then, Thadarth had a president, volunteers. But a few assemblies were held and very few people came. Those who came, came to brutally defend their newly-born political parties. In front of the monsters dwelling in Thadarth, Thajmath would not have done much.

People were threatened, frightened. Cafés and shops closed before sunset. Girls, little girls, were prevented from going to school. Foreign language teachers were threatened.

"Teaching the enemies' languages is a big sin," stated the monsters. The enemies were the West. Everything coming from the Western world was a sin. Nevertheless, the monsters wore Nike shoes, nice leather jackets and used arms fabricated in enemy countries.

Windows and doors were sealed with steel bars. People were terrorised and drank their bitterness in silence.

Should we wait, receive threats and watch? The authorities seemed overwhelmed by the reach and the roughness of those monsters. On TV, the radio and in the newspapers, assassinations were reported daily. Things worsened. Should we stay home and let them do whatever they want?

Thadarth is quite cold in winters. I used to stay home almost the entire day, for the whole week. My bones were losing their firmness. But I could not stay motionless. So, I used to take, twice or three times a week, my sheep and Lulu to the neighbouring fields, next to the woods up Thadarth's hills. They had to stretch their legs and, of course, be fed fresh grass. During certain times, I felt observed. Mainly in Thadarth's avenues. I noticed that I never crossed with any of the bearded youths. I wanted to meet at least one, to see him up close. Because of the *gendarmes'* visits, they stopped praying at Thadarth's mosque and held a low profile. Did I want to provoke things? If so, I probably did it unconsciously. I then started going out every evening, pretending to take Lulu for walks. Then, what was supposed to happen, happened. It was dark. Walking down to Lqahwa, Lulu suddenly started barking so ferociously. That was unusual. Whenever she was with me, she never barked as loud as she did. I instinctively looked to where she was barking. Down the road, two men were coming up. Their pace was alert, threatening. They had rifles. I calmed Lulu down.

"Holy thunders! Where do you think you are?" I shouted at them. They were young, not more than twenty-two or twenty-three years. They had ridiculous beards. They had inflated torsos, chins up. Their eyes were scary. I recognised them. They were my neighbours.

"Who do you think you are to terrorise the villagers this way?" I said.

"The villagers must help us," replied one of them. "*Jihad* is the duty of all believers."

"What *jihad* are you talking about? Look at you! You are your fathers' shame," I shouted. "You are Musa's son. Your father is a martyr. He died for this country…"

They tried to interrupt me. I did not give them any chance to do so. I was perturbed. I shouted who in hell knows what. They looked at me. They did not reply. Lulu was so nervous. She could not stay still. The armed boys went off, silent but provoked.

"Things won't stay like this," I shouted at them.

A few nights later, I heard knocks on the main door. Lulu started barking. Zira was so concerned. I had told her what happened with the armed boys. I did not tell her that I stood up against them, though. Before I went to open, I took the axe from the pantry, hid it behind my back and walked towards the door. When it comes to my house, fear is a shame.

"Who is there?" I asked.

"We are Thadarth's children. We want to talk to you," calmly replied a young voice.

I opened the door. There were two young people.

"What do you want?" I asked looking into their eyes, one after the other. They weren't the boys I had met the previous night. They were avoiding my firm looks. I checked behind them to see if there was anyone else. Not far, I saw two shadows hiding in the dark.

"Listen..." But I was soon interrupted by one of the two shadows that came closer. I recognised him. It was... Musa... his expressions, his look, his looks. No doubt, it was his son. Musa's son.

"Akh Akli," he intervened.

"What's the..."

I stopped him. "You! Yes, you! You are Musa's son. What is the... this beard, my son? Your father..."

Then, moved, I could not articulate any further word.

"Akh Akli," he tried again.

I looked at him. I breathed in and I firmly said:

"Dada Akli! No *Akh* with me. *Akh* in Saudi Arabia or Yemen, not here.

"But you are a Muslim, aren't you?" said someone from behind.

"This is between me and my creator," I answered. "There are traditions and laws in this village. Those who don't want to respect them should go away..."

"Man! What is happening?" Zira interrupted us from within the house.

140

"Nothing is happening," I answered. "I am coming."

"Do you understand?" I continued.

"Our people are gone astray," said some young man in a frail voice. "They don't follow Allah's *Sharia* anymore."

"No one cares about your *Sharia*, little boy. We always lived in peace here. Islam or not, Thadarth principles must be respected. You want to follow Islam, follow Islam but don't force people to be what you want them to be."

"Dada Akli!" said Musa's son in a fierce tone, his eyes reddened. Musa's eyes. Oh, Musa! See! Your son came to my house, an arm at the hands, to threaten me.

"Let's go," I heard the frail voice again saying.

I held on to the axe I hid under my jacket. Musa's son's stares were unyielding.

"Our emirate has decreed a *jihad* tax," he said solemnly. Each family must pay a thousand dinars per month."

"Is what I'm hearing true? A *jihad* tax? A tax?"

I stared at them for a moment then, unexpectedly, loudly, I laughed. They looked at me. Some had a stupid gaze, others hateful stares, others astonished eyes. I stopped laughing then I abruptly spurt: "*Bla rebbi* (Without God)! If you come again here…" I took out the axe… They stepped back pointing their weapons at me.

"May Allah be our witness! We have informed you," said Musa's son who walked away immediately, followed by his acolytes.

It was a threat. Provoked by their immediate departure, I began shouting into the darkness things I didn't want to say.

"I am an atheist!" I shouted to their backs. "Shame on you! You dirty the memory of your fathers… If anyone gets close to my house, his head will be cut off!" I ended there, closing the door.

Zira was so worried. The following day, early in the morning, I went to talk to the members of Thajmath.

"We can't do anything," said Slimane Uhemu. "Our families will be killed if we denounce them."

Without hesitation, I headed towards the police station in Thizi and told them what happened in details. I thought about it the whole night. It was unbearable for Thadarth to live in terror. I have always avoided any contact with the officials from whatever institution, military forces, *gendarmes*, the police, the Mayor. But, in the face of the terror Thadarth endured, a solution had to be found. What are the soldiers, the police and the *gendarmes* for, if not to protect the citizens? What are they for, if not to do their job?

Rombo, the *gendarmerie* captain, listened to me with interest and humility.

"Worms should get out of the apple before it gets rotten," I told him. That same morning, even before I got back home, two military trucks along with three *gendarmerie* vans were sent to Thadarth. The soldiers and *gendarmes* combed Thadarth, all the surrounding villages, and even the neighbouring forest.

Once back from Thizi, I decided to sit at Lqahwa's terrace and read the newspaper. I saw the military trucks and the *gendarme* vans passing by, going back. The sun was at its noon position. In the past months, Thadarth had, once a week, the visit of three *gendarme* vans. They just drove by, without stopping.

"What if things get worse?" I asked myself. Better cut the rope for these monsters before they emerge. Until when will Thadarth be terrorised?"

"The soldiers arrested two of them," said Nana Ldju when she came to visit us.

"Did they arrest Musa's son?" I asked.

"He fled, brother Akli. He is the head of the hydra, my brother. His father doesn't deserve this. How can a lion give birth to a monster?"

Zira was scared.

142

"The whole country is plunged in terror. Bombs, fights, blood everywhere. On TV and in the newspapers, they don't stop talking about that."

"What's his name again?" I asked Nana Ldju. "Kamal," she answered, "but he changed his name to Abu Baker."

"Abu Baker," I echoed, nodding.

"You should be careful," said Zira.

"You wife is right," agreed Nana Ldju. "Those people will punish those who denounced them."

I was the one who denounced them. I carefully locked my doors that night. I regretted not having any gun or weapon. I took the axe, carefully hid it under the bed and tried to sleep. I looked at Zira's face. She always went to bed before me.

"Is she sleeping?" I wondered. I sat at the edge of the bed just beside her. I looked again at her closed eyes. I never could overcome that feeling of guilt I had whenever I joined her there.

"And now I put myself and her in a hazardous and fearsome situation," I thought.

I lay down, covered my body with our blanket. I suddenly had an urgent need to feel her, to touch her, to be in her. My soul, my heart, my body wanted it. But Le Peine and his soldiers wanted something else. Why did God put a whole focus of pleasure in one organ, one member? One could caress, cuddle, kiss, fondle but it gets bitter, frustrating when the culmination comes then nothing happens. Dead. Flabby.

I stretched a hand towards Zira. I reached hers. We seldom shared physical affection. I used to hold her for a moment between my arms whenever she cried her dead parents. She was more like a sister than a wife. I wish I could show her more affection. To kiss her little nose, to caress her hair, to tenderly bite her lips. But the remembrance of this flabby thing killed my desires even before they were born.

I took back my hand to my heart and closed my eyes. I had barely slept for one hour when I heard Lulu barking. A few seconds after, I heard gunshots.

"What's happening," asked Zira in panic.

"Gunshots," I answered taking the axe from under the bed and went out to the courtyard. "Stay here," I told Zira.

Lulu didn't stop barking. It was the first time that Thadarth had been targeted.

"These are threat shots," I told Zira, trying to calm her a while after the shooting had stopped. We went back to bed again but we didn't sleep. Worried, we kept speaking the whole night. The soldiers did not come until the first sunrays. The sun did not come to awaken Thadarth. Thadarth did not sleep the whole night. The sunrays came to stamp on it a new destiny. An odious destiny.

"I am going out," I told Zira. "I will not be long. Stay home and close the doors carefully."

I rushed out to check what happened last night. As soon as I put a foot out, Slimane Uhemu greeted me. He was accompanied by some soldiers.

"I want to talk to you," Akli, he said. "Things are getting bad and the soldiers want to set up camp to watch Thadarth. We must gather and discuss the matter as soon as possible."

Two days later, a camp (barracks and containers, surrounded by a fence) was built at the exit of Thadarth. About twenty soldiers were positioned there. They raked Thadarth and its surroundings four or three times a day. Tension at Thadarth rose. Thajmath was convened. People were divided into two groups. Those who agreed with the idea of having a military camp. Those who were against because "it's even more dangerous to have the soldiers within the village." We all convened to have a military camp but not within the village.

Curious, I took Lulu and walked towards the newly set up military camp. It was more a shanty than a camp. The soldiers were young. They looked frightened. They were, for the

144

majority, forced to fulfil their military service. They weren't professionally trained. War was not their business. Whose business is war? It is the business of those who, from their safe balconies, watch the people's children kill each other. War is the business of those who provoke it and watch people do it. War is the business of the masters who get richer through it.

Weeks later, a few women went back to Thala and the little girls went back to school. Since the beginning of all that fuss, I neglected my sheep and left them in the small barn I had in the courtyard. Zira took care of them.

"Are you out of your mind?" asked Zira when I decided to take the sheep out. It was seven in the morning. Spring was sending its soft breeze. We could smell its scents.

"Life must go on," I told her.

"Lulu did not stop barking all night long," she said.

"She is as worried as we are," I replied, sipping Zira's coffee. "She barks because it's spring time. She is celebrating."

I looked at Zira. She was cooking some cakes. She slightly, with no conviction, smiled at my bad joke. I smiled too. With no conviction. At the very moment I made it, I realised how displaced and silly the joke was. It wasn't the best moment to say such things. How did it come out? I don't know.

I looked at Zira again. All of a sudden, hard and insistent knocks on the main door made us both jolt.

"I am coming!" I shouted.

"Who would visit us at this hour?" said Zira, startled.

The sky was cloudy when I crossed the courtyard towards the main door.

Lulu was already by the door, barking and moving vigorously. I pressed her to stay back and be quiet. She did.

"Who is it?" I asked holding tightly my axe.

"It's me, Dada Akli," answered a sharp voice.

"Yes, but who are 'you'?" I insisted.

"I am Lieutenant Djamel, the military camp officer," replied the voice again.

I remembered him. He was invited to Thajmath when we spoke about the camp.

I opened. He was not alone. He evidently was escorted by an entire troop. After the usual greetings, he handed me a humid folded paper. I opened it. It was written in Arabic.

"I can't read Arabic, my son," I said. "What is this about?" I added.

"Please, let me read it for you."

I looked at him then at the boys behind him. They were preoccupied.

"Something bad has happened," I thought.

He hence started reading:

"In the name of Allah the most gracious,

Mister Akli son of... for having denounced our brothers the mujahedeen in the village, and for refusing to pay the jihad tax, we, Abu El Hawl group, order his execution. This execution will serve as an example to... bla bla bla..."

The letter was signed by Abu Baker. Kamal. Musa's son.

What should I have done, Musa? What would have you done? I came to your tomb, brother. I wanted to be relieved. I'm sorry, brother Musa! How would I not be sorry? May your bones rest in peace. Your son ordered my death, Musa. What can I say to alleviate my pain? You died. You, Rabah... Almost all my companions. You all left me. Said-My-Book, my unique confidant, had moved to Algiers. He seldom visits Thadarth. You all fled the past's ghosts. But I couldn't. I couldn't flee them. I didn't flee them. I can't flee them. See, Musa! Me, threatened by your son? Didn't we fight together for him, for the children of this land? Shall I ask you for forgiveness, Musa, or ask God for it? Shall I ask you to forgive your son or shall God forgive him? Oh, Musa, we are living in absurd times. But, in the name of these tears I'm shedding before your tomb, I will never abdicate. In the name of the unjust bullets that pierced your body, I will never give up. Thus, I spoke before your tomb, my brother, when war was over. Thus, I spoke before your tomb when war started again.

When the officer finished reading, I laughed. Yes, I laughed. Stunned and puzzled, the soldiers looked at me.

"We were wrong," I stated. "When we were under the French boots, we thought that there was nothing worse than the French. We thought that colonisation was the worst thing that this country could endure. But, thirty years after we kicked out the French, the worse…"

At that stage, it was useless to carry on speaking.

My voice tone was calm and wise, deep. I then went silent. The officer offered his assistance and promised to do everything possible to keep Thadarth and its inhabitants safe. He executed a military salutation then they withdrew.

I closed the door. Lulu was hanging to my leg. Zira rushed towards me.

"What's going on?" she asked.

"The bearded men want to kill me," I replied, cynically handing her what remained of the paper I unconsciously crushed with my hand. I headed to the kitchen. Zira followed me. Lulu was standing outside by the door. They both were waiting for an answer, an explanation. They both seemed at a loss because of my calmness and silence.

"What are we going to do now?" she asked undecidedly.

"Was it right for her to marry me?" I thought at that same moment. "Was it right for me to have married her?"

She was sixteen years younger. Fetta, my previous wife, got married and had children with her new husband. At that time, I tried everything to have a child. Traditional medicine made from uncanny herbs and spices. I even tried Qara Aderwish abilities. Thadarth's sorcerer. I visited him, secretly. One should avoid curious eyes and bewildered tongues.

"Future or amulet?" he asked once I was sat in front of him. "I know your secret, Dada Akli," he added without waiting for my answer.

Qara Aderwish had a special way to say things. Concisely, never direct. He was a poet too. A poet, seer and amulets maker. He lived in a dirty and half-destroyed hut. He may still be living there. He pretends solving people's problems, but seems unable to solve his own. However, no one can explain his success. People visit him from faraway lands. Is he not capable of chasing out the *djins* and the bad spirits that dwell in their bodies? He used to organise (at Sidi Hiyun, the mausoleum) dancing sessions where many people were conveyed. He plays the *bendir* and a dervish friend of his played the flute. Those who are said to be possessed go into the circle and start dancing. The *bendir* and the flute's rhythm instantly attract them. They dance during a long, tiring, dizzying time, until trance. The *bendir* and the flute's rhythm accelerates, people twirl, flinging the dusty soil under their feet. Men and women wave, contort, scream, like demons. Women's hair wind up and over, floating snakes. At the end, those who are said to be possessed by *djins* spin around until they fall down, speaking eerie and vague words. Thenceforth, Qara Aderwish gets to them, holds them by the wrists or the hair, and speaks to them. Speaks to the *djins*, as he pretends.

"Where are you from? Why are you in this man? Get out of him! I order you to get out. Get away or in hell forever you will dwell!"

He keeps talking, ordering, threatening, screaming. People, the 'sane' ones, stand at a distance watching, eyes wide open. When the *djin* is gone, Qara Aderwish gives orders to the flute player to douse with water, the heads of the 'possessed'. I never knew how he could know that the *djin* was Muslim or Christian, black or white, from this land or another.

"How can you tell, Shikh Qara?" "The djin told me," he would reply.

Those sessions ended by the fire dance. Qara Aderwish walked on coal, put a hot sickle on his tongue, and pierced his jaws with a long needle. No burn, no scorch, no blood.

"How did you learn that, Shikh Qara?"

"I am Shikh Qara, my knowledge is not human. To my left, there is a black woman *djin*, and to my right, a white one. They taught me what no human can do or understand." Thus, spoke Qara Aderwish. Qara Aderwish is right.

But Qara Aderwish didn't do that for free. Aha! He received a lot of money in return.

"The salt of the hand," he used to say.

"How much, Shikh Qara?"

"God forbids, I never choose. Give me, in good intention, however much you want."

He had a lot of money, but has never lived or been rich. He amassed the money but only used it for necessary things. Well, he could at least rebuild his hut! But thus is Qara Aderwish. Qara Aderwish never wrongs.

"An amulet," I replied.

"You are afraid, my brother, he said. Your life has never been easy."

"We all don't have it easy, Shikh Qara."

"An amulet, my brother. Even if you, one day, will ask me to read your future, I wouldn't do it," he said firmly.

I wanted to leave at that very instant. That was already an answer of how terrible my future would be.

"An amulet," I asserted with no fervour in the heart.

"Stretch your hand."

I got closer. The old man was wrapped in his dirty white *burnous*. He was sitting behind his always-lit *kanoun* dug into the soil, at the corner of the main room.

"Your hands are cold. Your belly is cold," he whispered.

He took a glass from under his *burnous* and ordered his wife to bring him something I cannot remember. She came with a jar in hand. She then poured some dubious yellow liquid in the glass held by her husband. As soon as the glass was filled, Qara put it close to his mouth and uttered an unintelligible string of words. Then, seven thunders, he spat twice into it. I stood there dumbfounded.

"Drink this," he ordered.

With a trembling hand, I took the glass. I felt disgusted, sick. I looked at him. His eyes were red, his beard grey. His mouth covered by his moustache. He was devilish. I felt my stomach coming out of my throat. My knees wobbled. Then quickly, I dropped the glass into the *kanoun* and rushed out. Once at the main door of his hut, I vomited all that I ate that day. Then, feeling stupid, I ran away hearing Qara's Aderwish cries.

"Your amulet," he shouted whilst I was running. "Come back to take your amulet!"

"Rather die than drink that donkey pee mixed to your spit, damned warlock!" I told myself laughing.

Time went by. I started accepting myself as I am. I am made that way and it is, maybe, my fate. For years and years, I lived alone. I tried as I could (often I could not) to occupy my spirit with other preoccupations.

Nevertheless, Qara Aderwish had sent his son to my house.

"My father says," the little boy held, "the 'thing' is ready and you owe him forty dinars for the glass and the… " I don't recall the liquid's name.

The 'thing' was the amulet. Avoiding gossip and problems with the old warlock, I took sixty dinars from my wallet and handed them to the boy. Peace!

"Tell your father that I will, whenever I have time, come to take the thing". I lied.

"I'd better postpone it indefinitely until oblivion," I thought.

I hope he didn't throw any curse on me though!

The problem was inside me. Therefore, I didn't want to give myself any false hope. Neither by getting married nor by going to any witch or to a dingy sorcerer.

"You mustn't stay alone, Akli," advised Nana Ldju.

I used to cook by myself. I washed my clothes myself. Then things became unbearable. My house became chaotic. So, I accepted Nana Ldju's advice. I married Zira. We both were divorced. We were a good match. At least that was what I thought.

"Being divorced, she has no suitor," I was told by Nana Ldju.

"Can she give birth?" I asked. I didn't want to compromise her future with me if she could give birth.

I didn't have any convincing answer.

"She is a good woman, Akli," said the old woman. "She won't find anyone to ask for her hand."

Zira made my life easier. I was happy and tried my best to make her happy too. We didn't expect anything from each other than respect and attention. I was fifty-four or five when I married her. She was thirty-six.

"No, I like doing that," she said whenever I tried to explain to her: "Sorry, I'm not good at doing all that."

"It keeps me busy. Your task is to take care of the sheep," she consoled me.

Thus, it was decided. The truth is, I only helped when I bought sardines. Sardines are the unique food I can cook, along with fried potatoes and eggs.

I loved Zira's succulent food. She made her way to my heart through my stomach. Hahaha! We got used to each other despite the floppy thing standing between us. I wonder how she lived her sexuality. We never spoke about that. Speaking about sex is still a taboo in our society. For me, sex was a double taboo. With Zira, I shared the bed, the talks and the food. We never touched each other. The unique contact our bodies had was when we married. We kissed on the cheeks. That was the unique time our bodies were in contact, if I may call it so.

Is this part of me being a bitter man?

151

With Zira, we almost never fought. Why did I marry her? Probably, because I was scared. Afraid of being alone. She was my family. My unique family in Thadarth. Was she unhappy with me? She never showed any sign of dissatisfaction. We lived as we could.

"I asked you what we are going to do," she repeated, drawing me back to the present.

I loved the 'we' she used. She was part of my life. At that moment, we were both in danger. And my duty, as a man, as her husband, was to protect her.

I thought about the hunting rifle that I had given back to the authorities. I wish I hadn't. What would a rifle have done anyway?

"The military camp is about two hundred meters away," I thought trying to hold to some comfort.

"The officer promised to protect us. Now that the soldiers are here, there is no fear," I said with little belief.

"I am not reassured at all," replied Zira. "Why can't they stop all the attacks happening in the country? God knows how savage those people are."

"God seems to have forgotten this land," I said sighing deeply.

"Don't say that. God knows what he is doing".

"Yes, he knows, he is almighty, he... whatever... but I would have liked him to stop all this. Now".

Then, I stood up, walked towards the kitchen door leading to the courtyard. Lulu, wagged her tail, looked at me then got up. Whimpering, she came towards me and as if she felt my worries, she rubbed her back against my leg. A breeze from the high mountains of Djurdjura caressed my face.

"I need a walk," I thought. Walking helps me a lot. It helps me to clear up my thoughts, put things in order.

"I'm going out," I looked at Zira.

"Are you out of your mind? You want to be killed?"

She stood up and got closer to me. I looked at her. Our eyes crossed for a few seconds. She avoided my gaze. Tears suddenly filled her eyes. Her voice went frail.

"Sit down," she kindly insisted going back to her task. "Don't go out, please. At least, for some days," she ended.

I went back to my chair and slowly sat down. She served me a cup of coffee and a piece of bread she used to prepare every morning. A delicious bread made with wheat semolina, raisins and olive oil. The best and natural preventative medicine against colds. She then sat on her chair facing me. She sighed and looked out sadly. I felt that my silence surprised her. However, she didn't interrupt it. She knew that I would soon take a stand.

"It's useless to wait at home. I shall take up arms again," I spurt briskly, grimly.

"Take up what...?" she mumbled in astonishment.

"I will go to the *gendarmes* on Saturday and get a weapon to defend my house and family".

I waited for a moment. I rubbed my knees. I waited and hoped to hear her say something. She didn't. Did I want her to approve of my decision? To dissuade me?

She didn't say anything else. Helpless, she wiped the tears falling down her cheeks. I didn't say anything. I felt week, guilty. Was I guilty? That feeling of weakness and guilt made me so uncomfortable, awkward. I wanted to stretch a hand and... hold hers... I didn't dare to.

Zira stood up, walked out. She went to the living room. I wanted to follow her, talk to her, hold her in my arms and calm her down. But I didn't. I didn't. I didn't...

I didn't finish my coffee. I left the cup on the table and went out to the courtyard. Lulu followed me. Together we went into the little barn. I gave some dry bread and wheat grains to the sheep. I heard someone walking behind. Zira. She joined us.

"Poor little sheep!" she said.

"Poor us," I replied. "These sheep are lucky. Their unique concern is to eat and reproduce. They don't think, they don't suffer; they don't cause any suffering. Humans are the most savage race ever known on the face of the earth," I ended.

"Thus is life. And God knows better," said Zira.

"God!" I echoed her. "I don't know… He seems away, far away".

"Curse Satan," she frowned.

"Satan is Man," I replied going back to the kitchen.

I took my coat then came back to Zira.

"I want some air. I am going out. I will tell Nana Ldju to come and keep you company. I won't be long".

"Will you leave me here alone?" asked Zira anxiously.

"Come with me to Nana Ldju's house then," I replied.

"No, I have a lot of chores to do here. Leave Nana Ldju in peace. She already did a lot for us".

"Then close the door and don't open to anyone. I won't be long," I repeated.

"But…" Zira hesitated for a while… "Where are you going?"

"I don't know," I answered. "I will probably go to Thizi".

"I… I don't understand. Aren't you afraid?" she asked.

"You know my answer," I replied. "Stay home and lock the doors".

"I… Be careful… " She mumbled.

"Stay in peace," I held and started walking down to Lqahwa's, from where I should take the transport vans towards Thizi.

The door locked behind me.

Thadarth seemed in deep sleep. Not even the shadow of a cat. I felt light. My steps were light. That was what I needed. Walk. I felt peaceful and calm. I took a deep breath, savoured the fresh air.

When I felt old age's pain at the knees, I wanted to stop running from a town to another. I wanted to spend the rest of my life at Thadarth, as a shepherd. I bought three sheep, and dedicated my daytime to them. I loved taking them to graze in the forest or on the hills, not far from the village. I loved contemplating the beauty of the surrounding mountains and hills, full of olive, fig, pine, oak trees, eucalyptus trees…

I just have to close my eyes to see that enchanting scenery. In the quietest moments of life, one never suspects misfortune to be at the corner of the road, waiting for him. Even the short moments of pleasure cannot exist without a bitter aftertaste. Fear made everything soar. Fear of death. Fear of failure. But the worse in all of this is the loss of one's hope for freedom. Freedom to move, to live, to be, to dream.

That morning, walking with no destination (Thizi was just an excuse to walk), I realised that my life took another course. Not the one I wished, for sure.

"I should watch every step I took, every word I said. I thus should lessen my contacts with people at the very most".

When I arrived to Thajmath, my eyes fell on the papers fixed to the walls. They were copies of the one the officer had read to me. I got closer to look at them. The same ones, indeed. I sighed. I lifted a hand…

"No, I won't," I thought, dissuading myself to take them off. "Leave them there," I thought. Then, I walked on to Lqahwa. The café was not yet open. I stood at the terrace, looked around. There was no sign of a van.

"Let's walk," I decided. By then, anguish seized me. I didn't feel peaceful anymore. With a cold bosom and an anxious mind, I walked down to Thizi.

"Down, down, God hasn't yet shown," I sung Ferragui's song. Down, down, I found myself in Thizi at the terrace of my usual café. The road was short. The five kilometres separating Thadart from Thizi seemed short. Plunged in my thoughts, doubts and feelings, I sat at my usual table. Sometime later, the waiter came to me.

"Yes, tea," I confirmed.

"Why wouldn't I go to the *gendarme* camp right now?" I wondered. Then I remembered that it was a Friday.

"Tomorrow," I told myself resolutely. Came the tea, I sipped a dribble or two and looked away to the top of the Djurdjura mountains. Snow was covering its peaks. A few moments later, some acquaintances joined my table. Once tired of chitchatting, "let's go for dominos," confirmed someone.

How lovely is it when someone you don't even know, just comes to your table, sits down and starts talking to you, smiling, sharing a coffee, a piece of information, a joke... Whatever. A 'good morning' to an acquaintance or a stranger, a little hand to a friend or a stranger, a visit to a relative or a neighbour, is a little effort but helps a lot in painful moments. It chases that awful feeling of loneliness. We all are human, wherever we are, and despite our differences, we share the same pain, sorrow or joy. At different doses, we swallow the same sip of pain, sorrow or joy to show that we are able to resist, to live. Isn't it then better to resist together, to share with each other, and to live together?

The men at the terrace with whom I played dominos changed the course of my thoughts. We laughed, drank more tea. I felt fine for a while. The sound of the dominos pounded on the table stirred my enthusiasm. I felt stronger.

Because it was a Friday, Thizi wasn't as crowded as on weekdays. Only a few businesses were open. But as soon as the call for the prayer was heard, they would close.

"Double-blank," I shouted, laying down my domino on the table. My opponent shouted in frustration whilst I laughed, as did the watching crowd surrounding our table.

All of a sudden, we heard children shouting. We turned and saw, coming from a distance, a man followed by a crowd of kids.

"Batulis," said someone.

"He seems on fire today," said someone else.

"Heads rolling from above the hills…" we heard Batulis shouting.

"Batulis, *mashi d arkhis*," joyfully said the children behind him. "Batulis, a man not a coward!"

Wrapped in his dirty coat, Batulis, barefoot, was waving his arms, jabbering, walking without greeting anyone that day.

We used to see him in Thizi wandering around, asking for a cigarette or a coin. He talked to himself most of the time. Whenever he became agitated, he insulted everyone, spitting and shouting. People said that he was an orphan, but we never knew from which village he was, from which family he came.

"Human heads! Picked like watermelons!"

"Batulis! Even the devil he can stop," shouted the children all over again.

"He has gone crazy," said someone.

"In a country like this, how wouldn't we go crazy?" said someone else.

"Leave him alone, bad mannered kids!" shouted an old man towards the kids, waving his cane. The kids did not listen to him and kept trotting behind Batulis, clapping and singing.

"Batulis is brave, born brave, lives as one, until the grave!"

"This land is cursed," said the old man. So, a frantic discussion, without a tail or a head, started.

"The generals have another say," said a young man, called Democratoz ('Democra' stands for democracy and 'Toz' is the sound of a fart).

"All the problems come from Allah's lovers," stated another one.

"All the politicians are hypocrites," sprung someone.

"The unique problem we have is this sinister regime," claimed a furtive voice from behind.

"Stop it! Stop it!" urged some old man. "We all are responsible."

"He is right," said some in unison.

"We gave them the whip with which they are hitting us," added another man.

"What should we do then?" asked someone else.

"Democracy…" tried Democratoz.

"Stop it with your 'democracy'," uttered the man at the table next to his. "See where your 'democracy' has led us. People are killed like flies, if not by the army, by the dirty monkeys".

Suddenly, the café owner, a seventy-something year old man, came out to calm down the uptight clients.

"Do you want my café to be burnt or forever closed?" He said. "The things you are talking about are big," he added. "Aren't you afraid for your lives?"

By then, the tables begun to empty. The muezzin's calls started whilst Batulis, passing by again, was still speaking about the human heads.

"Talking is the only thing we can do," concluded the old man, hands on his cane, looking around.

"Talk, Ammi Sa, talk!" added the café owner. "But be careful where and with whom you talk. You know better than I what I mean, right?"

At that time, when one spoke about 'those things', he should do so quietly. One should talk about them secretly. Because one never knew who was an ally of these ones, who was with the others. Who was with the terrorists, who was with the military services? Avoid raising suspicion. How many people were taken, kidnapped by the secret services before even opening their mouth? The secret services, like the terrorists, were hidden. They dwelled among the ordinary people. A secret agent could be a café waiter, a bartender, a beggar, a vagabond, a tramp, your neighbour, your colleague, your friend, your brother, your son. Be very, very careful. If ever your heart or mind itches, keep silent. Kill your thought! Kill your feeling! If ever your mind or heart stifles you, whisper your thought or feeling and pray that no one has heard you. If you dare assert yourself, do it in a cell, on a torture chair; or assert it drenched in the blood dripping from your slaughtered throat, in any forest or in front of your children, in front of your house. So, whenever you are asked about 'those things', be blind, deaf and ignorant. Say: "I didn't see, I didn't hear, I don't know".

"Did you hear that?" exclaimed some persons around the table. Some stood up. The passers-by stopped, looked at the neighbouring hills.

"That must be an assault," acknowledged the café owner.

As the clashes between the soldiers and the terrorists were frequent, we, every now and then, here and there, heard gunshots. At the beginning of the war, we were taken aback. But after the first spikes of alarm, we only had a true concern when it was very close.

"As if you never heard gunshots before," mocked the waiter, collecting the glasses and the dominos. Before he even finished his sentence, a heavy gunfight, not so far this time, came to muzzle the café's hubbub and brought to a standstill everyone in the vicinity. Then Batulis ran by, shouting louder and louder: "Human heads! Human heads!"

He was alone. The children weren't behind him this time.

"That was so close," I said, standing up.

"It's in Thadarth, Dada Akli," added the waiter, a hand over his eyes to see clearer.

"Smoke!" nodded a teenager. "Smoke... from Thadarth..."

"This is a bad omen, good men!" said the old man, holding his cane. He then, in frail steps, throwing back a "Safe is he who flees," went away, followed by his fellows.

A strange and yawning anxiety seized my soul. I was already up trying to see where the smoke was. I couldn't see it. However, the gunshots became heavier and heavier. I could feel that they came from Thadarth. Intuition? Fear?

"It's nothing serious," I tried to convince myself. "It's a gunfight like the ones we used to hear. The terrorists wouldn't dare to attack Thadarth since the military camp is not far from there. The officer himself reassured me, didn't he?"

I looked around me. The café was already empty. People were gone.

"What am I doing here?" I thought.

"Come in, Dada Akli! We should hide and wait inside," advised the café's owner standing by the café's main door.

I looked at him. I didn't say anything.

"I must go home!" I told myself. "It's useless to stay here and wait. They came for me," I stated, looking into the eyes of the old man who invited me to go in again.

I hopped onto the terrace's steps. I looked around then walked. No car, no men, no children... I instantly looked for Batulis. He wasn't there either. I closed my eyes for a while, and then I started running. At the station, at the town's exit, I didn't find any van or taxi. Who would transport people to hell? Fear forced Thizi's inhabitants to lock their doors without delay.

"What am I doing away from my house? Why didn't I listen to my wife?" I reproached myself when running.

My feet felt heavy. The road became shaky.

"Human heads... from above the hills..." I heard again, when I stopped to collect my breath. Batulis stayed at a distance for a while, then howled in my direction: "Good man, whether you run or not, things are already set! Good man, things are written, no one can change them..."

"Go away, bad omen!" I shouted at him fiercely. He didn't stop talking. In which world was he dwelling?

I looked towards Thadarth. A long streak of dark smoke was swirling up to the sky. I couldn't run anymore. I stopped for an instant.

"Old man, do you want a cigarette?" asked Batulis, coming closer to me.

"Curse you! Go away, son of…"

I was exhausted. I couldn't finish my sentence. Batulis jumped back and disappeared. As if I wasn't already in enough trouble.

After about fifteen minutes, the gunfire stopped, but I could still hear some distant and scattered shots.

"Retreat shots," I guessed. The heavy fire came from the military camp. The terrorists couldn't have so many ammunitions. They never faced the soldiers head-on. Guerrilla is the perfect technique when a group is outnumbered. The cowards imitated our technique during the revolution against the French. Cursed be them all!

"I must carry on," I encouraged myself. Then I started walking. I walked hurriedly for about three kilometres.

"Where did all my vigour go?" I thought. I felt weak, old. Suddenly, images, faces, memories came flooding back to me. Rabah, Musa, Said, war, my father, my childhood… Then Zira, my wife.

"I should have stayed home," I repeated to myself.

I was running, the past catching up to me because of war, wars. I was running. I was running towards my own demise. I had a premonition. I stopped, crouched down and rubbed my knees. I looked up. The road towards Thadarth became all at once longer, heavier. I went on. I walked up looking, from time to time behind, if ever a car would come up.

"The *gendarmes* and the police would come shortly," I wanted to believe. Not one shadow of a car. I heard a helicopter flying over. I looked up. It was flying over Thadarth.

"They want my head!" I thought. "They want my head, Batulis!" I said, remembering his words.

Unexpectedly, fast like thunder, a 4 by 4 pick-up, overloaded, drove down. I waved at them to stop. The people in the pick-up, looked alarmed. Some hands waved at me. I shouted twice: "Stop!" Then I heard others shouting: "Stop! Stop!" The pick-up stopped about a hundred meters away.

Someone opened the door and came, rushing towards me, shouting: "Dada Akli! Thadarth is on fire! The terrorists attacked..." He gathered his breath and added: "Do not go there! Civilians and soldiers were killed... They looted... They kidnapped girls and women... Don't go..."

Then, the driver jumped out and shouted: "Come with us, Dada Akli! Let's go! They were looking for you! We have found notices calling for your death on the village's walls."

"Zira!" I said.

"Come with us!" many added.

"My wife..."

"They attacked your house..."

"Zira! How stupid was I?" I thought, distressed. How didn't I realise it? How didn't I feel it coming?

"Zira... Zira," I whispered repeatedly, running towards Thadarth. Her words resonated into my ears: "Are you out of your mind? Your life... Danger... I... alone here?"

I didn't hear the people calling my name behind. I didn't want to hear them.

"Zira... Lulu... My house!" I should have stayed home. "Zira, what did those bastards do to you?"

I impulsively and unconsciously hurried. I didn't feel my feet, my knees. Everything became vague. My heart, my eyes, my life was there, home. I saw people between the trees, walking or running behind their donkeys loaded with what they could save. They were fleeing, in silence. Urging their donkeys, cattle or children to walk faster. Silent shadows. They were miserable, looking down. They lost the gift to look at the horizons over the hills and the mountains. They didn't need to talk. Pain was heavier than words. What are words in the face of horror? The horror they would carry within themselves during their entire life. What would they have said? Why would they have spoken about? Is there anything left to be spoken about? I didn't look at them. I didn't have time to stop and call them. They didn't see me. They were preoccupied with survival.

"What if Zira is among them?" I thought for a moment.

"Zira! I called. Ziraaaa!"

"Dada Akli, come with us," replied a woman.

"Ziraaa!" I called again. "Are you there?"

"She isn't here," responded the same woman. "Don't go to Thadarth."

Deep fear got into my soul. "What if those savages raped her and left her there, bleeding in the middle of the courtyard?" I was afraid to find her body, without a breath of life.

When I arrived to Thajmath, I found it full of soldiers.

"Stop there!" I heard. "Hands up!"

I raised my arms, immediately saying: "Let me go! Let me go!"

Some soldiers recognised me.

"Let him go!" stated someone. I ran. I stood in horror once in front of my house. The flames and the smoke had already darkened its facade. I held my hands up and slapped my face. The house I dedicated my energy and time to was burnt. The soldiers who had extinguished the fire had sweaty faces, and black smoke stained their uniforms. They were standing outside.

"My wife!" I shouted.

"Please calm down, sir," someone tried to retain me. I pushed him away. Then I ran through the main door. It was broken down. The barn was in ashes. Some sheep were lying under the olive tree. The tree's leaves were browned by the smoke but the tree survived. The furniture, the doors had been burnt. I could see no more. I had seen more than I could stand.

"They kidnapped women and girls," I recalled the runaways' words. I knew it! I knew whilst running up to Thadarth that Zira would be the instrument of their vengeance. But I didn't give my feeling credit. I didn't want to believe it, to think about it. I wanted to give myself hope. It was fake hope.

I collapsed under the olive tree and closed my eyes to avoid looking at that disaster. My own disaster. I felt empty. Tired. The soldiers did not dare to come in. They silently watched me.

"What if Zira fled to Nana Ldju's house?" I dared to wish. I stood up.

"Lulu! Lulu!" I called looking for her. No answer. No yapping. I searched among the sheep, in the rooms. No trace. "No, not Lulu too! Zira took her and fled to Nana Ldju or somewhere else!" I wished, once more.

I then decided to go straight to Nana Ldju's house. "If they aren't there, they wouldn't be anywhere else."

All of a sudden, I heard a dog barking. "Lulu!" She came through the ruins of the front door. She came towards me, jumping all around. I kneeled and caressed her. Then I instantaneously looked towards the approaching silhouette. "Zira?" I... smiled for an instant but... it wasn't her. It wasn't her. It was Nana Ldju. Her face was sad, her eyes perplexed.

"Nana Ldju, where is Zira?" I asked. "Ziraaa!"

"Calm down, my brother," she uttered.

Her tone expressed my woe. Woe! Lulu didn't stop jumping around.

"They took all the women they found," she started telling me. "They were... they took two women and the girls... three girls."

I wanted to stop her. To take her by the shoulders, shake her and shout to her face, "Where is my wife?" But I couldn't. She was old and shocked enough by what happened. I owe that woman a lot and the respect I had for her was stronger than my emotion. The fault was mine. Mine, not anyone else.

"One among them, his face was covered, came along towards us and looked fixedly at Zira. I couldn't do anything, my brother!" she said, crying out her bitterness. She then awkwardly sat down on the dust, overwhelmed by her emotion. She took a breath and talked hardly.

"They took her!" I thought. Pain entered my heart silently.

Then she carried on, "He asked her if she was your wife… I got up begging him but he pushed me back so roughly. These people aren't afraid of God, my brother! They took her. They took them." Nana Ldju started sobbing. "I'm sorry. I'm sorry!" She repeated.

I didn't know what to say. I had nothing to say. I went back to my place, under the olive tree, and sat down. I was confused. Guilt, sorrow and rage were tearing up my soul. How could all that happen so fast? Savageness occurred in Thadarth. They wanted to punish me. They punished me. But why did they take the other girls and women? Am I not the only responsible? Am I not the one who denounced them to the authorities? I held my head between my hands, elbows on my knees and cried. I cried not because of what happened that day but I cried about it being another day adding to my regrets. A day… or an instant…an instant marked by the stamp of cowardice and abjectness. We went to Qiyas' house. We knew that it was him who sold us out when we came to visit our families. A visit during which Rabah and fourteen other fighters were killed. We were full of wrath. We wanted to avenge our comrades. Qiyas was home. We could see smoke coming out from his roof. He fled with his family to live in a hamlet situated on a little hill, not far from a French military camp. A kind of village around which the French put an electrified barbed wire fence and forced people into confinement, watching their "movement". Watching their wretchedness and agony too. They weren't allowed to go out of the village without a pass from the camp officer. They had a lot of pleasure watching the villagers, those savage indigenous barbarians, suffering in their own land. Didn't they come to bring about civilisation and enlightenment?

We made our way through the high fence already cut open by an informer we had in the confined village. We met him at the huge eucalyptus tree as convened. The soldiers were preoccupied with what was happening in Algiers, where the partisans of *Algérie Française* rebelled against De Gaulle and were now in charge. That night, they were listening to one of his speeches on the radio. They put on loud speakers out to allow the population to listen. We could hear his husky and charismatic voice through the loudspeakers. We went through the hamlet's paths until we arrived in front of Qiyas' shack. Said-My-Book and I broke in, smashing the front door easily.

"He is a collaborator. He must pay for what he did," I thought pitilessly. If we let these people do what they want, the revolution will not succeed."

Wartime was not propitious to a lot of reflexion. Many of us were ignorant, tired, hungry and full of rage. It is not an excuse for any abuse but it plays a big role in shaping the minds of the fighters. The man and his family were scared as hell. The little children and their mother were screaming and Qiyas shouted: "Please, don't kill me! Don't kill me". Said-My-Book, with one shot to the head, killed him. I didn't want to allow myself any doubt at that moment. I didn't want to think about what we were doing. We pushed the children and the wife out. Then the shack... I... I put fire to the shack... Qiyas' corpse burnt in his shack. Then we fled. De Gaulle's voice covered the cries of the children and the screams of Qiyas' wife. Huge flames soon spread up to the sky. Alerted, the soldiers started shooting with no precise target. We had risked our lives for a foolish operation. We fulfilled our objective. We killed Qiyas. But was our deed an act of courage? Can revenge be a victory?

I didn't sleep that night. I realised that I had repressed my empathy. I had repressed the calls of my conscience during the entire operation. Once the night's silence came, it brought shame and contriteness. I couldn't sleep that night. We could have avoided that abominable revenge. We could have left the man in peace. He was harmless and afraid. He was not allowed to even go out of that concentration camp. But, for God's sake, why did we make Qiyas' wife a widow? Why did we make his children fatherless? Would it bring our comrades back to life? No. Why did I put fire to that house? Not even a house. The man was in there. Burnt! Why? The answer was in front of my eyes. My house. Burnt.

That night, I left the little tent we had set up in the middle of the huge rocks at Thazruth. I refused the handful of acorn and some wild herbs that Said offered me. That was our meal for weeks. I wanted to get away from my comrades. Too tired, so hungry and tormented by remorse, I was like in an altered state of mind. I huddled up, like a foetus in his mother's womb, under an olive tree until the sun came up illuminating the treetops. I didn't sleep for days. I had endured sorrow and remorse for years. However, one day, I decided to make peace with my past. Especially with Qiyas' family. I thus started searching for them. I found them in the same hamlet. There was no fence. They had built another shack. Qiyas' collaboration with the enemy brought another suffering to his family, even years after the liberation. Their neighbours constantly harassed them and wanted to kick them out. They were a collaborator's family. Many collaborators had been executed after the liberation. It was a hidden horror. A secret horror that a whole country has kept quiet about. Is still keeping quiet about. Speeches about a perfect revolution were the most welcome. The most welcome. In any revolution, in any war, horrors and errors happen. There is no perfect revolution, no perfect war because it is simply a war. We must accept the past horrors, face them and try to repair them and above all, give to those who were damaged, some relief.

When I was about to knock on their frail front door, I remembered that regretful night. I awkwardly knocked and a female voice shouted: "Knock or send your children to stone the house! We won't leave this village! May God bring curse on you! Go away!"

"Good woman, it's me, Dada Akli," I said. "I am your husband's friend. I came to see you."

The silence I heard behind the door indicated her suspicion and surprise. She finally opened.

"Who are you? He never told us about any friend," she replied. The woman's face was pale and tired. She invited me to come in. I kindly refused to have coffee. She however forced me to. It was strange for me to find myself again in that place. I didn't stop thinking about that night. Said-My-Book shooting down the husband, the kids and their mother screaming, De Gaulle's speech, my coldness, my ignominious rage, the flames... But I was there, visiting them. I was there sipping that coffee to please my host, animated by a desire to do the right thing. Aware about the suffering of Qiyas' family, I was even more motivated to do something for them. Reassured, his wife started telling me what she endured with her children. They stood up at distance, looking at that stranger who offered them the candies they were happily eating. They were skinny and dirty but they had an earnest spark in their eyes.

"They send their children to throw stones on our frail roof every morning," said the woman. The school principal didn't want my children to be enrolled.

"My husband didn't do anything," she said. "His family was decimated by the FLN during the war. They didn't do anything. Let's suppose he did something, wasn't he killed and our house burnt? Let's suppose he did something, what did his children and I do? But, no. For how many years now, have they wanted to kick us out? But, by God willing, I won't go anywhere. I don't have any family, I don't have any land. What Qiyas inherited from his parents was taken by Birita. He is a killer. Everyone knows that he killed many people, wrongly accused to be collaborators, to take their land. This happened not during the war. It happened after. Why don't they stone his house? Because he isn't weak. They provoke a weak widow and her starving children. You know what? If Qiyas were still alive, we could have been all killed. They know that there is no man in this house; this is why they don't dare to come and face a widow and her orphans. I don't know if they still have even a drib of honour in their hearts. If Qiyas were here they would have come to assassinate us all," she repeated.

I listened devotedly, silently.

I looked around and asked, "How do you do to survive?"

"Thanks to some good people," she answered. "They send us food in secret. Don't think that good people don't exist anymore. They still exist."

Then she started crying and swearing. I tried to calm her down, but she didn't until her children gathered around her.

"Take this," I said getting up and handing her some money. "I owe your husband a lot," I lied. She didn't accept my money at the beginning, but when I insisted, she took it. She thanked me a thousand times.

Before I left, the kids kissed me one by one.

"I will come back to visit you," I promised.

"Our door is open, my brother," she spoke. Go well!"

"Stay well, my sister! Stay well!"

I then went to Slimane Uhemu asking for advice.

"They are relatives of mine," I told him when he asked.

"You know very well what the traditions are, Akli," he answered. "Whenever someone offers protection, would it be to an enemy, the entire village should accept."

"I have an old house at the entrance of Thadarth," said Slimane, the idea brilliant. "If you repair it, they can live there," he added. I offered to pay him but he strongly opposed it.

"In the name of the revolution, I will never accept money from you," he replied.

The next week, I took my wife and visited Qiyas' family. They were happy to see me and cheered a lot. We spoke about the house in Thadarth and they, immediately, accepted to move there. Some weeks after, they moved. The children were enrolled in school and everything was arranged. Qiyas' wife started working. She brought water from Thala to some families and helped others with their cattle.

A big part of the weight, which was oppressing my conscience for years, was taken off. Malika my first wife visited them often and kept me informed about them.

So, there I was, watching my burnt house.

"Dada Akli!" the voice of the military camp officer brought me back. I had drifted far in my memories. Djamal... That's his name.

"I don't want to hear anything," I said. I don't want to talk to anyone. Then, I got up and called Lulu. Nana Ldju stood silently, looking at us both. Maybe she talked to me whilst I was buried in my thoughts. I didn't hear her. I went out to the yard and walked through to... I didn't know where to. I only walked, walked. I wanted to forget. But can one forget his horrors by just giving a ride to his knees?

Why didn't I die during the revolution? Why did I survive to see my own house burnt, my wife kidnapped, my dignity trodden. I stopped walking.

"Where am I going like this?" I told myself. I sat down on the grass. "Where is this life leading to? Is all this written, as Batulis said, as we say? Could my life not be better written? Why is my fate's writer so cruel?"

Filled with anger towards myself, towards my fate's writer too, I went back home and started cleaning the mess. I didn't find anyone. I nevertheless found some food.

"Nana Ldju," I thought.

The soldiers announced curfew earlier than usual. Far away, explosions were heard. When the night fell, I went into a room I managed to clean a bit and fell into deep sleep, Lulu by my side.

The next day, Nana Ldju and Slimane Uhemu came together, each one bringing some food. I didn't even dare to put a crumb into my mouth. Nonetheless, I gave Lulu some.

"Come and sleep at my house until you repair yours," the man offered. I kindly refused.

"I won't add to what you already have to deal with, brother Slimane," I told him.

"My brother's daughter was killed," said Slimane Uhemu. "She is fifteen years old. They killed her because she didn't want to be their prey."

"Si Muh, the shepherd, was also killed," said Nana Ldju. "When a terrorist assaulted his daughter, he fiercely attacked him with a dagger he had kept hidden. They shot him."

I was too absorbed in my own pain and distress. I didn't realise that other people were going through worse. Five soldiers were killed during the terrorist attack. The terrorists created a diversion. One group attacked the military camp and two others came into the village to destroy my house, collect money and kidnap women.

"We must stand by each other," said Slimane Uhemu.

"Stand by each other! How?" I thought. Waiting for them to come, attack, rob, kidnap, kill? Stand by each other to shed tears? To listen to our wives shrieks? To bemoan our fate? To mourn and accept that 'thus it is written!' Until when will we stand by and watch? When do we defend ourselves, since the state (though applying this concept to our country is an insult to the human intelligence) isn't defending us?"

For every disaster, there is a tomorrow. To stand by each other, yes, bury the dead, console the families and show them some solidarity. This is how we were raised. We gathered the next morning at the cemetery to cry Slimane Uhemu's niece and Muh, the shepherd. No one dared to look in the eyes of each other. The gazes seemed absent, distant. We were there without being there. No one dared to talk about what happened. Why talk? Fear was clutching the souls. Did the disaster consume the ultimate seeds of our resistance? That attack blotted Thadarth's conscience forever. The mouths spoke differently, the feet walked hesitantly, the minds thought gloomily. Smiles deserted the faces. And those children! Look at how afraid they are. They don't dare step further than the brinks of their houses. See how strange and anxious they look. They don't run, they don't play, they don't dare anymore. How can we send them into the future? How can the future be brought to them? How to make them understand what is happening? They are unaware. They opened their eyes to see blood, death, fear, threats. They are afraid without knowing why and how. They will definitely bear that fear and insecurity in their hearts for the rest of their life. Life, love and hope are robbed from them. Future? Another disaster to weigh down their heads and kill the light in their eyes? Life in Thadarth seemed to be wrecked. We had lost the capacity to dream of good things. Fear had replaced everything. Fear had overcome life.

During the following days, many of Thadarth's inhabitants fled. Thadarth became a shadow.

"Death is inevitable," I thought. "Here or there. Today or tomorrow. Better die in my village than in any far away shack or barrack."

Coming back from the cemetery, I went to my house and carried on cleaning. Images from the recent past flirted with my mind. Zira. Her smiles. Her silences. Her things all around the house. My memory was soon interrupted by Lulu's barking. I looked towards the entrance. Slimane Uhemu. He was standing there and by his side, were three young men. His neighbours.

"We came to help you, Dada Akli," said one of them after greeting me. I thanked them and told them what they should do.

The young men who came to help didn't speak a lot and stayed until noon. At noon, unfailingly, Nana Ldju brought some food. I invited the young men to eat. We sat and ate together.

172

When Nana Ldju was about to go back home, I took her hand, "Here is some money for the food you have been offering me these days," I told her.

"*Jmaa liman*," she replied, her hand up, waving her index finger. "I will never take your money. We must stand by each other. We are friends and neighbours."

"Yes," I said, holding her hand, "but listen to me, please." She listened. "I'm not good at cooking, so I'd like you or your daughter-in-law to cook for me. In compensation, you or she will have some money every week or month."

"Oh, my dear brother," she said. She was weeping. "I'm sorry, my tears don't want to stop pouring these days. I cannot control them these days."

"Don't worry, Nana Ldju."

"I don't mind cooking for you, but let me speak to my daughter-in-law," she replied.

One week after the disaster, my house was cleaned and repaired. For days, I did not stop dreaming about war and fights. One and unique idea was scampering in my mind then. Start fighting against the savages. It was time. Thus, I went to the *gendarmerie* station and got a weapon.

When I joined the resistance against the French, it was all or nothing. It meant dying, win or lose. But against our own children, what was it for? Win what already has been lost? Lose what already has been lost? It was a nameless war. Both victory and failure were ignominious in that war.

A Kalashnikov hanging on my shoulder, I went to the village assembly where I found Nana Ldju. She greeted me and after a little chat that ended with "Stay well, Akli!," she went to tell Thadarth about what I decided to do.

Fold my arms and watch was not for me. I did not play any hero or victim games. I know that finding Zira was an improbable thing. However, hunt down the terrorists and protect Thadarth was worth doing, in the name of justice, in the name of my rage. After having lost almost everything, rage

173

had replaced my hopes. I then started surviving. Things went quicker than I expected. Life taught us: "Only bad things happen faster."

"I heard that you took the arms again," said Slimane Uhemu during his next visit. I couldn't find any better example of sympathy and solidarity than in Slimane. I expected him to be surprised by my resolution, but he continued: "My brother wants to take up the arms too. He didn't sleep a single night since his daughter's death."

The next day, Slimane Uhemu came to my house accompanied by his brother. I explained to him the procedures and the whole process. Two days later, he got a gun too. He then became the first member of the group I led since other young men joined us. We were about ten people taking up arms. We had ammunitions and a salary every month. We then started doing what the state could not do: Protect its citizens.

I was happy but also sad for the young people in my group. Happy because they could earn some money through it; sad because they were risking their lives. But was it not better for Thadarth's young men to take arms and fight than wander around the whole day long? Was it not better than laying their backs against the village's walls waiting for things to happen or waiting for nothing to happen? Between bad and worse, bad is a better option. Our choices are limited to worse or bad. Good and better were out of order. "Not written." Not for us.

Along with the young men, we planned our activities. We held briefings everyday and used to split into groups whenever we wanted to rake Thadarth and its neighbouring woods. We sometimes worked together with the armed forces at the camp, but we were not under their commandment.

The young men in the group had all accomplished their military service, so they had the elementary training to carry out these kinds of tasks. At the strategic points in Thadarth, permanent vigils were placed. Another team patrolled day and night. My house became our meeting point. Our operations weren't limited to Thadarth. We often went out of Thadarth to inspect any suspicious activity.

The inevitable, written or not, happened in the afternoon of a stifling August day. We were scouting in the forest. I know every nook, every stone, and every tree in that forest. The previous day, I had a dispute with the lieutenant. I heard rumours that the soldiers were sent to light fires in the forest.

"Those are none of my orders, Dada Akli," he said apologetically.

"This forest is our life source," I told him. "It's true that it is infested with terrorists but the villages need this forest."

"I received orders," he added.

"You are adding fire to nature's fire. The sun is already burning us. I will shoot anyone who sets fire to that forest," I threatened, "if it is one of your soldiers," I added angrily.

So, we were scouting after the previous day's fire when, unexpectedly, three terrorists ran towards us. "FIRE!" shouted Ali.

We fired. One among them fell and the others ran away in two different directions.

"After them," I shouted running.

The young men ran behind them as fast as they could.

"Take them down," I heard.

I tried to run for a while, but my knees betrayed me. We chased them. They retaliated but not for long. Another terrorist fell down.

"Get the other down!" Cried someone.

The pain in my knees increased. I stopped walking. I leaned against a tree to rest. I was out of breath. My vision was blurry. I looked at the young men chasing the terrorists. I felt confused. I watched those young men hunting down people who could be their brothers, cousins, or neighbours. How could it end up this way? Who deserves the blame? Those young extremists fighting against the regime but also turning the country into ruins? Those who indoctrinated them? The regime that created all this confusion? God? Satan? What am I doing? Running after these kids? If I had children, they could have been as old as them.

I suddenly heard a scream. Ali! It was his voice. No doubt. I recognised it. Ali was the youngest member in our unit. Twenty-three years old. He had just finished his military service.

I hurried towards him.

"*Ayemma! Yemma!*" he shouted, calling his mother. He was lying on the ground.

The third terrorist had shot him and fled. We hurriedly gathered around Ali.

"Oh, how cruel is life, my son! Who else would you have called? Who could be caring and loving to a son more than a mother? But what could a mother do to a son pierced by the bullets of savageness and absurdity?"

Blood covered Ali's clothes. He didn't move. No breath. Closed were his eyes. I lifted his head up. He was lifeless. He was gone.

"From God we came, towards him shall we return," I said mechanically, gently laying his head down.

But where was God at that moment? Where was God when all that was happening? Why was it not I who had been killed? Why a twenty-three year old boy?

A helicopter arrived and flew over the area.

"Where are the birds?" I thought. I don't know why and how I noticed their absence at that exact moment. Yes, birds! The birds flew away when the weapons started flinging. Nature is certainly horrified by human savageness. Why didn't God send some angels to save Ali before he fell? Why did he not send his angels to save Thadarth? Is he not the Almighty? All powerful! Let them sing! All powerful! So, why did he not save all those innocent people? Why all those widows, orphans, raped women, killed babies and men? We do not need the angels once dead! Send them NOW! We do not need your promises of heaven. With the blink of an eye, make this life good to live. That's a true power. That's life? God is not responsible? He made things like this. He made men like this. He is not as 'almighty' as he pretends. He is not as 'almighty' as people make him to seem.

I got up. My companions were appalled. A while after, the vigil team and the soldiers arrived. They transported the corpses towards the camp.

I sat down on the ground and watched them. I couldn't walk.

"Are you alright, Dada Akli?" asked lieutenant Djamal.

"Nothing serious," I replied. "Pain in the knees."

"Let me help you," he proposed. Then, together with Karim, we walked to his van and drove towards Thadarth. Once in the van, I closed my eyes and didn't utter a word. The lieutenant, probably understanding the situation, did not speak to me.

We killed three terrorists but we lost a man. Ali. We lost a boy. Is is about counting the dead?

"What am I doing?" I asked myself. "Why are these absurd things happening to me?" Suffering was deep and tears became useless. Once more, Thadarth cried one of its children. We stood by each other, sharing nothing else but misery and death.

"Cry, oh, mother of his! You were the last one he called. Shed those warm tears over his corpse and slap your chest with those hands that took care of him. Slap that chest which fed him! Then let him go the way of all flesh, down that horrible hole. See! See all these people coming to share your pain. You are not alone in this. No, they cannot bring your son back. Would your tears do? No! But cry if you want to. Cry, but don't add pain to your heart. Your son is dead for something noble. Be proud of him! Let him go."

Last kisses, ultimate caresses of an inert twenty-three year body wrapped in a white shroud.

"Come, good people! Take him now. Take him to that traitorous hole."

We accompanied Ali to his grave. People helped to carry his coffin on their shoulders. We walked behind his coffin. We were tens, hundreds. Other villages came to share Thadarth's pain. We arrived to the cemetery.

"Ali, may your bones rest in peace! May God open the heavens' gate to you. We are from earth, to earth shall we go back. We are from God, to God shall we go back," held the Imam in a sad and cavernous voice.

The corpses of the three terrorists were taken to Thizi where they were publicly exhibited. People from many villages and cities came to see them. The authorities called that a 'psychological operation'. Whatever it was, it was rather, 'See what our country is up to'.

"Did we kill enemies? Misled brothers?" I thought in all sincerity. "But… they are men. Human beings. Souls. Like you and me."

New militants, even from other hamlets, joined my group. I therefore could rest from time to time and leave the hard missions to the young men. I never knew how I became the head of the group. Maybe because I was the first to take up the arms? Because I was a known veteran? Because of the respect I had among people? Yet, I was getting older.

The terrorist attacks lessened. We didn't have a lot of work to do. The occult forces holding the throne were in secret discussions with 'the misled men', as they then called them. They substituted the old vocabulary with a new one. From 'terrorists, blood suckers, etc…' to 'misled, gone astray'. That was not an innocent change. It was a change to prepare the population to what no one asked for: The Civil Concord. In other words: Give the chance to the slaughterers to repent. Or reconcile the killers with the population. "A high act of faith in brotherhood," they pretended it to be. But, in truth, it was reconciliation between the monsters and the snakes. They didn't need them anymore. The chaos they caused brought huge returns. The most important one: Maintain the lie-makers in power. They fabricate lies as they fabricate our misery, our reactions and even our days. Even Allah is out of their games. Nevertheless, they use his name to support their lies. Allah is a labelled brand for more submission and acceptance. It often works. Thus how the Civil Concord was fabricated. In the name of Allah and his prophet. Some verses on the issue were found in the holy book. The president, the politicians, the ministers, the Imams, the teachers, the 'dog-journalists' threw them to the people. People had to vote and the 'cheating YES' made up about ninety-five percent of the count. The new president, with the status of 'Neo-Prophet', had the pawns at his disposition; he moved them as it suited him. The pawns: Justice, Laws, the Constitution. They served him, his family, his friends, and the clan of snakes that was behind him. The 'Neo-Prophet' fabricated laws and got eternity. Shut up and applaud!

gain? I am now used to his screaming. However, better take my headphones. Haha. I say 'my'. I got used to them. Good God, they are a very good idea, aren't they? I never thought I'd one day use this kind of thing. But they are efficient.

"Whenever he starts shouting, plug these into your radio then put them into your ears," said the nurse, handing them to me.

Ha! When the prisoner in the neighbour cell starts shouting, I put them on. It felt odd at the beginning. I smiled the first time I had them on. It worked.

"Technology, brother! These are not made by those who are preoccupied by growing their beards or those who keep watching if their wives are well veiled or not. Made in… '*Ze gouud* life, my brother.' Let me increase the volume. '*Ze gouuuud*' life, brother. Scream now if you'd like! I'll lie down for a while."

On the radio, on TV, the terrorists were received with embraces and *youyous*, smiles and handshakes. They spoke about repenting in the name of Allah and his prophet. Weren't they killing people in the name of Allah and the prophet? Now, they admit their mistakes. Plus, tears on the cheeks, they incited their brothers to abandon the *jihad*.

"We were gone astray and we ask our people to forgive us."

Yes, as easy as it sounds. If your family, wife, father, son or whoever was killed, raped or kidnapped, shut up! They would slap God and the state's laws right at your face. Shut up! If you keep arguing, jail or a fine would be a least reward. Yes, it is as easy as I say. As easy as it seems. Is it not written? Written in God's scriptures. Written in the state's scriptures. You must look down whenever you meet a terrorist, now called 'The repentant'.

"Embrace and kiss the butchers and keep your mouths shut! Embrace and kiss the killers and thank us for this divine invention: Reconciliation."

Pardon, YES! I agree. Reconciliation, YES! I agree. But not without justice. It was inconceivable for me to pardon a killer. Well, if it were only one killer, it would be somehow easy to justify his savageness. But they were killers, thousands.

Our discussions at Thadarth became recurrent. The voted law: The Civil Concord.

"How are we going to deal with them?" we often wondered.

My wife has been kidnapped, my house burnt. How about Thadarth? Would we receive the killers, those who desecrated our village, as if nothing happened?

My men and I stood against the killers for more than four years. What now? Put down our weapons and watch the killers come back home?

Whenever I thought of Zira, my pain increased and my rage plunged me into a deep sadness. My will for revenge didn't lessen during that period. I didn't want to think or imagine what could have happened to her. Nevertheless, unexpectedly, life had a surprise in store for me. I never thought that I'd live such a thing in my life. I never thought that life was able of such a thing.

Whilst we were making the rounds in the neighbouring woods, we heard a baby's cries coming out from behind a bush.

"Who is there?" asked Karim, his weapon pointed towards the bush.

No answer. The baby did not stop crying. We surrounded the area. One never knows what could happen. Didn't those killers put a baby into an oven and leave a notice behind saying that by doing so, they have saved him from society's decay?

We cleared the path towards the bush.

"If you don't answer..."

"Go away! Go away!" yelled a woman, interrupting Karim.

We got closer to her. She didn't move.

"Who are you, woman?" I asked.

"Faruja!" she said.

"She was among the kidnapped women," asserted Karim.

"Leave me alone! Go away!" she screamed again when we tried to get nearer.

Faruja's clothes were torn. She was half-naked. Her feet were dirty and bloody. Her legs, full of scratches. She was pregnant. Swinging, she held the crying baby to her chest so tight. We didn't dare to get closer.

"Are you, Faruja?" asked Karim.

"Go awaaay!" she repeated frenetically.

The baby's cries increased.

"Come with us, my daughter," I tried. "I'm your uncle Akli. Don't you remember me? Come with us! You are safe now. Let's go home now."

She didn't answer and did not stand up.

"Don't touch me!" she finally said. "Don't touch me!

We walked some meters away to speak and find a solution. Faruja was traumatised.

"We shall call a woman from Thadarth," suggested Aqshish. That was a brilliant idea.

"Nana Ldju," held Karim. "She is the best one at these matters." He was right. Who else was good at those things?

Bakhi offered his mobile phone. We called the vigil team and about twenty minutes later, Nana Ldju came up through the trees, escorted by two men of the team.

"Come, my daughter!" she said to Faruja. "I'm your aunt Ldju," she added, holding her by the shoulders this time. Faruja calmed down. She started mumbling something to the little baby. Right away, Nana Ldju, with tenderness and grace, took her *fouta* from around her hips and covered the little baby with it. She then took, from her bag, the clothes we told her to bring and helped Faruja to put them on. Shortly afterwards, we saw the two women coming out from the bushes.

"A car is waiting for you," said Karim, who had already arranged everything necessary.

I was eager to know what happened to Zira. I wanted to ask Faruja about her, about... Thousands of questions were trotting in my mind. But the time was not for questions.

"The poor woman needs rest," I thought, repressing myself. She was weak and fragile. Nana Ldju helped her to walk. We looked at her in shame, in regret, in rage. We didn't dare to look into each other's eyes for a long while. What we witnessed was unbearable, indescribable, unspeakable.

Then, a thousand images and thoughts assaulted me. "The baby she is holding and the one into her womb are a result of long nights of rape and savageness," I supposed.

Those bloodsuckers used the kidnapped women to satisfy their animal desires. We heard countless stories about God's madmen. Horror in Faruja's eyes, on her body told us how cruel and inhuman they could be.

I looked at the two women walking towards the car. I was proud of Nana Ldju. She succeeded in what we failed. We walked at a distance behind them.

Before they got into the car, Faruja turned towards us. We were standing not far away. She looked at me. Her gaze was insistent, strange.

"Does she want to tell me something? Zira..." I couldn't help thinking.

Her eyes were red, filled with tears. She was pale like snow.

"Why is she looking at me?"

I felt extremely embarrassed. I waited a moment for her mouth to open and articulate some word.

"Are you well, my daughter," I was about to pronounce. But how can she be well, I dissuaded myself.

I looked at Nana Ldju.

"Come with me now," she told her.

Faruja was still looking at me. I didn't look into her eyes. I didn't dare. I couldn't stand the situation anymore. I suddenly felt so warm.

"Something is wrong," I told myself.

"Go, my daughter," I told her. "This car will take you with Nana Ldju to the hospital."

She looked at the baby. I was, for a heartbeat, released. But she looked at me again. Thus far, my puzzlement and intricacy grew higher when I saw her walking, in frail paces, towards me.

"Didn't she recognise me when I talked to her? Is it only now that she recognises me? I never remember having talked to her before."

"What do you want to tell me, my daughter?" I asked her gently.

Faruja didn't say anything. There was about a meter between her and me. She looked at me and handed me the baby. I took the baby between my arms and... I didn't know what to say, what to do, how to hold him or her... It was the first time I held a baby between my arms.

"Zira..." she pronounced in a slurred voice.

I opened wide both my eyes and mouth.

"Zira's daughter..." she added pointing at the baby.

Drops of sweat formed on my front.

"Zira's daughter?"

I looked at the little creature. A drop of sweat fell on my nose and then, on the *fouta* covering the baby. As I was about to turn to Faruja, she fell unconscious.

"Be careful!" we all shouted.

I was holding the baby. I couldn't help her. I didn't move. My knees went cold. I held the baby tight to my belly. Nana Ldju hurried towards her, followed immediately by my companions.

"Her water broke," Nana Ldju said startlingly.

185

"We must take her to the hospital!" Karim shouted. "Help me! Hurry up!"

The little creature I had between the arms started crying.

"Hush…" I said lulling her and talking to her.

"Zira's daughter, she said," I thought.

Noticing my embarrassment, Nana Ldju came and carefully took the baby I handed her.

"I will stay with the baby," I heard her saying.

Relieved, I thanked the skies for having sent me Nana Ldju at that very moment.

"Did I hear Faruja correctly?" I thought. Would I dare to ask Nana Ldju if she heard what I doubted having heard?

I dared.

"This is Zira's daughter," she confirmed. Nana Ldju seemed happily surprised. She kept cradling the baby.

I didn't know what to say, what to think.

"Shall I believe what I heard? Believe what I am living?"

Nana Ldju's easy and undoubted cheerfulness struck me and put me in more confusion.

"Is she as naïve as to believe all a sudden that this little baby is Zira's daughter?"

"No!" I shouted unintendedly. My mouth betrayed me.

My knees shivered. I had to sit down. I sat down. I closed my eyes.

"What did this woman go through? She fled from her captors and God knows how many hours she walked. Then she arrived there, in the middle of the bushes, holding a baby, pretending that it was Zira's daughter. My wife's daughter. She was pregnant… Her water broke…

"Are you fine, Dada Akli?" I felt a hand on my shoulder.

"May God make sure that she doesn't lose her child," I held.

She left that small creature. She left behind her, consternation and a lot of doubt. She left that creature along

186

with the most improbable declaration: "Zira has a child". Hence, ugly images assaulted me. Bearded terrorists jumping onto her... she screams... she waves her arms, she gets a slap on the face, insults... shouts, she becomes powerless, weapons are pointed towards her, insults, cries, shouts... silence, moans, sighs, an ultimate attempt to grunt, pain...

"Chase them! Chase these images away!"

I couldn't chase them.

Zira's eyes are shut, they put a handkerchief into her mouth, she moans, can't get her moans out, her hands are tied, she is naked, they don't take off their clothes, she is lying on her back, unconscious... one after the other they jump on her... dogs... they abuse her, brutalise her, violate her, dirty her!

I got up and walked until exhaustion. I heard some echoes behind me but I didn't pay any attention. I wanted to walk.

"A bottle of whisky," I told the barman as soon as I sat at the table of that secret smoke-filled bar in Thizi.

"The mosque seemed unable to transmit my prayers to the creator. So, let me drink, to repletion, my bitterness in this bar."

I ordered a bottle of red wine.

"I give you the best wine," replied the barman. "It's national. The best in the world," he added as he served me a first glass. "No one speaks about it, not even those so-called open newspapers." He seemed proud of holding such a piece of information.

I shut my mouth. I didn't reply. I lifted my glass. "In the name of Allah," I said. The barman laughed out loudly.

"Don't insult our God," I heard a drunken voice behind me.

"God is not your private property," I swiftly answered, as I emptied the whole glass into my mouth.

It did me good to feel the first stimulating flow of alcohol in my body. I paid, thanked the barman, took the bottle of whisky and went to a hotel. Hotel or brothel? I didn't care. I wanted to drink and sleep. I rented a room. I drank until I passed out. Everything was submerged in a sort of mist. My childhood, my life, Thadarth, people's faces. I felt as if I could not step out of it. For days, I ate very little but drank litres of alcohol. I wanted to forget, to kill my pain. But neither my prayers nor the bottles I gulped down could be of any help. Nothing could change what happened and what was about to occur.

The responsibility was too high to escape. What was I supposed to do? The price I had paid was already high. My wife had been kidnapped, raped, and now I found out that she had a baby. Where on earth can my wife be right now? Has she been killed? Why didn't she flee with Faruja? I'm not the father of that baby. I am not my wife's baby's father… Who on earth can tell who is the father? How could God allow that to happen? The monsters raped my wife. She bore their seeds, damn it! And gave birth to…a bastard. I hate this word. Bastard. The little baby is innocent. She is innocent and unaware of what was happening to her, to what was happening around her. What about when she is grown up?

"But what now?" I asked myself, half-sober. "Where can that little creature be? Who would take care of her? I never knew how to deal with children, even less with babies. I am too old to take care of a baby," I thought.

When I finally got back home, I found my companions in a tremendous state of panic. I didn't tell anyone about my escapade.

"I visited family," I lied disinterestedly.

"We were worried," said Karim. "You should have called us, Dada Akli."

I looked at him. I felt uncomfortable.

"You are right. I'm sorry… I wasn't… I was tired."

Karim went on and told me what happened during my absence. I was shaken and mortified when I heard that Faruja passed away, a baby in her womb. God knows the suffering she went through. What did fate want to tell us? Is there a suffering beyond that? Poor woman. Poor creatures! Zira! The tiny and unique light I had to know what happened to Zira went off.

Straightaway, I went to visit Nana Ldju.

"The little baby was in her house," Karim had told me.

"I will take care of her," she assured. "My daughter-in-law will help."

I consented to it. Could I have found a better solution? I took out my wallet and handed Nana Ldju some banknotes. She refused. I then went to her daughter-in-law and forced her to take them.

"You have already done a lot for me," I said.

"We are a family," the old woman said when I came to sit beside her. She was holding the baby into her lap. I didn't dare look at that little creature. Nana Ldju didn't say anything at that moment. She was lulling that baby.

I then, unexpectedly, opened my heart and spoke: "If she is Zira's daughter I shall treat her like my daughter."

"Listen, brother Akli," Nana Ldju explained reverently, "this baby is a gift to you from God. It is Zira's baby. Zira was your wife. This baby comes from her blood, from her flesh."

"Is it a sign? A divine sign? Hope? My lifelong wish?" I dreamed.

I closed my eyes for a while. I felt so frail for a moment. I sighed. I thanked God. I thanked God to put on my path a woman like Nana Ldju. She opened my eyes to something I couldn't see, or rather, something that I was seeing differently. There was goodness on this earth still.

I sighed again and took a deep breath. I felt enthusiastic. In a fit of a renewed hope, I decided to take care of that baby and protect it until my last breath.

"She is not my blood, but why would she not be my daughter?" I thought excitedly.

But suddenly something trotted in my mind.

"We didn't name her yet, Nana Ldju," I shook my head.

"I already named her," she said in a poised voice.

I frowned. "She already named her?"

"What is it?" I asked impatiently.

"Zira," she replied looking into my eyes, smiling.

I smiled back at her thinking how marvellous and witty was that.

"Zira," I mumbled and finally got closer to her. I peeped at her. She was like a little doll, lovely, shinning. I poked her little nose. "Zira, Zira…"

Whenever Nana Ldju came to visit me, she did it with her grandsons and granddaughters. They all kept that little creature company. Zira. My house became full and joyful. I felt happy and enthusiastic. I observed them. I didn't expect myself to be as patient about the noise that children could make as I was. The kids ran all around, screaming, laughing, playing, and jumping with Lulu. They made me smile, laugh, talk. Finally I had hope. My hope was her. Zira.

11

"**F**orgiveness is something good, brother Akli," maintained the Imam whom I suspected to be sent by Thizi's Mayor.

He never talked to me before. There was, between us, no more than an exchange of "Good day, go well." Yet, that time, he even paid me a visit. I had a good reputation and influence in Thadarth. Our resistance group gained a lot of respect and fame in the whole region.

"What does he want? To preach the new farce of 'reconciliation'? To persuade me to go and vote in favour of it? Is he here to incite me to go and pray at the new mosque he is leading?"

A mosque was built in Thadarth. We didn't have even a medical centre or a space for cultural or sport activities for our teenagers. Thadarth had many rich people, all of them retired from France. They had Euros. Some of them left Thadarth and went to invest elsewhere. Those who remained were limited to showing off to each other, buying expensive cars and expanding their houses. No common public project for our teenagers, to save them from the grip of unemployment and drugs. Values had changed. So fast. The tragedy lessened but its aftermaths were devastating. Our society lost its marks, its values, and its principles. The tragedy became a foul farce.

"Voting this law is a huge deed on Allah's accounting balance," said the Imam.

"Listen, Shikh! I have a lot of respect for you, but I won't vote," I boldly replied. "And you know as well as I do, that whether we vote or not, the results are already known."

"Pardon is in our religion…"

"Listen, Shikh! If pardon is in Islam, is killing in Islam too? Aren't these people killing in the name of Islam? If pardon is in

Islam, then why vote it? Pardon them and it's over? But for me, things are as clear as the falling snow outside."

"God says…"

"I won't put this down," I interrupted him, showing him my weapon.

The Imam went back with his tail between the legs. Too many lies, too much pain, anger and frustration had planted cynicism in me. I became cynical. Bitterness is no more than mental death. So, between bitterness and cynicism, I chose the latter.

Did the killers ask for forgiveness? Why are the lie makers asking for pardon on their behalf? They provoked the civil war to instil ambiguity and slay the intelligent resistance. They slayed the intelligent resistance and went on a fake fight against terrorism. Then, they made up another lie. The 'terrorism' the snakes claimed was happening was fought by people's children. Policemen and women, soldiers, *gendarmes*, resistance groups here and there, ordinary citizens, journalists, teachers. What did the snakes do? Perpetuate terrorism and weep in front of the international community, telling them that the country was left unaided and helpless.

The new life you are leading us to is more ambiguous than the ones we walked through. Our conscience and our intelligence are not yet appeased. Denying justice is renouncing human dignity. Denying justice is an insult to human intelligence. Denying justice is the prospect of future injustices. What dignity do I have behind these walls? However, I will not write a letter to implore the President's mercy. I will not send a letter to those newspapers, lies promoters, working for the lie makers, to publish it. Let them dispense their mercy to whomsoever they want. I do not need it. The victims, the civil war, blood, bones, history, justice…are a mere business for the lie makers and the lie promoters. They are like torturers. They keep torturing until you, by yourself, affirm what they want to hear.

My words will not change anything. They are mere words. We are reduced to gauge our pain and misfortune. Cry beloved children of this land! I pity you. The misfortunes that this land witnessed, we saw them coming. Yes, we grew up with our misfortunes. And today, you are carrying both our and your misfortune. Nevertheless, we call for you to think about the glorious past and keep up the revolution's promise. What is left of glory and promises? Ashes.

Every new day was like putting embers on our still fresh wounds. The fugitive terrorists' families came back to Thadarth. They seemed more arrogant and provocative than before.

The terrorists' activities decreased a lot. This is why my companions didn't show up often. Furthermore, a rumour about stopping our activities and firing us was heard in the higher circles.

"Calm down, Lulu," I urged her, and went to open the door. "It should be Yidir," I told Lulu. Yidir is Nana Ldju's grandson. "He is bringing us some food, little girl!"

"Here is your food, Dada Akli," said Yidir. He kissed me on the forehead as he used to do.

"Better shake hands," I told him.

"I can't do that, Dada Akli. It is good to kiss you on the head because then one may gain some of your wisdom," he said wittily, with a mischievous smile on the face.

"Who told you that, villain?" I joked with him. He is an intelligent kid. Let me prove it. Hear what he said: "Dada Akli, I don't wait for the others to tell me what to do. I have a head and I use it."

Today's generation is so smart. Smarter than we were. Yidir was about fifteen years old. He already had an adult's brain and attitude.

193

"Before I forget," he said, "Uncle Lwenas sent you this letter."

"Lwenas? You mean Ali Lwenas, the shopkeeper whom you used to provoke?"

Another malicious smile was on his face.

"We just like laughing with him. He is a good man. He offers us sweets, sings for us and tells us that weird and unique tale he knows. The funniest thing with him is when he repeats the last word of every sentence he pronounces."

He then went on imitating the old Ali Lwenas. I laughed.

One might be surprised about how often funny little things pop up to cheer the spirits up. We just have to look for them, to look at them, to detect them. They are around us, sometimes, within us. Instead of charging our hearts with burdens, let's make them light and more emotive. Why are we afraid of emotions? Why are we more and more interested in the brain and the mind, whereas the heart is stifling? Heart. From the heart come natural ethics capable to improve our life, our relationships. We plan a lot and forget that there are thousands of things that we can enjoy in mere spontaneity, without putting them in this or that pot, in this or that box. Without philosophising about them, the way I am doing now. Hahaha!

I am naturally a serious man. I do not really know what being a 'serious man' means. It didn't help me a lot, even through trials and tribulations. I ought to think less and feel more. That is the conclusion I reached. In every tragic, serious and painful situation, there are scattered moments of happiness. One should appreciate them. Am I becoming sentimental? Is it because of age? However, nothing is bad with sentiments. We are more human when we are sentimental.

"What is the song you used to sing, hiding at the back of his shop?" I asked Yidir. I, more eagerly, wanted to see him laughing and speaking rather than singing the song itself.

Yet, he started singing: "Uncle Lwenas is short and sweet, in his pants there's a lot of heat!"

There and then, we laughed together in full joy.

We served Lulu first. Then we sat down, ate and talked. Lulu liked him. She often went out with him for walks along Thadarth's streets.

The letter Yidir handed me was wet. I took it once we finished eating. It couldn't be my brothers' since they had sent me one two weeks ago. They didn't write a lot. They preferred calling me. Whenever they wanted, they called Karim who then came to me with his mobile phone. We didn't talk much. We didn't share much. "How are you? Everything is fine." A little chitchat. The weather. "We miss the sun, we miss the air, we miss you." "Me too." "It's not safe enough to come, kidnappings, fine, be careful, take care, stay well."

I took the letter and examined it. It was an official letter. The last official letter I received, as far as I remembered, was around five years ago when they used to convey me to the Party's meeting. The Party I quit decades ago. The Party they should send to the museum instead of using it for their interests.

I opened the letter. It was written in French. I looked at the signature at the bottom. Mister the Mayor. "Dear... bla bla bla...· to the meeting with the *gendarmerie* brigade officer at bla bla bla..."

"What on the earth am I going to discuss with these sinister individuals?" I asked myself. Corrupted to the marrow, we all knew what they were capable of. Both the Mayor and Rombo were the devil's associates in many dirty businesses. Odious, they had large hands in the entire district. God in the skies, the Mayor and Rombo on earth.

I tore the letter up into pieces and threw it into the bin.

"Not for me," I frowned. Even before the last piece of the letter landed in the basket, I heard the main door opening.

"Karim," I guessed. He has my house key.

195

"The Mayor wants to talk to you," he said after the usual greetings and handshake. He handed me his mobile phone. This goes without saying that I knew what the intentions of the man calling me were.

The phone rang. "Bla bla, the meeting... an important decision coming from higher up... You should come tomorrow."

Against my will, I went to the meeting. At Lwenas' shop, I waited for more than an hour for a van. The roads were covered with snow and Mister the Mayor didn't bother to send a snowplough to clear the streets. He certainly had other important matters to attend to.

"What am I going to speak about with that sinister man?" I was angry. In front of Lwenas' shop, there was a long queue waiting for the gas delivery van to come and sell them, so expensively in the country of gas and oil, a bottle or two. Freezing and unsure whether the gas delivery van would come or not, you wait for hours, watching your empty bottle so as not to be thrown back in the queue by any cheater who wants to, stealthily, take your place, cursing the skies, which, among hundreds of countries, sent you to a dull and poor village. You freeze for hours, insulting vehemently, the state, the third or fourth largest gas exporter in the world. What about that parading bench of ministers! They keep promising heaven on earth. Promises they are uttering for decades whilst they keep sending billions of dollars to Palestine, Western Sahara and other countries, in the name of solidarity and other values. Everything is a fuss!

"You, citizen of this land, queue up for what is yours. You queue up for days whilst the gas pipeline serving the Spaniards is laughing at you under the Mediterranean Sea, where your children are dying in search of a drop of dignity. You also queue up for hours at the municipality for a mere birth certificate or whatever document. You queue up in shops for a loaf of bread, a litre of oil, a bag of milk. You queue up at the post office for even to retrieve your own salary whilst the bench of ministers are robbing public money by the billions, placing the money in tax havens, sending their children to live in foreign, developed countries."

"Damned be the Mayor and the men of his fibre!" I whispered, getting onto Muh's tractor.

"There are no vans," he had waved at me, inviting me to jump on. He was on his way to clear the road toward Thizi. His tractor had thick wheels and could at least trace a string into the snow covering the road, therefore allowing Thadarth's cars to circulate.

"As a good Muslim and a patriot," started mister the Mayor under the appreciating eye of Rombo, "we have no doubt about your collaboration, Dada Akli."

"He is preparing for something huge," I shook my head. "Are they trying to stop our resistance group? Muslim and patriot," I wondered, secretly rejecting that political vomit that was coming out of his mouth. "Pure demagogy," I thought, serving the man an interrogative glance.

"You know that our misled brothers are coming back to their homes," he verbosely said, "and we count a lot on you to…"

"To what?" I asked, finally guessing what that arrangement was about.

"We have orders from higher positions, Dada Akli," nodded Rombo, supporting the hesitant Mayor who already knew my opinion about those laws of the Concord and Reconciliation. "You, as a leader of the resistance group in Thadarth, me, as the brigade officer, and our Mayor have been assigned the task of receiving our misled brothers. They are here right now, in our brigade, and next Friday, after the Friday prayer, we will all meet at Thadarth."

I froze on my seat. Words itched in my throat but I remained quiet. I swallowed Rombo's words with disgust and internal ire. I raised a hand and reflexively brushed my moustache.

"We will send a TV team to Thadarth," stated the Mayor.

The Mayor's comment drove a sardonic laugh out of my throat. The men's eyes went wide at that outburst. An idiotic air had sketched on their faces.

"You will send the TV, ha?" I cynically said as soon as I rose up. "Thadarth doesn't need a TV team," I rumbled. "We need a bulldozer to clear the road, the van of gas, and peace. We don't need TV, we don't need your Concord, we need your justice…" I hesitated for a moment and stopped talking, knowing that my word would fall into hollow ears, shallow minds. "I'd better spare my saliva," I thought.

I got up and walked out. I expected the Mayor or Rombo to rush behind me or try something to dissuade me, but they didn't dare.

Once home, I invited my companions to my house. We talked about why the Mayor and Rombo wanted to meet me. Tension raised so high. I told them my decision and my fear of the authorities' revenge through dismantling our group.

"We will stand by you," raised some.

"If it depends on me, I will put down the arms," I assured.

"We already know that our turn will come, Dada Akli," said Wali. "It doesn't have anything to do with your decision concerning those bearded apes."

Some days after, the municipality notified me, through a letter, about the dissolution of our defence group. The Mayor and his acolyte, seemingly touched in their pride, if ever they had some, got their revenge. We were thus fired and were asked to give back our weapons. My companions did, but, stubborn as I was, I didn't. I kept my weapon on me.

"We will integrate the neighbouring municipalities' vigils," suggested Bakhi.

I had forgotten about that. The authorities gave the right to the defence groups founded during the height of terrorism, to integrate those improvised vigil groups, depending on which municipalities they were located in. These groups were doing the same job we did, but more in the cities than in the villages.

How could they dare to bend this way and be so vile as to organise a reception for the killers! I'd rather kill myself than accept to participate in their sordid parade!

"The Mayor and his dog Rombo held the ceremony in their honour this morning," reported Karim, when he came to visit me during the evening. "Didn't you see them on the news at one o'clock?"

"I hate their TV, their radio, and all their shit," I replied angrily. "I heard the police siren though," I added.

"I don't know how we are going to live with those assassins after all that happened," pondered Karim. "Some people are moving away from Thadarth."

"Were you there?" I wanted to hear more about the Mayor's parade.

"Yes, I was just curious but didn't stay long. They were disgusting. There were a lot of military authorities, their 'doggy-media' and boot lickers from the masses and politicians. They brought four or three terrorists, kissed them in front of the camera, and things were done. No war, no blood, nothing happened."

"Where did they do that?"

"In front of the new mosque."

"They always have what they want," I nodded, remembering the face of those who came for the *jihad* tax. Musa's son, Kamal, and his friends.

"Did you recognise any of them," I asked Karim.

"Two of them are from Thadarth," Karim asserted, but suddenly, his voice was shrouded by the *youyous* and bursts of joy coming from the neighbourhood.

Karim looked at me and seemed saying: "Do you hear what I am hearing?" I glanced back: "Don't tell me that they are doing what I think they are doing!"

Yidir came in. He had been walking Lulu.

"Times are terrible," pronounced the kid looking at us, surprised and quiet. "The killers are received like heroes," he declared.

I got up from my chair and went to the bathroom. I sat down, absorbed in my thoughts.

"Tell Dada Akli that my father called me," I heard Karim telling Yidir. "I will come back tomorrow."

The *youyous* didn't stop for a long time. As soon as they stopped, the *bendir* and flute replaced them. That was unbearable indeed. A dire provocation I could not consent to.

I took my gun and hurried out. By then, they started their '*Allah akber*' calls. Women, moving under their black tarps as if they were coming back from hell, were parading with their children in Thadarth streets. I never saw a *burqa* so close. I never hated the *burqa* as I did that day. Alienation was in action. Why do they put their wives, daughters or sisters under those moving cloth jails? Because they are sick. Because they are afraid that their wives, daughters or sisters would cast shame on them, the husbands, fathers, brothers. Because the only thing they limit a woman to is having reproductive organs, what she has between her legs, her body. As if she has no ability to think, feel, work, and be by herself. Because those men have a penis in the head instead of a brain. They veil them because they believe that women are of little brain, referring to the prophet's saying. Because they are sinners and easily attracted to women, they castrate them. Why do some women accept those breath-killing tents? Because of the certainty to get a better life after-death. Because of the certainty that Allah wants them to bow to their men. Because of their permissiveness, because of misery, because of stupidity...

"Stop your circus!" I shouted at them as soon as I went closer. "Away!"

The children screamed and ran behind the black moving things. They stepped away and walked silently. Then, forthwith, five white shadows moved towards me. At that precise moment, I realised that Lulu was not with me. The men were wearing the strange *qamis*. I then knew who they could be.

Karim didn't answer my question about... But the face of Musa's son, smiling oddly at me, gave me an answer.

It was him. I didn't recognise his mates. They weren't from Thadarth, I think. He looked stronger and grown up. The unique sign of evolution was his long beard, his leather jacket and those American shoes. Nike. It's ironic indeed. They were wearing the brands and clothing made in the very countries they called to fight against.

"Satan never dies," I thought, looking at him.

The young man looked straight into my eyes. He wasn't smiling anymore. Something in my core told me that he was responsible for what happened to my wife and house. I could read mockery and hatred into his eyes. He was indeed challenging me.

"Dada Akli," Karim's voice came from behind me. He was with Wali and Bakhi. As I turned to him, the bearded men walked by and went off.

"Is everything well?" whispered Karim.

Everything that was happening was beyond belief.

"It feels like everything we did was futile," said Wali.

I looked at Wali, then, in slow motion, at my weapon. Pointlessness. What else could come after a sacrifice? Reward? Disgrace? I could not understand. What else could there be after war? Something that means that our sacrifices were not useless, that those who died did not give their life vainly. What remained after all our sacrifices?

"I don't know, my son," I addressed him thoughtfully, handing my weapon to Karim.

"I'm going to visit Nana Ldju," I told him, asking him to take the weapon home.

I did not go to Nana Ldju's house. Absorbed, I ended up at Lqahwa's, which I had found full of Thadarth's jobless young men. Surprisingly, I found Ali Lwenas sitting with Jabril, his 'best enemy', himself running a rival nearby grocery. I wonder how a cat could sit down with a dog. I greeted them all. It was warm to hear tens of greetings back. Ali Lwenas invited me to a domino game, but I refused. I sat down at their table though and watched them playing. As soon as I sipped the last drop of my tea, I said to them: "Stay well, sleep well". I walked back home. I felt so tired. I slept peacefully until Yidir came the following day to bring lunch. We had shook hands.

"Better this way, my friend," I told him cheerfully.

It was a pleasure hearing him talking. The boy did not stop asking questions. Many questions about life, history, people, Thadarth. "Dada Akli" in his mouth sounded so jovial. No, I was not lonely. I had around me such nice people. I was too blind. Blinded by my rage and hatred, I could not see that people were lovely to me and helped me a lot during my years of solitude.

"The truth, Dada Akli, why aren't we like the kids on TV?" he questioned me as he switched the TV off. "I see on foreign channels, fathers and mothers taking their well-clothed children to school in nice cars…"

"This is life, I awkwardly replied. "There are rich and poor people. Good and bad countries." Then I stared at him, I went on, telling what seemed to be a lie: "Succeed in your studies, you will get whatever you want."

Yidir looked at me suspiciously and said: "Then why are the cafés and the streets full of young jobless people, old and new graduates? You know that, Dada Akli," he shrugged.

Should I have told him that in this country, whatever one does is useless?

"Better flee from this country," Yidir said enthusiastically.

"Where to?"

"France or wherever," he replied, unsure.

"How?

"A visa, hide on a boat or pay a boatman," the boy's eyes widened. "Everyone wants to go to Europe now."

"Even in Europe, if you don't study you won't succeed in life," I said again.

"Europe is something else, Dada Akli. They have buses to take them to school, and if not, their parents take them. They eat well, they have nice clothes. We, from Thadarth, walk five kilometres every morning and every evening to school. We aren't allowed to eat at the school canteen when even those who live five meters from the school eat there. Is this just? Before they moved to a private school, the Mayor's children used to eat there. His son was in my class. They have a personal driver."

"Those are the untouchables, my son," I sighed. "Do you still eat at Ammi Rezki's, the grocer in Thizi?" I asked.

"Where else? Bread and soda. The best of us eat a piece of cheese with a whole baguette," he added, amused.

I smiled.

Yidir's questions were innocent but relevant and often put me in uncanny positions. I often wonder how one would raise his children in this country. Yidir, like the majority of the children of his age, lived in permanent doubt. He was trying to find not only his purpose, but also the meaning of his life in a country full of doubt and lies. Fear is embedded in those children's souls who, instead of enjoying life's delights, were staying at the margins, expecting nothing more than unhappiness. When we are used to hardship, whenever a nice moment comes, we feel lost, we stare at it half-paralysed thinking: "It is too good to be true!" Then the moment goes by and we miss out on enjoying it. Our children become cognizant beyond their age. When the future proposes them frustration after frustration, they become full of anger and hatred. This is why they become violent. What did school do? Nothing more than ruining them. Their language is ostracised; their creativity and opinions are silenced. What are they taught in school?

They are taught to be afraid, to be blindly submissive to God, to the teachers, to the parents, to the policemen, to the Imam, to all authorities. They are taught fear and obedience. They are taught hatred for difference. They are taught to hate everything different from the established ideologies they are stuffed with. At home, all the same. Fathers, for the majority, are machos, treating their wives like slaves and their children like asses. "Shut up! A little bird can't teach his parents how to pick the grain" has been forever our biggest mistake. We never conversed with them. We never gave them the chance to make mistakes. Never spoke to them. We denigrated and underestimated our children all the time. And why? Because of their age, of their inexperience. Rightfulness can never come from age or experience. It comes from work, love and competence. Democracy starts at home, at school, in the minds, before going to the streets to shout against the dictator. We must first stop being dictators in our houses with our wives, our children, and our families. We should first stop being dictators at school, to our pupils, in the factories and the administrations, to our employees. Or else, dethroning a dictator to place another one isn't the solution.

Let our children play, sing, learn, work, be themselves, make their dreams come true. Let them doubt, let them make mistakes, let them love and build their self-esteem and confidence. This is the true revolution. And, for God's sake, let us stop thinking that we are the best nation on earth! We are, whether we like it or not, just as human as the others are. And our duty is to live together, to be better in a better world.

Oh my God, I feel as if I suddenly became an orator. God forbids! On second thought, I think that what I'm thinking is not as idealistic as it seems. Is it? If Abel and Cain... Well, better nature's laws of survival? God, Adam was fine in the heavens, was he not? Why all those other complications? Eva, the snake, the apple... Well, if ever all these are not mere myth, of course. Well, well! From politics, I went to philosophy stuff.

God knows I do not have any knowledge about all these things, except what life has taught me, so little, and what I can remember from the newspapers and the radio. This is me. I put a lot of heart in my dream. However, are my requests extreme? I do not think so, though fate is too harsh with me.

"It's getting dark," said Yidir. "I must go."

"I'm coming with you," I said. We then went together with Lulu to Nana Ldju's house.

"I'm too old, Akli," said the old woman whilst adjusting the sheepskin she was sitting on. "In wintertime, cold freezes all my bones." She sighed.

"But you refuse to wear shoes," I told her.

"Oh dear! Never. Winter or summer."

"Why, grandmother?" asked one of Yidir's brothers.

"She is strong," replied his mother who was tickling little Zira, trying to make her laugh.

"She is strong because she is of the olive oil generation!" exclaimed Yidir, embracing his grandmother.

"You? Which generation do you belong to?" asked Nana Ldju cheerily.

"We are the yoghurt generation," laughed Yidir and his brother.

"Better olive oil!"

"I don't like it," grimaced Yidir.

"Olive oil is natural and healthy," explained his mother.

"Yoghurt is sweet and yummy!" said a little girl, a cousin of theirs.

I was sitting on my stool, cheerfully listening to those lovely creatures talk whilst Nana Ldju's daughter-in-law stood up and headed towards me.

"Hold her for a while, Dada Akli," she smiled, handing me little Zira.

"I…"

The good woman didn't give me time to hesitate. Zira was already in my arms. I lulled her. Spoke to her in childish words, caressing her pinkish face with my fingertips. I felt heat on my cheeks. Zira's fragility made me more flimsy. Only life's beauty has the magic ability to soften our hearts and lull our souls.

When I was about to go back home, the kids ran and made a circle around me.

"A tale, Dada Akli! A tale!" They echoed each other.

I sat down, on sheepskin this time. Excited, the kids sat around me. Lulu was surely happy to finally have some peace. The children didn't stop making her jump and run in the courtyard.

"*Mashahu...*" I started. They altogether repeated after me: "*Mashahu... tella m shahu ...*"

"May my tale be nice and spread like a long thread. Once upon a time, there was a smart kid, called Vulajud. He used to make up stories only to laugh and make his fellows laugh. One day, he attacked Teryel, the ogress, who, for many years haunted the entire country. Teryel, because of senility, became blind and voracious..."

The kids' eyes hung to my mouth. They looked like they were seeing on my face the images my words projected in their minds. I was interrupted several times to answer their questions and ease their doubts. Then I ended my tale: "They lived happy and had..." "*Mashahu...*" The kids finished: "May my tales, as wheat and barley, never end."

Lulu, who was lying beside Yidir, sighed.

"Another one! Another one!" started the kids.

"No," objected their mother. "Dada Akli is tired now."

"May God bless you, Dada Akli," said Nana Ldju thanking me. She then started telling the kids, who had already gathered around her, some riddles.

Zira was peacefully sleeping in Nana Ldju's lap. I stooped and kissed her on the tip of her nose. I wished good night to the kids and the two women and went back home.

I was happy. I felt young, light. I only had one wish: to be under my blankets, dream, think and reminisce that moment I had with those kids. Zira's face illuminated my night, my dreams. Curled up like a baby in her mother's womb, I slept peacefully.

12

Days passed by. Apart from a few visits, nothing special happened. I often went to Nana Ldju's house and spent hours there enjoying their company. I didn't carry my weapon on me anymore. It became heavier. My soul wanted something else. Something calm, deep, good. Peace within myself.

I was determined to carry on living with no fear and no change in my routine.

Terrorist activities decreased a lot but still, we read and heard about false checkpoints, run by terrorists or mafia groups wearing military uniforms, where people were stolen from. We were, since then, in the grip of gangs of all sorts. In the streets, in state institutions...everywhere.

A few weeks after their release, the rats came out of their holes. After that night of celebration, I saw them on my way to Ali Lwenas' shop. They were probably walking towards the mosque.

"*Jmaa liman...liman...*" was shouting Ali Lwenas when I arrived to his shop. "If one of them comes here, I will chase him...him! I don't care about their law! Let them put it where I think...think. Terrorists are not allowed in this shop!"

He was sitting in front of his shop along with the Imam. There was also some young men, Ali Lwenas' clients, for whom he had put a bench outside, "to kill time," as they said of their idleness. They became, with time that was killing them and thanks to unemployment and school failure, part of the scenery. It was strange to find the Imam there. Ali Lwenas was known to be fond of red wine, mainly the local one.

The rumour was that he also sold it under the counter.

"Curse Satan, Ali!" the Imam told the old man. He seemingly came to 'reason' with him. Well, his own reasoning since it wasn't Ali Lwenas' reason at all and that was felt in his gestures and the tension in the air.

The young men, one after another, preferred to go somewhere else.

"They are Satan... Satan..."

Ali Lwenas had a verbal tic. He repeated the last word of any sentence he uttered.

"Our country needs peace," said the Imam, whose speech rhymed very well with the political speeches we heard on TV and the radio.

"Listen, Shikh," Ali Lwenas told him, tripping over his own words, "I don't believe in your God...God. I don't believe in your law... but I have respect... for... everyone here in Thadarth. So...I pray you to, to... go and... and let me in peace...peace."

Disconcerted, the Imam took his cane and stood up. He looked at the old man for a moment and then abruptly threw: "By God, you definitely are stubborn and one can't even talk with you."

"Go find your God...God," Ali Lwenas told him angrily. "Yes... yes... I am donkey-headed!" He did not stop. "This is my business. I do what I want here... here. If you... you come here again, I will smash your head with a bottle... bottle."

The Imam was already far away.

"My shop is dirty. Why do they come and buy here... here? Let them go to the other shops. Or it's because they don't find there what I have here... here?" he asked me when I was trying to calm him down, inviting him to sit.

"I will be right back, Dada Akli...Akli," he said, his breath heavy. He went inside the shop. A while later, I heard him gulping what was, no doubt, the liquid he cherished the most.

"That's it, Ammi Ali!" I whispered, smiling. "A sip of wine will chase your anger away."

"They dare to invade people's houses... houses!" he said, sitting down beside me on the bench...bench... Hahaha! I'm contaminated. I wonder why he had that tic.

"Don't pay attention to them, Ammi Ali," I uttered.

"How? Even the Imam is getting involved...involved. In the old days, the Imam was a citizen like the others...others. He had no authority. He voted at Thajmath like all the others. See today! He is poking his...ass...ass... even in people's things...things."

I didn't comment on what he was saying. I secretly smiled at his tic, but I immediately blamed myself because of the seriousness of the situation. The old Lwenas, hardly breathing and with no respite, said: "Do you know what this Imam of bad omen did...did, ah? He invited the killers to do their prayers in the mosque...mosque, ah. The whole of Thadarth knows that...that, ah. He speaks about reconciliation and brotherhood every Friday through those loud speakers for one hour...hour, ah! My favourite time to take a nap. They don't let us rest...rest, ah. Moreover, this new luxurious mosque! We need a hospital not a mosque... mosque, ah. They, up there, the President, the generals, the ministers, they go to Paris for their healthcare, ah. Instead of having a hospital, will we go and pray to not fall ill... ill? And what, ah! Every morning, at five, he wakes all Thadarth...Thadarth. Everyone has a watch, a clock, a mobile phone and can get up at the exact time...time. Why disturb people at five in the morning...morning, ah? We aren't in the prophet's time. If Mumu was here, now...now... do you think he will grow a long beard and wear the ugly clothes these sick people wear...wear, ah? He would have worn a suit and a tie...tie, ah!"

I was sitting there listening to Ali Lwenas' disrupted words. He didn't stop: "Why don't they stop using cars? Why do they not use camels or donkeys...donkeys? They should live in tents, not houses. *Sunna... Sunna*, ah. They want to be like their prophet...Profit. If Mumu lived in these times, he would have

211

been jobless and unable to do anything... anything. The prophet is dead. He is enjoying himself with the virgins and the rivers of wine and sweet milk...milk. They only think about their stomachs and dicks...dicks. They think that they are the best...but they kill babies and slaughter throats, rape women, ah. You know the story...story. I'm not afraid of them. I'm not afraid of their God! With people like these one must cut ties straight away...away, ah!"

"Aren't you afraid your shop will be closed?" I asked him.

"I have a nephew at the district's police," he answered. "Still, without their God's intervention, I won't shut up. Fifteen years of civil war, *basta*, Dada...Dada Akli."

I left the old man speaking to himself, getting out everything that he had in the heart. From time to time, he went back in to gulp down some wine.

My wife's shadow struck me more often. Kamal's bold looks awakened in me the revengeful beast I had quietened with time. I had the feeling that Kamal and his group were responsible for the kidnapping of my wife. Things were obvious. I denounced them, they burned my house and kidnapped my wife. I went into war against them; they are now free, here among us, as if nothing happened.

I had two Ziras in my life. My wife, gone, but whom I couldn't keep in the past. Zira, my little daughter, my hope, my future. I clung to the latter because I believed that she was a sign, or maybe a message from my wife, from God. A message that said that, after all, I have something to live for in this life. A message that said that even from evil, good could come. Zira had been kidnapped, raped, but she gave birth to a lovely creature, she gave birth to my hope, my joy. And it was there, at my reach. I could see it, feel it, live it. I could finally exult. I did it whenever I saw the little Zira. Zira, her mother's name. My wife's name. So, I decided not to spoil that bliss with past ills. I silenced that revengeful voice within me. Thus, I did everything I could to avoid crossing the path of the devils.

Noticing my absence at the mosque, the Imam came to visit me some days after. I remembered Lwenas' words: "He pokes his ass…ass everywhere."

In eloquent words and a poetic tone, he explained to me the weight that a collective prayer has on the balance of good retributions. How can one weigh faith? This, I couldn't understand. Oh, do they not know the art of giving an explanation to every worldly and heavenly thing!

"Your advice is precious, Shikh," I answered, "but I have my reasons, which God would surely understand."

"May Allah guide you, my brother. But…"

I looked into his eyes and said in a firm tone: "Listen, Shikh. These things are between him and me!" I raised a finger to the sky.

After a long pause, the Imam dared another issue.

"I came to talk to you about something else too."

I gave him a questioning look.

"Some people in Thadarth abandoned their religion. They gather in a secret room transformed into a church in Thizi."

I shook my head.

"This is serious, Dada Akli. Can you imagine that? Apostasy! It's the biggest sin ever. As good Muslims, we can't permit that."

"What do I have to do with all that?" I enquired.

"I was thinking of denouncing them to the police," he said hesitantly. "I talked to Slimane Uhemu about it. He says that this is none of his concern. He is the village leader, he must do something."

"Wait! Wait!" I stopped him. I'm out of this and Slimane Uhemu is right. It's their choice and no one should interfere in their life or choices. They want Allah's path, they follow Allah's path. They want Jesus' path, they follow it. I don't care about that. You are the Imam here, so just do your work. Preach for the goodness of Muslims and that's all. There were Christians even before the coming of Islam!"

"What you say is weird, Akli," he looked at me in surprise. "I never thought you were like this."

"What I am concerns me and me alone," I said dryly. Then after a short silence, I added: "You are Muslim, aren't you?"

"Yes."

"Does anyone come and ask you why you are Muslim?"

"No…"

"Does anyone force you to be a Christian or a Jew?"

"No… but we are in an Islamic state…"

"The entire problem, Shikh, comes from there. People are free to be what they want."

He interrupted me: "These are European thoughts! We are not Europeans!"

"We are not Europeans but we are humans. Do you think that we, Kabyles, can't think by ourselves? Are we such idiots? Do you think that whenever we think, when we think differently, it's because of a foreign hand or a foreign head? Aren't we all humans and able to think? Aren't we humans and humans are different? There are Muslims, Jews, Christians, Atheists… Just like in nature, there are different colours, shapes…"

The Imam's eyes were wide open. He couldn't believe his ears.

"And where is the problem in European or Chinese thoughts, if they are good?"

"But we are Muslims…"

"So what? Our society has good traditions and is well organised. Religion replaced all of this: in the mosque and people's hearts. You are a man of science, Shikh, aren't you?" I tried to explain without knowing how I could arrive to that. I was myself surprised by what I was saying. I was also surprised by the capacity and the way in which I explained my thoughts at that moment.

"Yes," he said with verve.

"Before Islam, didn't Northern Africa have different religions?

"But Islam came to sweep away the ignorance spread by the other religions."

"Why don't you accept that the others may be different?"

"In the constitution of our country, Islam is our religion," he tried to justify.

"*Toz* on that constitution! We also are Amazighs, but your constitution doesn't even recognise your language, your identity."

"We are Amazighs arabised by Islam," he said hesitantly.

He swiftly held my hand and added: "These are political things. I don't do politics."

"Everything is politics, Shikh," I replied. "When you say that we are arabised by Islam…what about those who aren't arabised? 'Arabised by Islam' means being in deep alienation. Worse than anything else. You know how the tale goes."

He looked puzzled and struck.

"Once, Teryel, the ogress, helped a widow to get out of poverty. In return, she wanted to own the widow's children. Afraid the widow gave her children away. Nonetheless, she advised them to suckle at the ogress' breasts. Why? Because once they suck her milk, she would not eat them. Time went by, the widow died and the children became the ogress' children."

"May God bless you," the Imam said when I finished. "How can you know all this?" He asked.

"Do you understand what the tale means, Shikh?"

Confused, he exclaimed: "By God, no!"

"We became the children of Teryel, Shikh."

"May God preserve us. Do you mean that Islam is an ogress?"

"I don't know. Look at how subjugated our children are. If not by the Arabs, by the French."

"No, Dada Akli. Not politics again."

215

I smiled. Of course, stupid and proud people hate politics. They don't know that everything depends on political decisions. From our ignorance, come corruption, prostitution, poverty, war. This is why our systems want us to be ignorant, stupid and silly. This is why they want us to hate politics and do whatever it takes to prevent us from taking part in decision-making. From our ignorance, comes their wealth, comes our wretchedness too. "I hate politics!" Yes, it is the easiest way to be an accomplice of the calamity falling upon us.

"Anyway, Akli, I must go do my duty. Apostasy…"

"Are you truly going to denounce them?"

"Not to the police. They already know everything. Next Friday, I will talk about it in my sermon. The sermons come from higher up!"

"Up, you mean your minister?"

"Who else?"

I hummed for an instant.

"*Allah akber*," said the Shikh. "Time for me to go."

Then stood up and after a while, asked: "Did you go to school, Dada Akli?"

"Life is a school, my brother. Life is a school."

"But life's knowledge is different."

"One must think about the past and understand it. There is a lot of knowledge about us, about life, about humans in the past of this land."

"Do you read books?" he insisted.

"I used to read newspapers and listen to the radio," I replied.

We exchanged farewells, he then left.

With eloquence and an inexplicable rage during his Friday sermon, synchronised with the mosques of the entire country, he sent to hell the Christians, the Jews, the atheists, the drunkards and all those the minister of the religious affairs cited in the paper he read.

I was sitting at Lqahwa's when the Djurdjura Mountains were sending a breeze that refreshed that summer evening. Slimane Uhemu, who was sitting beside me, had been as silent as were those mountains. I was quietly sipping some coffee, hearing, without listening to, the voices around me. The clients who were playing dominoes and cards made a lot of noise though. They shouted, accused each other of cheating and laughed with all their foolishness and innocence. I barely heard them. My mind blocked them out.

"What if I bought a house somewhere else and left Thadarth?" I rumbled again the idea that was trotting in my mind for days now. "I have seen enough. I have lived here enough," I thought.

Unexpectedly, the clients' voices lowered.

"They are here! They are here!" someone murmured.

I returned and saw three men coming by.

"*Salam alikum*," they greeted.

Only some scattered and hesitant voices greeted back.

"Dada Akli, stay in peace," Slimane Uhemu said as he stood up. He looked furious.

"Already? What about the domino game we agreed to play?" I lamented.

"It smells rotten here," he pointed to the newcomers who were entering the café.

"This is our village, Slimane," I said to him, almost shouting. "For decades, we didn't give up and now what? Shall we give up?"

This sentence swept away all my thoughts of leaving Thadarth.

Nevertheless, Slimane Uhemu left Lqahwa's. One, two, three, more people followed him.

The remaining clients seemed tense and fearful but they quietly continued what they were doing. In a few minutes, Lqahwa lost its joviality. It was unbearable for me to see all of

Lqahwa clients' attitude change by the arrival of those insignificant rats. I was at the end of my tether.

"How is it that you suddenly became dumb?" I exclaimed loudly. "Have you swallowed your tongues?"

The three sinister men were sitting inside. They could however see and hear everything since the windows and the large door were wide open.

"This is your village!" I unwillingly started sermonising. I almost cried. "You have the right to live freely. Play, laugh, shout. Send the rest to hell!"

I lived my life with no pretence to change the world. No pretence to change things or people. But I lived with the deepest conviction that I was part of the world, responsible of my people. Therefore, I firmly decided not to shut up whenever I would be confronted to any evil or injustice. If I did so, I would be less of a human. I did not play the hero, much less the victim. I just had the duty to be responsible as a citizen, as a human.

"Stop speaking nonsense!" said someone through the café's door.

It was him. He walked towards the café's porch.

Seethed with anger, I shouted at him: "It is a sin to go to a café! Was this not what you were preaching not long ago? What are you doing here then?"

His two companions stood up, got closer to him. They were seemingly trying to calm him down. I heard some chairs moving. Some clients stood up in surprise expecting the worse to happen.

The three of them left. The monster's eyes were on fire. Some steps away, he turned around, took a gun from under his jacket and shouted: "If you don't shut up... " He waved the gun towards me but not for long since his mates rushed to him, snatched it and hurried him away.

I regretted not having my weapon on me at that instant. I would have loaded his bulging chest with bullets.

I calmed down. Looked disgustedly at the people in Lqahwa's. Then, I swore to never go back there again. "God, open the ground and let it swallow my last drop of pride. What did that mean? Are we that cowardly?"

I went home.

"How is Nana Ldju?" I asked Yidir.

He was the only one to whom I opened my door. I locked myself for days.

"She is too old and can't walk anymore," he replied.

"Zira?"

"She can walk now," he said excitedly. "She holds onto the wall and walks. She can also mumble some words."

"That's good. That's good," I smiled.

Even if I could leave Thadarth, could I have left that little creature? Zira became my unique source of enthusiasm. No, I couldn't have left her. I couldn't leave those mountains because I grew up there, because, there, I felt my first joys, experienced my first love and my first aches. In this land, I saw my comrades dying, watering the soil with their blood. I saw a lot of tears, smiles, laughter, resistance, and pride, although painful was our life. My tears, blood, sweat watered this land. I won't... I can't live elsewhere.

"Dada Akli, everyone is speaking about what happened at Lqahwa's. You should be careful," innocently uttered the young boy.

At that very moment, calls and knocks came to interrupt us. It was Slimane Uhemu and Karim.

"Yidir would go and bring him food, so, let's go and try to meet him if ever he opens the door," I imagined them saying.

"You should open the door," stated Slimane Uhemu as soon as I was about to open. "Are you angry with us too or what?

I smiled. I tried to make up an excuse. It didn't help. We sat down and talked about what happened at Lqahwa's.

"We are truly trapped in an absurd situation," concluded Slimane.

"It's not that absurd, Ammi Slimane," replied Karim. "It's what they want us to be in."

"Right, my son. You are right."

"What about work, Karim?" I asked.

"A lot of problems. We are on strike. They want to force us into retirement without a decent wage or any basic rights."

"Things in this country cannot get worse than this."

"I lost my energy, brothers," I confessed.

"I heard you have bought a ewe," said Slimane. "Back to shepherd life?"

"Instead of staying at Lqahwa's playing dominoes or being idle, I prefer taking care of my ewe and Lulu."

The ewe bleated in agreement. Lulu wagged her tail.

"She understood you," remarked Yidir.

We laughed at both the ewe and Lulu's response and at the boy's remark.

"Should I tell the police what happened?" I reflected on the idea for days before I finally went to report the incident and the threat.

I had found a young officer to whom I explained what happened. He trembled when he heard Kamal's name. He mumbled some words and said: "It's a delicate situation, sir."

"Delicate or not I want to report what happened with that man," I insisted.

"I'm afraid we can't do anything in this respect…"

"Listen, dear! I don't want to be saucy with you. I'm just asking you to do your work."

The young man panicked and asked me to wait. He then went out of the office and disappeared in the corridor. A few minutes later, he came back.

"The boss asks you to go to his office," he announced. I followed the officer to Rombo's office. Rombo, Rombo. I was offering him the chance to take his revenge. Didn't I refuse to take part in their farce? Rombo was relishing his ass being on a huge leather chair. A throne. I doubt if even Berlusconi had such an office. Rombo became Thizi's Berlusconi. They resembled each other a lot. A malicious look, a perverse smile.

"Sorry, *signori* Berlusconi! *Liberti ezprezioni!*" Hahaha!

Everyone knew about the bribes he received from the town's richest traders to keep their trade, legal and illegal, going on. Everyone in Thizi knew about his regular visits to the capital's brothels.

He was holding a newspaper when I got into his office.

"When did he learn to read?" I wondered.

Rombo got up, walked towards me, shook my hand.

"No, things aren't alright!" I answered when he asked, "Is everything alright?"

"I have already heard what happened in Thadarth," he replied with an air of self-confidence.

"I'm impressed," I said.

"We have eyes everywhere, Dada Akli. You know that."

"I won't take much of your time," I pressed. "I just want to report what happened and I want to do it properly. On paper."

"Listen, Dada Akli," he started a sort of a political speech. "We don't want problems with those people. Our president initiated a law to recover peace and security. You and I know very well how much this country needs that. Am I not right?"

"This man threatened me with a gun," I responded. "The gun he threatened me with has been given by the state itself. You and I know very well that those people have blood on their hands. Today, they are free."

"I'm sorry, Dada Akli, but this case is so delicate. You just had an insignificant quarrel with that guy. He wouldn't do anything."

"I'm here to ask you to do your job," I cut him short. "I would like to file a complaint."

"It's impossible," he replied sweating. "I risk a lot if I do that and you know it very well."

"If you risk your job, I risk my life."

"I understand you."

"Then let me file a complaint."

"Please, Dada Akli... Well, what if we calm down and talk... Sit down first!" He tried. "We didn't even 'sit down and... Sit down, please."

"I won't get out of here until I get my complaint filed," I claimed again.

He went back to his throne and threw his ass on it. He held his head between his hands for a while and said: "This is a dilemma! This is a difficult situation!"

Then he looked at the officer and asked him to take me to the other room: "I need to make some calls."

He was confused. We went to the officer's office. He offered me a chair. I sat down and waited. I refused his coffee. Fifteen minutes later, Rombo came in.

"I can't do what you are asking, Dada Akli," he declared. "I have received orders from higher authorities."

"You are alone in this, Akli," I told myself. "Alone."

I got up and left, ignoring the two men who were trying to talk to me.

13

Back to Thadarth, I went to visit Nana Ldju. The children were in school. I noticed how old and sick Nana Ldju was. I was sitting in the courtyard beside her whilst little Zira was playing under the big fig tree covering the entire yard, providing it with an agreeable shade.

"She can speak now," said Nana Ldju in a frail voice. "Come, my little child, come to see your father," she called her.

The word father sounded so strange in my ear. Father? Me? I was confused and didn't know how to react. The little child came towards Nana Ldju and embraced her. She looked at me, puzzled.

"Here is your father," the old woman smiled at her, kissing her on the cheek.

Zira, smiling, hid behind Nana Ldju for a while, peeping at me over her shoulder.

"Say it!" insisted the old woman. "*Vava*. Go to your *Vava*," she added.

Carefully, Zira walked towards me. I held her little hand: "Who am I? Say…"

"Vava," she whispered shyly in a fine soft voice.

I trembled. I heard her. I was looking at her, silent, happily surprised. I felt so fragile in front of her. She said it. She said '*Vava*'. I felt light. I could walk on air. I wanted to gloat. To cry out my joy. My eyes filled with tears. Some dropped down my cheeks. I realised that I hadn't cried for years. Real, enflamed tears of pain or joy. We weep less and less when we get older.

Zira looked at me innocently, a thumb in the mouth. "*Vava*." She said it innocently. She said it without knowing what it meant. Without knowing that it meant everything to me. To me, it meant the world, life, hope.

Zira's looks were heartwarming.

"I should go," I said, getting up from my chair, wishing a good day to Nana Ldju. I then bent over and kissed Zira on the forehead. She didn't run. A smile lit her face. I caressed her hair. Then, I left.

Zira! The fruit of an error. The fruit of violence done unto her mother, done to a woman, done to a human. The fruit of human barbarism. But, a fruit. A nice fruit destined to life, to beauty, to love. A fruit destined to learn from the beautiful and the ugly things of life. That was her destiny. The destiny of a woman is never easy in a society like ours. But it's her life and no one might prevent her from living. Because she is innocent. Innocent in a world where adults pretend owning the supreme truth, through their long beards and verses, if not through their hideous traditions.

Once in my yard, I looked up at the sky. Clear and blue.

"Let's take our ewe out," I said to Lulu.

She woofed and hopped in agreement. We then went up the hill, not far from the neighbouring woods. Thadarth looked calm. I could see all the villages around. I lay down on the grass and watched how the mountains were flirting with the sky. A deep sigh came out from my soul. I smiled at the sweet memory of Zira. "*Vava*". She said "*Vava*". I closed my eyes and stretched out my body on the grass. A moment later, I floated. A feathery cloud. It took me away from reality. Martine. The same sensation. I swayed gently in the air. I opened my eyes. The flute! I took my flute. I dried my lips, cleared my throat, I set my fingers on the right holes and started blowing. A note, then another, another again filled the instant, the atmosphere and my heart with nice tones. The tones waved out and went to meet those of the birds. I shut my eyes again and played.

"Come with me," she said. She was naked. My eyes widened in surprise. She laughed. Her breasts bounced. "Come with me!" she urged again, taking my hand this time. I followed her, watching her lower back moving splendidly. The water was warm and stunningly clear. We went into the water. Then I put my hands around her hips. She looked into my eyes and briskly kissed me on the cheek. She suddenly walked away, jumped into the water, and swam away. She laughed again and slowly came back towards me, keeping her head above the water. I smiled in response to her naughty gaze.

All of a sudden, Lulu's barking dragged me out of my daydream. A chill went through my spine. I stopped playing, opened my eyes and turned towards where Lulu was barking. As human stupidity can afford it, a heinous bearded man was standing right behind me. It was him again. I noticed the black stain of devotion on his forehead, labelled by the Saudi Imams, preached through a Qatari TV or other 'dog media' they had in the country. I angrily urged Lulu to calm down. She came beside me. Then, indifferent, I started playing again. I wasn't afraid anymore. I didn't want, at that moment, to allow anyone in the world to disturb me, my dreams, my sweet memories, by any means.

"Is this what you won, you, the regime's accessory?" I heard him saying.

"The regime's accessory," I repeated talking to myself. I stood up, swung towards that mass of a criminal in which I no longer saw any human traits: "Why then, did you stop your *jihad*?" I challenged him.

He smiled mockingly, and then puffed on my face. His breath carried the stink of his arrogance. Impatient, I almost spat on his face.

"*Jihad* is not over," he answered taking a step back.

About one meter was separating us.

"I'm not afraid of you," I sneered, searching in his eyes some sign of weakness.

"Your day will come!" he blurted and then walked away.

At full-tilt, I walked behind him, grabbed his arm.

"Do it now if you are man enough!" I shouted.

He turned back and violently pushed me back. I lost my balance and fell down. Lulu barked at the man who precipitately took out his gun and pointed at me: "I will explode your head!" he bleated. He seemed taking an eager pleasure in directing that gun at me.

"Do it! Do it, you coward!" I dared him. I got up, clenching my teeth and fists in wrath.

"I won't kill you," he said. "I will make your life bitter. And guess what? No one can stop me."

Then, he walked away hastily.

"I will end your days," I murmured between my clenched teeth.

How I went back home, I cannot tell. I was infuriated. Nothing could soothe my fuming soul. One thing could put out the fire within me. Only one thing. I rapidly took my Kalashnikov and walked towards the mosque.

"The *muezzin* had made the call for the penultimate prayer," I recalled. "The beast would be there."

I stood about fifty meters away from the mosque door and waited until the prayer ended and the worshipers came out.

"Come here!" I whispered when I finally saw him coming out. I walked, walked. Blind, deaf, dumb. Once in front of him, I pointed my weapon. Scared, his friends had already stepped aside. People fled, others screamed. Drops of sweat formed on his forehead, slipping down from his devotion stain. He looked pale, terrified. I did not give him the time to breathe, to sigh, to utter a word. I planted my bullets into his body and watched him fall down, down. I hardly heard some screams around me. The gunshots deafened my ears.

A pool of blood formed by him so quickly. I hung my weapon over on my shoulder. I walked towards his corpse. With rage and all my strength, I dragged it to a sewer: "Your blood shall not dirty this land... Your blood shall not dirty this land," I frantically repeated.

Things, I admit, went their own strange way. However, at that moment, standing up, riveted and empty, waiting for the military camp soldiers to come, I felt a weird satisfaction. The satisfaction of someone who has lost everything; the satisfaction of someone who has no more hope. My callous attitude at that point surprised me. I did not look at the crowd that had formed around me and around the bleeding corpse. I was in another world. I looked into the emptiness.

Call me insane, killer; call me assassin, never mind. I killed a man, YES. But I am not a killer. I killed a man but I did not kill him in a blaze of glory or out of some sort of heroic aim. I killed him because I have a human soul, and my soul was exasperated.

The soldiers arrived. They were confused. They did not detain me immediately.

Firmly, I told officer Djamal who came towards me: "I killed this man. You can arrest me now."

He did not say anything. They took my weapon.

A huge crowd formed around us. Curious, people came to do the best thing they were good at: Watch. The soldiers urged them to go home.

"Please, follow me to the camp, Dada Akli," ordered Djamal.

His voice tone was soft.

"I killed that man," I reiterated. "Aren't you going to arrest me?"

"Let's go to the camp," he said again in the same tone. "We will try to find a solution to all this."

I followed him to his jeep. Once in his office, he said: "I knew about what happened at Lqahwa's, Dada Akli". "Believe me! We are, like you, full of anger. But what can we do? We must follow orders. I spent my whole youth fighting terrorism and then, all of a sudden, they come out with a law that gives them the chance to come back and taunt us."

I did not utter a word.

227

"What would I tell that you don't know, Dada Akli," he ended with.

I sighed. I was ready to assume the consequences of my act. I was ready to spend the rest of my life in prison. My mind was resolved to it. I could not think of anything else than that corpse in blood. My eyelids went heavy. I felt so tired. I felt as if the chair I was sitting on was absorbing my strength.

About half an hour later, Rombo arrived.

"I..."

I inconsequently interrupted him saying furiously: "Would you do your job now? Arrest me!"

"I'm sorry..."

"Take me, now! Otherwise, you will have to explain much more to the higher authorities," I said sarcastically.

14

We never get used to the perfidy of circumstances. We then lose control. We lose control of ourselves, of our surroundings, of the situations we go through. We thus remain alone. Alone, empty and unable to change anything.

Watch how things happen and stay calm, cold. No need to act. It is useless to utter even a syllable. Consider how circumstances repress you, how fingers are pointed at you. Though your incapacity to react surprises you, you do not fight against it. Then you stop thinking about places, about persons. You just feel weakened by something or some feeling that you cannot name, you cannot control. Then you live that unidentified apprehension without knowing how to word or represent it. Words become useless. Your life becomes useless too. You should not scratch your wounds. Leave them. Do not try to explain the things that you cannot explain. Even time becomes an enemy. It flows slowly. Sloooow. Until some exterior factors come to shake it and to shake you forward so strongly.

Rombo arrested me and sent me, the same day, to the district's prison.

Time started to get slower when I first came in through this door.

I was then tossed around, from prison to court, from court to prison. The interrogatories were followed by tiresome cross-examinations. I tried my best to sidestep them. I thus answered the questions firmly, with no delay.

Visits were not allowed. I didn't need to meet anyone. I didn't want to meet anyone, though people were worried.

"People at Thadarth are protesting against your arrest," murmured officer Djamal, once close to me. We met in my first court appearance.

"A lot of them are organising sit-ins in front of the prison," he affirmed.

I knew afterwards that committees had been started everywhere in the country, in France, even in Canada, by my countrymen, to support me and protest against the court's sentences. I was torn between sorrow and joy. Is there any hope for the coming generations?

I smiled at Djamal's enthusiasm without giving it any credit.

"Now everything has gone to hell," I thought, when, for the first time, I appeared in front of a middle-aged man. His designation in that farce was "his Highness the Judge". He loudly and authoritatively held a long speech that he surely had rehearsed in advance. I listened to the judge, somehow half-awake, as if I were in a nightmare, and waited. I didn't hire a lawyer. I just wanted to be alone. I just wanted them to leave me in my cell and forget me forever. For them, it was a game, or, better, a business deal they had to win in the name of their 'justice'.

Thus, 'as stated in 'our religion', the judge outlined it solemnly, "he who kills one person kills the entire human species."

Crime against humanity. His highness, with eloquence and airs, spoke in a difficult Arabic I barely understood. When I wanted to, I nonchalantly said: "I am an old man, Your Highness. I can only speak Kabyle and some French."

"Arabic is the language of this country and our state…"

"My language, my ancestors and I did not come from Mars," I interjected. "Why don't you give this case to a judge who can speak Kabyle?"

The lawman, avoiding my request, spoke to me in a mix of French and Darija, which I could understand better. Nevertheless, abrupt and violent, the blade fell and dashed my hopes.

"…According to the articles number… amended in… signed by… His Highness… the President… of the democratic… tatabatata… the court condemns, Mister… to the death sentence."

"I did not hear well, did I?" I looked at those who attended the trial for explanations. I could not see their faces. People shouted. The judge repeated: "Death." My heart pounded. "Death," I repeated into the emptiness.

I was entangled in a web of situations I did not understand. How could justice be so cruel and unjust? Death? How would they kill me then? Hang me? Inject poison in my veins? Shoot me? In my own country? The country I served all my life? How could they so brutally erase all my merits in this land?

I flexed my fingers against the edge of the table I was sitting at. My strength dissipated. My mouth went dry, my hands trembled, my knees trembled. The ground started moving under my feet. I closed my eyes to gather some strength. I couldn't. I could do nothing about it. I couldn't even open my eyes.

Confined for about two years, I was forbidden to lodge an appeal. Two entire empty years. I thus took a lawyer.

"I can't understand how they can do that to you," he exclaimed.

He was even shocked when he knew that I never received visits until then.

"Two years without a visit? That's a huge infringement of the law," he explained, swearing to get reparations.

"To repair what?" I thought. I could not fight anymore. They sucked the last drop of my energy. They reached their aims.

Weeks later, I appeared before another judge. Other pleadings started. Another trial was started.

Fifteen minutes after the beginning of the trial, the sentence came: "Life imprisonment." Fifteen minutes. They did not want to bother themselves with that old man about whom national and international newspapers were writing.

"They are dogging me," I told my lawyer. "You can't do anything."

I was calm. Strangely calm. I watched what was happening in that diabolic and torturing configuration. Was I made an example? An example of the implacability of their law? To show that justice is applied whatever the circumstances are and to everybody, equally? Who had so much hatred towards me? Why? What for?

I had already spent five years in this prison. If justice were applied to the monster I killed, I wouldn't be here. "Crime against humanity" they said to justify their stupidity. Those who killed, raped, tortured and robbed, would they be terrorists, officials, ministers, administrators, are immune and untouchable.

Naïve and optimistic, my lawyer kept hoping for a presidential grace to get me out of prison.

"You should write a letter to the president," he insisted several times.

That was not going to happen. Of course, I refused.

"I won't court the pity of those who threw me in this hole," I answered.

I knew what was mine and what I would be able to lay claim to. I did not kill the human species but I killed a man who kept terrorising the human species. If I abdicated, I would have given the freed killers the right to abuse people over and over. If I abdicated, I would have given credit to the unjust law of my jailers. If I abdicated, I would have given up my dignity. I lost everything, my freedom, my wife, my hopes, my daughter, but not my dignity. No.

We lodged another appeal. They offered me a twenty-five year imprisonment sentence. Not bad. Not bad. Death, life imprisonment, twenty-five years… They did not transfer me, neither to another prison nor to another cell. Their scenario was a well-elaborated one. Keep him there. Make of him an example. Let him crawl. Consume all of his options. Silence him.

"You don't have any choice," asserted my lawyer. "At least try."

"Better die than bend before them," I answered.

"There are a lot of protests in your favour and many people are exhorting the authorities to liberate you."

I nodded.

"Well, let's talk about the letter another time. I have good news for you," he cheered.

I looked at him inquisitively.

"You are authorised to have visits henceforth."

We then shook hands and he left. My lawyer is a loyal middle-aged man. He is experienced and has a lot of energy. He also served as a contact person between me and Karim. And through Karim, Nana Ldju and Zira.

I charged Karim of taking care of Zira. I had sent him a signed procuration to be able to withdraw some money, every month, from my account and give it to Nana Ldju.

"For Zira," I told him in my letter.

"Yidir is taking care of the house," he wrote back. Nana Ldju is very ill and sends you her regards. People are worried and support you. Many journalists came and covered your story. People talked very well about you. No one forgets you even if years went by."

Was it a poor portion of consolation? Yet, it was enough to stir my noblest emotions.

"I am indeed grateful," I scribbled in a short letter.

The prison director came to my cell.

"You are having visits tomorrow," he confirmed my lawyer's words.

I was suffering in my cell. But knowing that people were supporting me, I didn't feel so lonely. I remembered Rabah's words: "We thank God because we are still alive. Because he gave us the force to accomplish our duty towards our land. Because he, right now, is giving us the courage to resist. Because we, all, are gathered here, sharing the same pain, the same chains. Nobody is suffering alone. How would one have felt if he were alone? Nothing's worse than suffering alone, my brothers."

"May you rest in peace, Rabah my brother."

Let me take these earphones off. Our neighbour is apparently asleep. I wonder what his name is. Shame! He is my neighbour and still I don't know his name.

Let's see what time is it. Five. I didn't shut an eye.

15

"Here you are, Yidir. Karim too. Good to see you. How are you? I'm doing fine. Thank you. Sit down. Everything is all right, my son. Between four walls. I'm getting old and tired. It's your time now to be adults and strong. How are your families? Good to hear that. Like everyone in Thadarth. Hahahaha! Like everyone in this country. How is Thadarth then? Nothing has changed? Hahahaha! You make me laugh, Karim. Nothing has changed! You are right. So, Yidir, you keep taking care of my house. I thank you. Is what Karim saying true? You are going to Canada? You never told me that. Is that true? You are going to marry too. Fresh love? I understand. Take your wife to my house. It's your house. It's no longer mine. It's yours and don't worry at all about that. You are my son and you are keeping it safe. Thanks to you, not me! So, Karim, how is work? Fine. Security agent? That's good. Oh! Food is not bad, but I sleep so bad. I don't tell you. I have a neighbour who drives me crazy. He shouts almost every night. Poor him! But I use those earphones. Good idea, Yidir, huh? The nurse gave them to me. Yes! I listen to the radio. Karim, you wrote that Nana Ldju was very ill. She is a good woman. I owe her a lot. Slimane Uhemu sends me greetings? He never failed sending me his greetings every time you wrote to me. Send him my regards. Tell me about Lulu. You said she was ill and couldn't eat. She recovered? She is old now. Just like me. Ah, dear Lulu. She refused to eat when I got arrested? She spent days and months waiting for me at the porch of the front door, you said. Yidir... look...he is a man now. You want me to be at your wedding? Thank you, my son. But you know about my situation. Of twenty-five years, I did six. Ah, the protests! I have heard about them. No, not in the newspapers. I refuse to read the newspapers. I listen to the radio and you know that on the

235

radio, they don't talk about these things. You are right, Karim. It's their radio, their TV. They never showed anything about me or the protests, you say? That is easy to understand. Thank them, please. All the protesters. Thank them a lot. They kept protesting after all this time. Ah, my son, be blessed. I know that you will never abandon me. They want me silenced or dead. Don't feel sorry. I'm so tired. I want all this to end. Don't be sorry I told you, my son. I'm used to it now. But the truth is that I'm so happy you came to visit me...Hummm...You have something for me? What is it? Ah, a letter? Who? Zira? How is she doing? She surely grew and became a woman. Of course, she is. I will read it later. Thank you. My brother in France? I received some letters lately. He is ill. France has sucked his blood, he says. He will, for sure, end up like my other brother, buried in Thadarth's cemetery. We will all end up there. Don't be sorry again! This is life. Every day is a new step to the grave. But you are young. You still have years ahead. Hahaha! See! I still smile. What else is there to do? My lawyer? Do not listen to him, Karim. He told you that? Yes. I refused. It's hard to explain, my son. I don't bargain my dignity. If ever they wanted to grant me the presidential grace, they should have done it years ago.

Oh! It's time to go. The visit comes to its end. Karim, stay a moment with me. Goodbye, Yidir. Take care of yourself and your fiancée. Don't forget Lulu. My greetings to your mother and Nana Ldju. Thank you for coming. Karim, I talked to my lawyer. As you already have access to my account... I know...I know...my money is safe with you... Listen now! I have put my house in Zira's name. Yidir can stay there until he goes to Canada. You have to open a bank account...you already did? Great! Then every month, withdraw my pension from my account to Zira's. And whenever you are in need, take from my account. I have enough but I don't need it. What would I do with it here? Nothing. I don't want to die and leave Zira with no security. If you have any problem, contact my lawyer. You have his number. Time is running. Listen. I would like you to watch over her and treat her as your sister. I know…I know… Go now! Give me a hug and go. Don't do that. Don't do that, I said. Crying is useless. Besides, if you cry I will cry too. See! Now, I'm crying! Go, my son and take care of yourself. Go well!"

"It's time, Yuva! I know. I'm not going to flee, am I? Hahaha. I know why you are laughing. Because you think that I'm too old to be able to flee. What if I tried? You are the guard. You are responsible. For how long have you been working here? Seven years! Aren't you tired of me? Hahaha! You are laughing again! Say the truth. You are tired of me. Will you arrest me or help me flee? You are still smiling. One cannot count on you, huh? If you help me, you will take my place? That's right. Well thought, Yuva, my son! Here we go. Welcome back to my cell. I will stay well, my son. Thank you. Go well too!"

Oh Zira's letter! How foolish was I! I'm trembling. She wrote me a letter! How old is she? Seven? Eight? How did she get the idea of sending me a letter?

"Open it. Open!"

I…

"Let me first put it on that table. Let me think a bit."

What has she written? Does she remember me? She was not yet able to speak when I saw her for the last time. I feel like a little child who is impatient to open his gift. What does she want to tell me?

"Take a breath. Calm down, Akli. Take it now. That's it. Yes. Open it."

Mmmm… It's written in Kabyle. For God's sake, she writes in Kabyle! Let's see what she says.

"*Vava* Akli…"

How sweeeeet is this word! I only heard it once from her lips. Didn't I weep that day? I did. No one called me "*Vava*". How would it sound in her mouth now?

"*Vava* Akli, I write to you this letter in Kabyle because my teacher says it's important to use our language because it has existed for centuries. I don't remember you very well but I… I…"

What's this word? Shame! I cannot read my own language.

"I don't remember you very well but I… I know that you take care of me. I wish you were here with me but people say that you will never go out from the prison. I…pray God a lot that you will come back home. I want you to tell me about the revolution. Last week, I… wrote an essay about…you and your friend Rabah. I presented it in the…classroom. Nana Ldju told me a lot about you and him. My brother didn't want me to come to visit you. He says it's far. I would like to come and visit you. He never lets me to go to protest for your liberation. I don't talk to him… When I grow up, I will be…a…lawyer…"

She wants to be a lawyer.

"I will help you to get out of prison."

How lovely. No. This shall not make me cry. This shall make me happy.

"Oh, my Zira. My daughter."

"I'm waiting for you to come back. Stay well and write me back. Take care of yourself. Zira."

This is the happiest thing I have ever lived. This is the happiest moment I have ever lived. How I wish I could embrace her for an instant, a tiny moment, and go. Go forever.

"Rabah, she wrote an essay about you and me and presented it to her class. Do you hear that, Rabah, my brother? An essay about us! See how excited I am. Rabah, my brother, there is hope. There is still hope for this land."

I wish I could be with her and see her grow up. What if she visits me next week? I need to call Karim or her brother Yidir.

I need to call him so that she comes with him next week. A telephone! I need a telephone. For heaven's sake, a telephone! Or... No. I won't call anyone. But...why not? It's becoming urgent now. I feel weird. I'm lost.

"Calm down, Akli! Calm down. Take a glass of water. Go! That's good."

Let me sit down now. I was calm and ready to carry on dwelling within these four walls. I am too old to finish the coming nineteen years. I may die soon. Zira's letter unsettles me. What if death knocks at my door before seeing Zira one last time? Before embracing her one last time?

Something within me rises. It's like I want bite, blow, scratch.

If only I can find something towards which I may direct my anger. But, HELL! This is my fate. I can't bite it. I can't blow it. I can't scream at it. I can't do anything against my fate except carry it quietly inside me, carry it on my shoulders, on my forehead, into my eyes. Cursed be it!

"I am waiting for you to come back," she has written. It's here.

"See! Read!"

Would my heart exult or bear pain?

"What can I tell you, Zira? What and how would this soul in torment answer you? Waiting for me, my little girl, is useless. Don't wait. I won't come. I can't come. So young you are, yet you wrote me a letter full of intelligence and lucidity."

Why did I kill that damned man? Why didn't I think about the consequences of what I did? Why? Why during all my years here, I never felt any remorse until today, until I read these words, written by a seven-year old girl? I don't regret having killed that man. But... Here I am. Away from my unique hope. And now what? My soul is tortured.

Let me lie down. Let me put this letter on my chest. Let me feel it.

16

I switch on the lamp. Seven. I want to hear something...someone else other than myself. The radio. Go! I want to distract myself from the stress that Zira's letter planted in me. It has been consuming me for three days now.

The newsreader is talking, talking about... nothing. I don't want to hear the night's sounds. Better the radio voices. However, right now, nothing would relieve me better than a long walk. I have an urgent need to walk.

Three days passed after I had received Zira's letter. I didn't dare to ask for a telephone to call Karim. I could have done it but I'm confused.

Are these knocks... Who could it be? Yuva. Breakfast? It's not nine yet. But why doesn't he open.

"Come in, Yuva. I am not naked. Come in. Yes!"

He is laughing again.

"Open it then."

It may not be him.

"Is it you, Yuva? It's not yet time for breakfast as far as my watch indicates. Who wants to meet me? Ah! Good morning, Mister Director. Good morning, Yuva. How I am doing? Waiting for my time to come."

Damn! Why is he smiling this way? As if he really wanted it to come.

"You seem in good shape today, Mr Director. You are smiling... Can I know the secret behind this smile? I let you explain. What will you explain? You have been a good man until now. Explain! What? I'm not going to what... not going to stay here anymore? Please... What did you say?... Released? What do you mean by released? Me? Are you serious? Let me sit down. I am calm. All this is going to drive me crazy. Let me gather my wits for a moment."

How come? He can't be joking. These are not matters for jokes. Yuva seems happy. He seems confirming what the director is saying. How would it be true? What does it mean? After all this time? No, it's not possible. Would the principal come so early to joke with me? He wouldn't have smiled this way... Released? It means I can see Thadarth again? It means I can find Zira again? Me, released?

"If I heard the radio? I didn't hear anything. They announced it? A presidential what? Decision? Please, give me some time to... I must calm down. Easy! Are you sure?"

Why would they release me after they threw me in here like a dirty, homeless dog forgotten for years? This is nothing more than another insult towards me. Towards justice. How could it be that my freedom was hanging to a signature? The President's signature. If I were a killer they should leave me here... Are they releasing me to appease their conscience? Are they releasing me to please some clans in power? Are they releasing me to show how merciful they are? Could they not have done that years ago?

"I should what? Be pleased? Right. You are right to think so, my brother. Fire is in my heart. I was the one confined here. These walls sucked my energy. You can't feel what I feel. I calm down. I sit down...I sit down. I know...I know you are doing your job. I'm sorry... I'm calm. I'm calm. I'm sorry, my brother. All this confuses me ... Never mind! Never mind... What should I do now? Get my things ready... Ah, my belongings... Sign papers? I come to your office. I come. Of course. I need to call. I need a telephone, if you don't mind. You want to give me a ride to Thadarth? No. You are a good man, brother. I shall just call Karim. Can I call him from your office? Thank you. Let me take my belongings. Definitely. Yuva will accompany me. Fine... Fine. See you in a few moments. Thank you. I still have a strong handshake? How not? This is...let's call it a surprise... I... I'm... All right. That's it. See you in a few minutes."

I must call Karim. I can already see his smile. Is all this true? It can't be a dream. Let me take a deep breath.

"Yuva! Thank you! Thank you. I really don't know what to think. Yes. It's incredible. You know, for a moment, I thought that you knocked for breakfast. See how I'm trembling. I can't understand. I don't understand. Enough suffering, my son. You are right."

"Dear God, I thank you. I thank you."

"You are right, my son. I mustn't cry... I...I cry the lost years I have spent here. Why until now? Why... You speak the truth, my son. I must think of home and my family. I will miss chatting with you. You are my favourite guard. You know that. Ah! Better go out and miss our chats? Oh, yes! Better that than... I think I'm lost in all this. Let me take my belongings. I don't have a lot of things. This... Help me with that. Thanks. So... I think we... we are done. Unbelievable! Let's go now. I just take these too."

17

It seemed to me as if time moved so swiftly forward again. The doors to the world in which I wanted to wake up into finally opened. The same world where, for a long time, my good intentions had been dissipated, my faith in better days abused, my hopes for peace trampled. Still, it is my world, my destiny.

I don't know what to name what happened. A dream? Some would call it a miracle. But it wasn't a miracle. It was nothing more than cynicism. Of course, it rejoices me to be free. But, believe in their pardon, I do not. I don't believe in their manipulating, fabricated miracles. A poisonous gift! They wouldn't have freed me if they didn't gain something from it.

Did my lawyer do what I refused to do? I called him before I signed the papers at the principal's office.

"No, I would never do that," he assumed.

I still don't believe him.

"The Minister of Justice wants to meet you," the principal informed me once he ended the call he has received.

Guess why? To make a public statement on their TV. What a genius idea! What a big day! What did they want to make out of my release? Demonstrate His Highness' probity and nobleness? After all those years?

"I don't accept to participate in their games," I told the principal, holding his shoulder warmly. "You have been a good man to me. Can I just ask you one last favour?"

"My pleasure!"

"I want to go out of here as discretely as possible."

He promised. He complied. We went through the offices' door.

"How do you feel, Dada Akli?" he asked me once we were in his car.

I looked at the sky, at the sun and spoke thoughtfully: "I can breathe. I can see the sky, the sun. It's beautiful."

He then drove me to the meeting point we arranged earlier with Karim. Happy for having some minutes of fame, my lawyer went to speak to the people and to the press at the prison's gate.

I was there. Outside. The town seemed busy. The streets were crowded. People were in a hurry. Life did not stop. No, it didn't. Mine had stopped for years. For years, I stopped living. But for years, I wasn't forgotten. I wiped the drops of sweat off my forehead and kept silent until we reached our meeting point. I thanked the prison principal and wished him good luck. Then, slowly, I walked towards Karim. He came towards me and helped me cross the street.

I looked at the buildings. There were more buildings. I looked at the sky; some white clouds were flirting with its blueness. I wished I could fly and catch up on the lost time. Catch up on all those missed occasions. But never mind, I still have some time to enjoy life. I just wanted to go home, to rest.

Karim led the way. He was holding my hand.

"I probably need a cane," I said half-smilingly.

"We will find one," Karim responded.

Before going into his car, I heard a familiar growl.

"Lulu!"

I looked at her through the window. She was jumping and yapping.

"She is happy to see you," commented Karim.

I opened the door. She jumped out and came to caress my leg. I couldn't kneel. I bent and caressed her back.

"You, my lovely girl!" I cuddled her warmly. "You were waiting for me, weren't you? You knew that I would come back, didn't you? Come! Let's go home now."

We then climbed into the car.

"Some people heard about it on the radio," Karim said about my release, driving back to Thadarth. "The whole of

Thadarth is waiting for you," he added with a huge smile on the face.

My heart was beating faster and faster.

"They are waiting for me?" I looked out through the window. It seemed as if nothing had changed.

"More stress, more riots, more repression, more economic scandals, more passivity, more beggars, more violence, more homeless people..." said Karim so morosely.

"Karim!" I called him, breaking the silence. "I want to see the sea. Can you do that for me? It's on our way, isn't it?"

"Let's go!" he stated.

I wanted to see that blue immensity. To feel the sea's fresh breeze gushing on my face. To breathe deeply and taste the salt in the air. To walk and feel the moist sand under my feet. Once there, I took my shoes off. How good it felt when the water flowed between my toes. I lay on the sand, closed my eyes and heard the waves caressing the sand. The sun, screening its rays on the water, caressed, regenerated my old body weakened by imprisonment. I was afraid to see Thadarth again. Afraid and eager. Eager to meet Zira and my people. But I should first assimilate what was happening. I should pause and think. I didn't want to meet people. I didn't want to 're-learn' life without understanding what was happening.

Lulu was heavenly happy. She was running around, chasing the seagulls.

"Come here, Lulu! "HOME!" I shouted.

It felt good, so good to shout. It had been a long time since I last was able to. A long time since I didn't hear my voice in a jubilant tone. Strange how things can change in a very short time. Strange how fate plays with our lives. Strange how suddenly I find myself here, free. I was waiting for death to reap my life. I was better prepared to die in my cell than to be thrown back to life.

We went home. We reached Thadarth by night. It was Karim's idea. People didn't know the exact day of my arrival. We went to Nana Ldju's house first. The kids were asleep.

"Should I wake up Zira?" asked Yidir's mother.

"No, let her sleep," I whispered. "I will see her tomorrow."

Nana Ldju was unable to move. She was dying.

"She can't hear you," said Yidir's mother who was taking care of her.

"She can't hear and she barely speaks," added Yidir.

"Akli," Nana Ldju sighed, her voice frail, holding my hand. "Here you are, my brother."

I kissed her hand. I cried. My voice was shaky. I didn't know what to say. Silence set in for a moment. Between Nana Ldju and I, there was always that kind of silence that reigns between true friends. The kind of silence where none of us needs to say anything and yet, everything is settled and restored. But that time, the silence was different. I don't know if it was because of old age, but I felt it. She was leaving us.

Karim, Yidir and I left Nana Ldju's house and went to mine. It was clean and it smelled good. Yidir showed me his good work. He bought a lot of furniture.

"Since you are here, Dada Akli, I will organise my wedding very soon," the young man voiced proudly.

"Go for it," I replied enthusiastically. "I promise you, I will dance."

We laughed.

Karim greeted me goodbye and went home. I hugged him and thanked him a lot.

"Where is my room, you the Canadian?" I asked Yidir.

"Your room is your room," he showed me.

It was painted, tidy, but he didn't change the way the furniture had been laid out when Zira was here. I stood on the porch for a moment.

"Zira". I bit my lip until it hurt.

248

I walked, with deafening pain in my heart, towards our bed. I lay down. I stretched a hand to where she used to sleep. Memories of her assaulted me. I felt exhausted. I couldn't sleep.

"Sorry, Zira. I am sorry," I sobbed.

18

Tens of people knocked at my door for the following days. Of course, I opened and received those whom I wanted to meet and see. Small chats, congratulations, thanks, coffees. Other people from all over the country came to visit me. I was very glad for that and it gave me a lot of hope. The authorities never showed up and I was also glad for that. But the TV and the Radio came. I didn't want to talk to them.

"He wants to take some time to rest," I heard Yidir answering them at the front door. I knew that with time, people would forget and carry on with their lives. But I will never forget. I will never forget and I will never forgive those who could not be indulgent towards me.

Cast them away now! Cast them like rubbish! Let me breed hope. Let me remember Zira and her innocence.

She came to my house on the second day I was home. She was more beautiful than I imagined her. She was ineffable. I know that the circumstances I was living had a lot to do with the depth of my feelings, but she had my heart, my eyes, my soul, all to herself... She wasn't my blood, but what does a blood bond mean? She was Zira, and loving her has nothing to do with blood.

"Loving you, Zira, is like building happiness in the present and plant hope in the future. Loving you is like living again with one condition: Believe in life and beauty, believe in intelligence and ability. And your eyes, your eyes reflect innocence and eagerness. Your eyes reflect back love. How lovely and fluently you speak! How full of energy you are! And that smile on your face!"

I told her about the revolution. I told her about Rabah. We even went to visit his grave. Together, we pulled off the weeds from it whilst she carefully listened to my stories and memories. She did not stop taking photos of me. She was so kind and I could not say no. Hahaha! I gave in to the game of pictures. And once home, she took that strange little pliable machine and showed me the photos she took of me.

"When I grow up, I will write a book about you, *Vava Akli*," she said.

I laughed and hugged her warmly.

"Yes, my life is perhaps a book. A story. But now, write your story, my daughter. Live your life. Go to the fields and see how beautiful and proud our mountains stand. See how beautiful spring is in this land. Run, free, after those butterflies. Pick a flower and smell its fragrances. Run, free! Run, smile, laugh. Run. Sing and celebrate love and beauty! Master your freedom. Even if there are risks and responsibilities, you will also find rewards. Rush with your schoolmates to school and study hard for good results. Stride confidently to make your way in this world. You will sometimes falter, maybe fall, but get up again and again, shake the dust off you and reach for the skies. Be the best, the prettiest, the nicest, the proudest, the noblest you can be! Zira, you are everything that I have. Your presence, your existence is enough for me to stay in this world."

I watched her running there in the fields not far from the neighbouring woods, witness of our first meeting, deliverer of my life's love, my life's hope. She was moving in circles, followed by Lulu. She was enthusiastic and blissful. I was admiring her as I never admired anything, anyone before. I was staring at her as if nothing else existed, before or after her. I was admiring her whilst a sweet tear ran down my cheek.

The End

Printed in the United States
By Bookmasters